A
TIME
TO
HOPE

BRENDA LOBBEZOO

CONTENTS

Once you choose hope,
anything's possible.

Christopher Reeve

Introduction

A *Time to Hope* takes place in a Frankfort of my imagining, although if you're looking for a beautiful place to experience Lake Michigan, Frankfort, Michigan is an excellent choice.

Some of the places mentioned in the novel do exist, in different capacities. Mackinac Island, in northern Michigan, truly is a "back in time" place with several inns that would make Sylvie proud. You can't buy a hammer at Frank's, but you can get a fantastic hotdog at FrankZ. For a latte, I highly recommend Bella's on Main Street.

In July 2020, after returning from a vacation near Frankfort, Michigan, I started working on a novel set in a beach town. Over the next few months as our world wondered about its own future, my story evolved from a "beach read" into something much deeper.

With A *Time to Hope*, I am so honored to bring you the stories of three courageous women and the community that saw them through.

Enjoy the read,
Brenda

Hope

CHAPTER 1

Hope scrolled through images of colorful butter-flies, seashells, flip-flops, rainbows, and compass rose tattoos and then lifted her finger off the screen. She frowned and tilted her head one way and then the other, trying to make sense of the series of open triangles each pointing in different directions.

After reading the caption "I am greater than my highs and lows," she got it. And she really did get it, like anyone else who constantly thought about their blood sugar.

Hope closed the tab. She had zero money for a tattoo, not until she got a car anyway. She couldn't use Maya's car forever—roommate privileges only go so far. And then there was the job situation, the whole point of the hospitality management degree she had worked on for almost two years. When she figured out where she would work, she had to actually get there.

"Hope, I firsty." At three, Lainie, her roommate's toddler, already had the same intense look in her dark eyes that Maya had. A look that said they knew what they wanted. A look that Hope did not see reflected in the mirror when she looked at her own eyes, which couldn't decide if they were Scheiner green like her mother's or her father's Vermeer blue.

"I think you had enough juice for today. How about some water in your crazy straw cup?"

"K. Can we go to the swings?"

The swings were Lainie's only break from their apartment, which was small but still bigger than the resort's staff quarters. Hope thought about the yard that she played in as a kid, so big it took the lawn care service two whole episodes of her favorite show to mow it. Two episodes she couldn't hear because the TV volume had to stay at seven and no louder if her father was working in his home office. What would Lainie do in a yard with real grass and a swing set of her own, with friends over to play soccer or run through the sprinkler?

Hope could spin out a whole story of fun that a little girl could have. Not that she had that herself. When Hope was little she had gone to the other girls' houses for birthday parties, but it was a one-way invitation. Some of her earlier birthdays were celebrated in the Fellowship Hall at church, a "perk" of being a pastor's

kid, but after a few years of that, she never asked for
another party. Inviting friends over was a hard no.

"Swings are closed for tonight," Hope said, letting the
water run cool. She handed Lainie the cup. "How about
a movie? Let's pick one we haven't watched in a while."

"Aw-right."

The one with the singing candlestick and teapot was
Lainie's current fave, but Hope had always liked the
princess movies where a fairy godmother knew just
what the girl needed. Hope put in the DVD, and Lainie
tucked in beside her on the couch. Hope hugged her
and hoped Maya wouldn't ask Lainie in the morning if
she had brushed her teeth before bed.

The little birds were bringing the final ribbon to decorate the princess's dress when Hope put Lainie to bed.
She went back to the couch and clicked off the movie.
If a fairy godmother did suddenly show up, Hope would
ask her to magic up a bigger apartment where each of
them could have a bed. Maya deserved it after sleeping
with a toddler who was as busy asleep as she was awake.

Her phone dinged with a message, and she picked it
up expecting a check-in from Maya.

*Hope, hi, it's Sylvie. I know, it's been two years, but
she's finished! Here's a picture of The Beachview Inn in
Frankfort, Michigan. I can't wait to show her to you.*

Hope enlarged the picture of a blue-gray Victorian
house with white accents, wrapped in a huge front
porch. She had been waiting for this text for a long time.
She hadn't intended to stay with the resort in Boyne for
so long, but it had gotten her through, and now Sylvie's
project was done. She wondered if Sylvie had recreated

her Mackinac inn on the mainland, or if The Beachview would have its own vibe.

Hope texted back. *She's beautiful! And I can't wait to see you both.*

She had checked Maya's work schedule and found a day they were both off before setting a date with Sylvie. Now she just had to figure out how to sell it to Maya, this perfect idea of scrapping their jobs at the resort and all of them moving to Frankfort so Hope could take a job with her former boss. Because even though they had only known each other for a year, Hope could not imagine living without these two people she now called family.

Technically, her own family still existed, although her Vermeer grandparents hadn't spoken to her or her mother since the trial. Her Scheiner grandparents had offered them both a place to stay while everything "blew over," but by then Hope was working for Sylvie on Mackinac and her mother had booked a one-way flight to Alaska. Her father would be in a cell wearing his orange jumpsuit for at least a few more years, not that Hope was counting.

Her testimony had been enough to convict, one of the few times in her life Hope had been "enough." Most of the time she faced The Consequences that followed whenever she didn't meet expectations. They could be her father's expectations that she would make only smart choices and excel at everything she did. They could be her mother's expectations that Hope not embarrass any of them with her questions or her behavior.

They could be her doctor's expectations that her test results were always in the normal range. See above, not embarrassing any of them. Like when seven-year-old Hope flooded the pew because she couldn't hold it until her father finished the sermon, and her parents didn't know she had diabetes. Or when thirteen-year-old Hope left school by ambulance because her blood sugar crashed somewhere between second hour gym and late lunch, and her parents didn't want anyone else to know she had diabetes.

They could be God's expectations that she follow all Ten Commandments even when her father didn't. They could be the college's expectations that the daughter of the mega-church pastor shown on the news every night would disappear and never come back.

She and her sophomore year roommate Bekka had joked about working jobs on Mackinac like the kids who came to the university on scholarship and had to work summers to pay for their education. It turned out to be a good thing Hope had applied at the Lilac Inn. It gave her somewhere to go when her life imploded and where the highest expectation anyone would have of her was to make a bed.

Even though she was happy to be one of the invisible service staff, the owner, Sylvie, had noticed her. More than that, she had been a friend when Hope had no one. Sylvie was the one who, over tea, helped her set a plan for what she would do when the entire island would shut down for the winter. Going back to her old life was not an option.

They talked about her college and her major, both picked by her father. Sylvie was the one who steered her into hospitality management. "I've watched you with the guests, Hope," she had said, "and hospitality is your gift. You care about them. You want the best for them." If a degree like that would open doors to a career doing what Sylvie did, Hope was all in.

Sylvie had told Hope her own plans to turn the house in a small beach town on Lake Michigan into another inn. "It will take some time, Hope, but when it's ready, I would love for you to come work for me again. No." She held up her hands and then crossed them over her heart. "No, not *for* me, *with* me."

CHAPTER 2

"Take the next left onto Lake Street and then right onto Main," Hope said, checking the map on her phone. "Sylvie's inn is three blocks from the beach. And how cool is this town?" She pointed out the car window to a playground with brightly colored plastic slides.

"We would be able to walk to most everything we need." Maya's subtext for *we are lucky this car got us all the way here,* and maybe a vote for everyone to move to Frankfort together?

Hope had already put in her notice at the resort. Maya was a little more "show me the money" about it all. She had to know that the next job was waiting before she would quit.

On the other side of the street between the library and the next building on the block, she caught a glimpse of boats in the marina. Signs over the sidewalk advertised a salon, a bank, and a dental office. Everything seemed so normal here. No franchise tourist spots or huge signs for area attractions. Just a sweet old main street of two-story brick buildings that ended at the shoreline of Lake Michigan, which seemed to go on forever.

Maya pulled into a spot in front of the huge Victorian house and turned off the motor. She nodded toward the back seat. "I'll wait with the sleeping princess. Take your time."

Hope quietly shut the car door, tightened her ponytail, and took a few breaths. Two years ago, she had stepped off the ferry onto the Mackinac Island dock with just her backpack and a duffle bag, and a letter from the owner of the Lilac Inn confirming Hope's employment for the season. Sylvie had given her more than a job that summer; she had believed in her. She had known then that with Sylvie's guidance, whatever she did would be so much better than the way she had grown up, shrinking into her father's cold shadow, hiding from people who waited for her to fail.

And here she was again, about to have tea with Sylvie and talk about her future. Hope walked up the brick path and climbed the four steps to the inn's wide porch complete with white columns and wicker furniture. She could imagine people a hundred years ago sitting out there with tall glasses of iced lemonade. Maybe they still did. She took another breath and pushed open the oversized wooden front door.

Inside, the inn was just as amazing as she'd expected. Just off the foyer a wide stairway gracefully curved up to the second floor. To her left a doorway led into a parlor with cozy chairs gathered around the fireplace and a grand piano waiting for someone to sit down and play. To her right was Sylvie.

"Hope!"

The first time they met, Sylvie had been draping fabric, and ever since then Hope's impression of her was of flowing color.

"Let me see you." Sylvie pulled back from the hug and studied her.

Sylvie herself was thinner than she remembered but still just as on point.

"Come, come," she said in the fabulous Greek accent Hope had missed so much, "I have tea ready in the dining room."

Sylvie led her through the lobby with its inviting settees covered in deep emerald velvet. Past the wooden reception desk was a sunny dining room that was perfect for the large oval table and antique sideboard that held the tea supplies. Sylvie obviously meant for her guests to interact instead of sitting at their own small tables.

Hope pulled out a chair and accepted the teacup and saucer from Sylvie. She chose an orange pekoe sachet and dropped it into her cup. "The house is so beautiful, Sylvie."

"You would not know it now, but she was in terrible shape. And with the weather in the fall and the early snow, it was a rush to get everything painted and ready for next month. I guess the weather is relative, though. I imagine the ski resort loved all the snow."

"Yeah, they said it was one of the busiest winters they've ever had."

Sylvie stirred a sugar cube into her tea and then tapped the spoon lightly on the cup's edge. Her elegant fingers were bedazzled by several rings. "Did you like working there?"

After Mackinac was Boyne. Not exactly the life Hope had wanted, but it was a job with a place to stay, and it paid for her online degree. "It was fine. I mean, none of the resorts can compare to your inn." Hope glanced around the room. "Inns."

"Thank you, that is very kind. So, would you like to see the rest of The Beachview Inn?" Sylvie sipped her tea and placed the cup on its saucer.

"Yes, please!" Out of habit, Hope glanced at the side-board for a tray to clear the dishes but Sylvie laid a hand on the table.

"You're not on duty yet." She smiled. "We'll catch those on our way back through, but first I want to show you my favorite space."

As she moved through the foyer and up to the second floor, Sylvie still had the flare Hope remembered, but each time she stopped to point out a detail Sylvie rested her hand on the stair rail or piece of furniture.

"So, for this project I wanted to embrace the lake but keep a secret get-away nuance. A little different from the 'back in time' feeling of the Lilac. Well, the whole island, really, as you know."

Hope remembered the suddenness of "horse" as she walked from the ferry to the inn on that first day on Mackinac. The island went vehicle free in 1898, a detail every hospitality employee was asked by a visitor at least three times daily during the season. Main Street had been full of wagons loaded with luggage or supplies, and carriages of guests, all pulled by huge horses. Where she grew up in GR everyone drove or at least rode a bus. The horses were just the first of all the things that changed about her life that summer.

"Here it is," Sylvie said, "the Green Room. I just went simple and called every room by its predominant color." She motioned to the windows. "This one faces the lake and that the channel, so lots of water. Did you know that in Michigan you are never more than six miles away from water and eighty-five miles away from a Great Lake?"

"Fun fact," Hope said.

"I'm from Chicago so Lake Michigan is nothing new, but I didn't really get the water thing until I moved up here."

They saw all the rooms and then went down the service stairs to the kitchen.

"I'm still in the process of hiring someone to do the food preparation. The Beachview is listed as a bed and breakfast, but I want to keep the teatime feature so we'll also need a few baked goods for that. Which brings me to you." She smiled.

Hope's stomach dropped. She knew nothing about baking and very little about making anything that didn't come with instructions on the package.

"I would like to have you as manager of guest services, Hope. You're in your final year of classes, so this could be a way for you to pull together all of what you have learned. I would love to hear your ideas for marketing the inn, maybe bundled with offers from the area restaurants or vineyards. What do you think?"

"I...wow. Manager? I mean, I thought I would be turning over rooms like before."

"Oh, Hope." Sylvie gently squeezed her arm. "You are so much more than that. Let's go back to the table and chat about my plans for all of this."

Over refreshed cups of tea, Sylvie outlined a soft launch with just two rooms full for the first weeks. Hope would be at the inn to oversee staff and daily operations while Sylvie kept track of the bigger picture.

"I may be traveling this summer, but I will always be available."

That made sense since the Lilac probably also needed Sylvie's attention, but some deep breathing would be necessary before she would feel anywhere near prepared to go it alone.

Hope's phone buzzed and she glanced at the display. *At the beach.*

Besides Sylvie, only her mother and Maya had her number, and it would only be 5:30 a.m. wherever in Alaska her mother was putting her life back together. "It's my roommate," she said. "Her daughter woke up from her nap."

"I am so glad they were able to come with you," Sylvie said. "I look forward to meeting them. Now, will two weeks be long enough for you to settle in? I will need to go to Chicago for some appointments, and I want you to feel comfortable here before I leave everything in your hands."

"Two weeks is great." Was it great? Hope had learned early on in life that the best way to avoid The Consequences was to let someone else make the decisions. Right now, she didn't have a car or a place to live. Maya might shoot her idea down and stay at the resort. Yeah, The Consequences were coming in hot.

"Fabulous." Sylvie wrapped her in a hug. "I will see you then."

CHAPTER 3

"Well, we won't lose anything in here," Hope said, scanning the garage attic apartment. They could always look for something bigger later. On the plus side, it was furnished, which was good since neither of them had any furniture.

Hope owed Marty big-time. A cook on Mackinac and part of the crew that moved to the cluster of resorts in Boyne for the winter, he had introduced Hope to Maya when she needed a roommate. A few months before Sylvie's text, Marty had left the resort to manage a restaurant, but Hope hadn't known where until she and Maya drove down to see The Beachview.

On the way back to Boyne that day, Maya had pointed out a restaurant a few blocks from the inn. "There's The Logslide. That's where Marty works now. What?" she said, glancing sideways at Hope. "What's that look?"

"I didn't know you guys were talking."

Maya looked straight ahead and then smiled to herself. "I don't have to tell you everything."

So, not only had Marty found this apartment for them, as manager at The Logslide, he could arrange Maya's schedule around Hope's so Maya wouldn't need a babysitter.

"What time do you work?" Hope asked.

"Four. Do you want to go to the store together before then?"

"She's too wired for that," she said, tipping her head toward the bed Lainie was using for a trampoline. "I think we should hit that park with all the slides. I'll take her shopping later when you're at work. It'll be an adventure."

Maya took out her phone and tapped on it. "I'll send you the list I started. Everything else to Lainie-proof this place might be at that hardware store across from the restaurant. I saw it when you were talking to Sylvie. Lainie, snack." She pulled a container of veggie puffs out of her bag, shook a few out onto a paper towel, and brought it back to the coffee table. "Stay here while we bring in the bags and then we'll go play, OK?"

Everywhere they went—the playground, Frank's hardware, the grocery store—Hope watched the people. Currently, the guy in front of them in the checkout line had an oversized cell phone clipped to his belt on one hip and a hammer looped through a metal ring on the other. The woman behind her verbally double-checked with her kids a list of food for that week's lunches, which apparently did not include the candy they tried to slip past her.

If this town was like most resort areas, Frankfort would soon be flooded with tourists whose brightly-colored clothes screamed vacation, but right now, all Hope saw were real people with real lives. Lives that had a purpose, had come from somewhere, were going somewhere. She had until the end of September when the inn closed to figure out where her own life was going.

When there was space on the conveyor belt, Hope unloaded the groceries that would get them by until their first paychecks: tuna fish, a carton of milk, cereal, four apples, boxes of mac and cheese. She came around to the front of the cart and took the juice boxes Lainie had been guarding in the kid seat. "Good job keeping an eye on these, munchkin."

The cashier, a little bit older than Hope, offered Lainie a sucker from a stash at her till. "Thanks," Hope said and then to Lainie, "It's OK, you can have it."

She swiped her card through the reader and ran a finger over the letters embossed on it. For months, the name Vermeer had been in the news while the accusations and charges were filed and the trial was held, the nightly exposé stories stopping only when the prison bus carried her father away.

College should have been a toe-dip in the pool of adulthood, but instead it had been a full-on shove right into the deep end. Every time she left her dorm room during the trial, Hope had felt the stares, heard the whispers. It wasn't the first time a conservative Christian campus had the daughter of a megachurch pastor as a student. The fact that the daughter sent her father to prison by refusing to lie for him, that was new.

She had considered not testifying. It would have been easier just to not say anything. But what he had done was so obviously wrong, she just couldn't let it go. Hope wasn't even sure who to tell at first, but then everything started rolling, and she couldn't have stopped it even if she wanted to. And then it was done. Sometimes she felt like she was in a movie where the main characters walk toward the camera and in the background a city is crumbling. Building after building falls, and they just keep walking.

The trial brought down her father, her family, and put a serious dent in the church. Nothing was the same anywhere. Hope had not been the one to commit fraud, had not sold religion to the highest bidder like some priest in the Dark Ages. It hadn't been her fault—none of it. And yet, for two years, she had also done the time, just in a different kind of prison.

"Bye fo' now," Lainie said and gave the cashier a wave.

Hope quickly stashed her card, flashed another smile at the woman, and took the receipt. Lainie broke into song about the sucker as Hope loaded the groceries and child into the car. She clicked the straps on the car seat, thinking about what her mother had written in a recent letter.

One thing I've learned through all of this is, you can't do life alone. As much as we think we can handle things, we can't, and we shouldn't expect anyone else to either. I've been spending a lot of time volunteering at a women's shelter, and I read something in their literature the other day that spoke to me: there is purpose in the pain.

Hope started the car and backed out of the parking spot. She wanted to sink into this little town and let it wash over her. She didn't want to think about what had happened, or what needed to happen. If she also had to think about the purpose of it, any of it, her head might just explode.

CHAPTER 4

"You're doing wonderfully." Sylvie perched on the edge of the stool watching Hope roll cinnamon and sugar up into a long tube of dough.

She wasn't used to either of those things, baking or having Sylvie stationary. Especially after Hope's diabetes diagnosis, her mother had done very little baking. It just wasn't a thing for her. They didn't decorate cookies at Christmas, or have more than just their three family birthday cakes in a year.

As for Sylvie sitting down—Hope knew there was something her boss wasn't telling, but it wasn't her place to ask. Be sympathetic but not nosy. That was the rule for anyone vaguely attached to ministry, including the pastor's kid.

She frowned as she cut off the spiraled slices and laid them in the baking pan. "I don't know about these. They look really flat."

"They'll rise up just fine. Give them time."

Sylvie slid carefully off the stool and padded to the stove in her slippers. Another unexpected thing; Hope was used to seeing her in heels.

Sylvie pushed a button and set the oven temperature. "Slide the pan in here, and we'll give it a boost." She rubbed her arms. "It's a little chilly in here for dough to work."

Hope raised her eyebrows. It was not actually chilly. If anything, it was tropical, especially for early May, so maybe the AC was not installed yet. She turned to Sylvie, smiled, and slid the dish into the waiting oven. "I'm feeling sort of accomplished, even if they do come out really wonky."

"A wonky cinnamon roll is still a good cinnamon roll." Sylvie closed the door to the oven and took a bottle of water from the refrigerator. "While these warm up, let's go to the parlor and sit for a while."

In the last week, Sylvie had walked her through not just baking and the online reservation process, but also the calendar of area events through the entire summer, inn packages, and ordering schedules. Things Hope wouldn't need to know working at the desk. Things Sylvie would usually handle.

"I have something to tell you, Hope." They had both eased into the chairs near the fireplace. "I hadn't planned things this way, but I have to go back to Chicago and it looks like I will be away for much of the summer."

Hope's stomach clenched. This could not be good. Was Sylvie OK? Would the inn be closing? What was going on?

"Is everything OK?"

Sylvie smiled. "I'm sure everything will be fine."

Hope fingered the end of her ponytail. Not "everything is OK," but "everything *will be* OK."

"And the inn?"

"Is in very good hands." Sylvie nodded. "Yours."

Hope dropped her hand. "Mine?"

Sylvie shifted her position, uncrossing and recrossing her ankles. "As I said, when I messaged you, I hadn't planned to be gone at all, let alone for several weeks. But I am convinced that you were, and are still, the right person for me to call on."

She should say something, but what? Thank you? No, thank you?

"The inn is brand new," Hope began. "I don't, I mean, I'm not—"

"You are, Hope. You have everything you need. You are enough."

"But, Sylvie..." She hesitated and then blurted out the words. "What if I mess it up?"

"I'll never be more than a phone call away. I promise."

In the foyer, the grandfather clock faithfully and steadily measured time. *Tick, tock, tick, tock.* At least

Sylvie could count on one of them to do their job right. *Tick, tock, tick, tock.* Actually, Hope did have experience working in several areas of the resort. *Tick, tock, tick, tock.* And she was nearly finished with a hospitality management degree. *Tick, tock, tick, tock.* With the intent to actually manage something, someday. *Tick, tock, tick, tock.* And Sylvie was waiting for an answer.

"OK. I mean, thank you. I mean…" Hope shook her head. "I don't know what I mean."

"Perfect." Sylvie laughed, her eyes twinkling. "It's not like I will drop everything in your lap and tell you, 'Good luck.' We will work through all of it together. In fact, this should earn you some credit for extra effort outside your class time. Like a co-op, getting practical experience to round out your book work. I'll tell you all the mistakes I made along the way." She laughed again. "Starting with rescuing those cinnamon rolls before they half bake."

Sylvie kept Hope next to her as she hired the rest of the staff, and explained Hope's role while Sylvie was away. Together they worked out schedules, menus, and set goals for the inn's inaugural season. Sylvie introduced Hope at the Chamber of Commerce Friday at Five. Finally, there was nothing left but to do the thing.

When her mother left for Alaska, just a week after Hope landed on Mackinac, it seemed like an overnight decision. They talked out the details, as many as her mother had known anyway, in a phone call just minutes before her mother boarded her plane. This was definitely a more organized leaving than Hope had with her mother, but losing Sylvie so soon after she had found her again was almost as hard.

"I have some concerns about one of the employees," Hope said.

"Oh?" Sylvie busied herself tying her signature Hermès scarf.

She was wearing a vibrant top and tailored pants that left no room to doubt her authority, even if they didn't hide how thin she had become. Her luggage waited in the Mercedes sedan, ready for whatever Sylvie had to do next. No details were given, and so Hope could think of only bad scenarios.

Sylvie looked at her reflection and patted the knot. "Which employee?"

"The manager of guest services. I don't know if she'll make the cut."

Sylvie nodded to her in the mirror and then settled the Louis Vuitton purse's handle on her forearm. "Let's keep her anyway. There's more to her than you know."

Hope gave her a small smile. "I hope so. I'm going to miss you so much."

"And I you." Sylvie pulled her into a strong hug. "Call me as often as you need. I'll look for the reports. Most of all, Hope, trust your gift of hospitality. It will serve you well."

CHAPTER 5

H ope stood in front of the rows and rows of little square openings, unlocked the one for the inn, and slid out the mail. With Sylvie leaving, all this was on her, even deciding whether or not to keep the weekly flier from Frank's hardware that advertised—what was it this week?—batteries. OK, taking care of the daily flow of the inn was the point of being the manager, but still.

She closed the little door and unlocked her own box. With surprise, she noted there was an envelope with her name printed in her mother's slanty handwriting. Hope had texted her the new address but hadn't known for sure if there was cell service in the Alaskan village so small she could not find it on a map. She slid the envelope into her bag, closed the door, and zipped away the keys.

In the three weeks she had been in town, the traffic had stepped up with RVs lumbering past the inn and out South Shore Drive toward the lighthouse. On her mail runs, Hope had walked both sides of Main Street, getting to know where the shops were in case guests asked. Not everything was open for the season yet, but that morning, the T-shirt shop across the street had put racks of shirts in the window for a soft opening before the weekend.

Her favorite of all the old brick buildings on this street was 408 Main. Hope traced the numbers that had been carved into the tan sandstone almost two hundred years earlier. Warmed by the early afternoon sun, the building felt like a living thing instead of just a historical landmark. She dusted off her fingers, readjusted her ponytail, and waited for the little bit of traffic to pass before crossing the street in eight long strides.

The grandfather clock chimed three times as she stowed her bag behind the antique desk. "Here we go." She took a deep breath and then laughed at herself. She had this. Everything would be fine.

She peeked one more time into the gift bags that she had prepared for the weekend guests. Each one contained wrapped toffees, coupons for ice cream, a tea sachet, and the schedule for the week's music at the park. As she straightened the bow on the last bag, there was a loud crash on the front walk. "That's not going to end well."

She hurried around the desk to open the door and found two women her grandparents' age trying to wrestle big suitcases up the porch steps.

"That thing never rolls right. I don't know why you keep using it," one said.

She was dressed all in black except for a white, loose-weave cover-up. Kind of dramatic for a beach weekend. The other woman seemed more with the program in her flowy top over denim wide-legged boho pants that were dotted with white daisies.

"Hi," Hope called from the doorway. "Can I give you a hand with that?"

"It's a good-sized bag. I can get a lot into it." The second woman lined up the wheels on her case and then smiled up at Hope. "Hello. We're Carla and Candace. I'm Carla."

"Hi," Hope said again. "I'm Hope. Welcome to The Beachview Inn. Sylvie asked me to watch for you." She opened the door wide.

"Oh, is she here?" Candace smoothly rolled her bag past them both into the foyer. "We didn't think we'd see her until next week."

"No, she had to go to Chicago," Hope said, watching Carla's struggle. Should she offer to help her?

Carla finally made it into the doorway. "She does stay busy. We've been to her other place, on Mackinac. The Lilac Inn, wasn't it?" She looked to Candace who nodded. "It was cute, but I already love this place." Carla took in the foyer, then went to the door of the parlor and stopped short. "There's a piano."

Hope moved Carla's bag farther inside and closed the door. "Do you play?"

"She'll tell you no," Candace said, "but don't believe her."

"Just now and then," Carla answered.

Candace tipped her head toward Carla and opened her eyes wide at Hope as if to say, "Don't doubt me. Ever."

"Well, it's yours, whenever." Hope smiled at Carla, wondering if her own face looked as maniacal as she felt. Sylvie liked to give each guest a personal welcome, but right now all Hope wanted was to get these ladies and their bags settled before any other guests arrived. "Would you like to see your rooms?"

"Sylvie sent us pictures," Carla said. "I'd like the blue room."

"Blue it is," Hope said. She glanced at Candace, suddenly feeling like she needed to clear the plan with her.

"Let her have it," Candace said. "She's the baby sister, so she always gets her way."

Hope bet that if there was a 60:40 scenario, Candace and not Carla would be on the winning side.

"Oh, stop it. I'm doing you a favor." Carla shook her head in a sassy way and leaned into Hope. "She hates blue," she said.

"I don't hate it. I just..."

"You hate it."

Hope went to the desk and retrieved the cards she had keyed to each room. She chose two of the gift bags and turned back to the women. "Well, the view is great from both rooms. If you want to leave your luggage down here, I can bring it up in a minute."

She handed a gift bag and keycard to each woman. "I hope the stairs will be OK for you both. Some of our guests have preferred the main floor rooms but Sylvie hand-picked these for you."

"They'll be fine," Candace said crisply. "We're used to steps."

Well, OK then.

Sylvie had done an amazing job with getting The Beachview rooms just right, each one inspired by a unique aspect of the lake. One had a gorgeous painting of the water done by a local artist. Another had a collection of beach glass. Candace's room had an incredible photograph of the lake at sunset.

Hope liked overhearing the guests' first comments about their rooms when they unlocked their doors. The Sisters, Hope decided to call them, were just as excited as she had expected. When she brought up their bags, they were telling each other about some new find. Hope stopped at the door to Carla's room. "Tea is every afternoon at four," she announced, and then added Sylvie's phrase. "I hope you can make it."

Carla glanced at her watch and then at her sister. "We should have time, don't you think?"

"We're staying through July," Candace said from her doorway across the hall. "I think we can fit it in."

Hope took a deep breath and put her face into what she hoped was a smile, but she felt Candace's eyes on her all the way down the stairs. Hope steadied herself

on the desk. Her first day alone, and the first guests
are not only her boss's friends but staying for a month.
Yeah, what could go wrong with that?

CHAPTER 6

Hope laughed as Lainie danced away from every wave and squealed whenever the water sprayed against her legs. With the public beach a short wagon ride from their apartment, she could swim and play in Lake Michigan whenever she wanted. So much better than making Lainie spend all day every day in the tiny, depressing room they had in Boyne.

Lainie was such a beach baby, but mermaid or not, she looked like she was going to be a stinker about bedtime, so Hope let her run along the beach as far as she wanted. Maybe the little muffin would even fall asleep as she bumped along in the wagon on the way home. Wishful thinking.

When Lainie came up to the blanket, Hope pulled out a packet of fruit snacks. She had forgotten to bring any wipes to clean her up, but at least the lake water was better than eating gummies with sandy hands. While Lainie snacked, Hope stretched her legs out and watched the boats come off the water.

For a Thursday night, the channel traffic was busy, and by the looks of it, the little town would be hopping that weekend. A few fishing boats powered down and turned in off the lake, impatiently crowded by the ridiculously yellow go-fast boat. A few minutes later, a couple of sailboats motored in, their empty masts echoing the dead calm of the water's surface.

Lainie grabbed her shovel and scooped sand into a mound. Her princess castles, decorated with shell pieces and pebbles, had become pretty epic. She wanted to be a queen when she grew up, but maybe architecture could be her fallback. Hope shielded her eyes against the sun with a raised hand. A bigger yacht at the channel entrance slowed its motor to limit the wake. Her stomach sank when she saw the flag, a red and white four square. Carsten's boat had flown the same flag, and even though he had never tried to contact her after the summer on Mackinac, she couldn't help the urge to hide.

Before she could stop it, the memory montage started playing. Her walking toward his boat at the Mackinac marina. Carsten standing on the deck looking away from her toward the boat in the next slip. The tan chick in the string bikini propped up on one elbow flirting with him. Her laugh. Her voice sliding the knife into Hope's heart.

Where's your ho'?

She had blocked his calls and not given him a chance to try to explain. It seemed pretty clear to Hope what was going on. *Where's your ho'?* Apparently, to Carsten, she had been more hookup than relationship, so another thing to add to the list of ways Hope was a disappointment.

She could have told Carsten that summer about the trial and her father. She could have explained why she needed whatever they had to be more, to fill in for all that Hope had lost in her life, but she hadn't. Maybe it would have made a difference.

Either way, it needed to be over. For two years she had carried the memory around like a seashell in her pocket, touching its sharp edges, thinking about what had once lived inside its empty chamber. It was time to chuck the memory as far away from her as she could and let it sink deep out of sight.

"Come on, chickie, time to go."

"No." Lainie patted the sand with her shovel. "I don't wanna."

Just as she thought. The little miss was going to be difficult. "If we never leave, we can't get ice cream."

"No." Lainie kept digging with her little shovel.

Hope held out Lainie's favorite purple towel to wrap her up and dry her off. "You don't want ice cream?"

"No. I wanna stay."

"We can't stay. I have to get to bed. Do you want me to be a crab tomorrow?"

Lainie shrugged and put more sand into her bucket. Hope sighed. She really did need to study before the next test. "Your castle is perfect," she said. "I think the princess wants to go to sleep, but she won't be able to if you're still building right outside her window." They had walked by the new lakefront resort going up near the channel, and Lainie rated the hammering, "Way too woud."

"*She* would be a crab," Lainie said.

"Exactly. Do you want me to help you pick up this stuff, or are you going to be a big girl?" The 'big girl' trick might work tonight. It was worth a shot anyway.

"I got this," Lainie said.

As they loaded the wagon, Hope smiled at how much Lainie was a tiny grown-up. At the last minute, Lainie decided she wanted to ride, so she pushed all the shovels and sand toys to one side, climbed in, and announced, "I ready."

"Then we're off, your highness."

Hope carried the little girl into Maya's room and peeled the clammy suit off her. It was too late for a bath, and Lainie's eyelids already fluttered against sleep, so Hope wiped at her sandy feet with a damp towel and pulled a long T-shirt over her head. Lainie rolled over and slid a thumb into her mouth. And, done.

If nothing else, this move would be good for Lainie. Her world was wide open and she had no fear of it. She tried to make friends with every other kid she met on the beach. After realizing the playground came with the amazing bonus of a school, Lainie started taking her crayons and a coloring book to the swings to "learn." Maya had already checked into the state-funded preschool for her.

Hope tucked the wagon and toys under the steps that led to their apartment, then stood on the tiny landing and watched the sun dip behind the houses on South Shore Drive. As far as her own life, this could work. For the first time in a long time, Hope felt like she belonged somewhere, like she could breathe for a minute, and she wanted the minute to last.

What she didn't want was the past to crowd in on her, but it was kind of hard with her mom unpacking their collective history. The end of her last letter had hit hard.

There's one more thing, and you can take all the time you need to decide. Your father wants to write to you. I'm sure your first thought is, absolutely not. But think on it. At least he's reaching out.

Her initial answer was a hard no. What could he possibly want to say now that he hadn't said before? What if he wanted to unload all the anger and venom she had seen on his face during the trial? Hope rubbed her arms against the chill. But, what if, by some miracle, he was actually sorry? She would want to read that, wouldn't she?

CHAPTER 7

Offering people dessert in the middle of the afternoon was win-win, and teatime had become Hope's favorite part of the day. She loved guessing right about which guests would choose tea over coffee and liked listening to their chatter as she set out the eats. The conversation earlier that afternoon had rocked her, though.

Since that first summer on the island, when she wanted distance from anything and everything people had known about Hope Vermeer, working the resort circuit had been perfect. The guests came and went. She didn't know their business, and they didn't know hers. She didn't have to think about the past or the future. But after hearing The Sisters' excitement that day about reliving some childhood memories of Frankfort, Hope wondered if, when she got to be their age, she would be able to look back and find anything she wanted to live over again.

She sighed, lifted a recently delivered package onto the desk, and slit open the top with a pair of scissors. Aside from confirming a September reservation for a guest, the late afternoon had been quiet. Nothing exciting, unless she counted the delivery of this large but lightweight box, which she saw now was just the pillows Sylvie had ordered a few weeks earlier.

Hope took off the packaging and carried the pillows upstairs to the green room that had the corner views of both the channel and the lake. She set the pillows on the bed and went to the window. Hope liked the water best in that last bit of day before the sun went down. A lot of nights there was a stillness that she could relate to as if the lake, too, had had a hard day.

She finished making the bed and was halfway down the stairs when Liam came from the dining room to start his shift. "Hey, how's it going?"

"Pretty slow," she said. "Just an email reservation—one of Sylvie's friends from Chicago." Hope went behind the desk to get her laptop and bag. "I'm going to take off, if you're good."

"Yep. Go for it."

Hope waited for a short Main Street parade of hipster Subarus with top mount bikes and a minivan whose rear mount rack barely corralled the spinning tires and pink and purple handlebar tassels, then crossed over to peek into the still-empty 408 Main Street. She loved so much about the building: the bay window, the high ceiling, the wood floors she guessed must be original. It was the perfect spot for a café.

She bypassed ice cream-holding teens, overstuffed racks of T-shirts, and tables from the sidewalk sale at Frank's. At the corner, she paused at the framed-in condos of the soon to be Harborview Resort. The sun, now low in the sky, struggled to shine through the steel structures whose shadows lay tangled on the ground like a giant spider web. Hope shook off the eerie feeling and turned toward the beach.

Her favorite bench at the beginning of the pier was occupied, this time by a sweet old couple, and it made her a little sad to watch them lean in. Would she ever have something like that? She walked past them to the tree at the edge of the sidewalk, as far from the water as anyone could get and still be at the beach. Hope dropped her bag and lowered herself to rest against the smooth bark of the trunk.

If she was honest, working for Sylvie for a summer was not going to slingshot Hope into the career she had mapped out when she and Sylvie talked on Mackinac. Hospitality management was about hotels, casinos, and resorts. It was not at all the romantic notion Hope had had when she started the degree.

During the trial, she studied for finals at a café in Eastown where no other students went, and it didn't matter that her name was just one syllable on a paper cup, even if it didn't really describe her situation all that well. In terms of actually applying all that she had learned in her HM classes, Hope pictured a place like that café where people could just be. Nothing fake or judgy, just a place to take a few deep breaths before getting back into it, whatever "it" was. A place where her mother could sit and write the letters that were helping her heal and make sense of a world she never meant to be part of.

Hope scooped up a handful of sand and let it slip through her fingers. She had to forget about this café thing. She had zero money for it, and it wasn't even really a thing. It was an infatuation with an old building. Starting a café was at best only a dream, and if she had learned anything growing up, it was that a dream was just another way to fail. She didn't need a dream, she needed to make something of herself. Stop mooching off Maya. Get a job, one that paid for a car and a place to live. After that, if she hadn't totally screwed up, she could look into opening a café. But until then, her primary goal had to be to finish her degree.

CHAPTER 8

Hope watched the fat raindrops plop onto the puddles that had formed for the last two days on the inn's soggy front lawn. There was no way she could ride the bike to get supplies. She actually liked riding the bike for errands, and the big front basket reminded her of working on the island where no cars were allowed. Spending that summer trying to steer around tourists and carriages with her basket full of packages had given Hope pretty good balance. But today, what she really wanted was a car, something she would need anyway.

Plus, she missed her baby blue Prius that had been confiscated with all of the other Vermeer assets.

Where would she look for a car? Honestly, she hadn't noticed if there were any car lots in town. Once they'd reached Frankfort, the farthest away she or Maya had gone was to the grocery store. She opened her phone. Maybe she should start with Marketplace?

She tapped the blue box on her phone screen and nothing happened. Resetting the Wi-Fi connection didn't help either. Her phone had been glitchy lately and apparently was not feeling it today, so Hope pocketed it and walked into the dining room. The week's *Benzie Record Patriot* lay on the sideboard. With all the online options, did people still use classified ads? She sat at the table and paged through the newspaper.

A picture of a black and white dog took up most of the front page, along with a story about a new animal shelter. Maybe someday she'd have a pet, but first things first. The inside pages had columns like "Today in History" and "Farm Report." Moving on. At the bottom of the next page, a border of shoes marched around a request for donations for a women's shelter in Frankfort. They specifically wanted shoes and clothes for the women to wear for interviews.

Hope sat back. More than once after a closet purge, she and her mother had dropped things off at a place in downtown GR, and some of the clothes still had the price tags attached. She sighed. Her father may have bent and broken commandments left and right, and even though anything she got had to pass through the filter of whether or not it would make him look good, she still had had all the bling. Her own credit card at sixteen, a new car at seventeen, private college paid for at eighteen. She went on trips and even had lined up a European study abroad for her junior year before she dropped out. Growing up, she had never been hungry, out of gas or out of clothes.

It was coming full circle now as she worked for every dollar in her account and chose her car based on how much it cost and not by how cute it was. She ripped out the corner of the page that listed the shelter's name and address. Maybe there would be something she could do to pay back the universe.

Finally, she came to the classified ads and found one car listed. The mileage was kind of high and the car was almost as old as she was, but she could afford it. Hope tore the ad out and laid it next to the shelter piece. There must be some kind of metaphor there about life, something like Hope Past and Hope Present. But what about Hope Future?

Her laptop was doing better with the Wi-Fi than her phone, so she opened the report she needed to edit for her class. A few minutes later, the notification of a new email slid onto the document. Subject: *You're Almost There.* Hope clicked open her email.

Dear Hope Vermeer:

With just one class to be completed, your degree is so close! Look for an email regarding a new tuition structure for fall semester, and keep up the good work! You're almost there!

Almost immediately, a second email hit her inbox. Hope read it and then reread it. One hundred and fifty dollars tacked onto the tuition? She opened another tab, checked the balance on her savings account, and scowled. What was going on?

It had been three months since she had last made a tuition payment out of the account, and an inactive account fee had been subtracted from her balance every month since then. That had to be a mistake. She scrolled down to the bottom of the statement where in small font, she found the answer: the balance was low enough to accrue monthly charges. She scrolled up and double-checked the balance. As if it would magically change. After the fees and the tuition increase, she would be short.

She needed that class, and if she didn't take it this semester, she would have to wait another year for it to be available. Hope took the elastic band out of her hair and pressed her fingertips into her scalp to rub out the pain. How could this be happening? And why now? In the lower corner of her screen, the tiny clock ticked away her life. It was time for afternoon tea.

As Hope arranged the different tea sachets in their compartments, she mentally sorted through her checking and savings accounts. No matter how she moved the figures around, there was not enough money. She stood up straight and lifted her hair off her neck, but it didn't give her any freedom from the lingering humidity, or the weight of The Consequences. Her plan to stay in Frankfort, living a real life—was an empty bank account The Consequence for that decision?

She could hear guests moving around upstairs. They would be on their way down in a few minutes. Hope put her hair back up in its high bun and pulled the newspaper ad from her pocket. Having no money meant she would definitely have to give up this café delusion of hers, and honestly, the whole Frankfort dream, starting first with the car. She crumpled the paper into a tiny ball and threw it away. By the time the inn closed in the early fall, she would need to move on with her life.

CHAPTER 9

Hope reached above the refrigerator for the tray, tucked it under her arm, and pushed through the swinging door into the dining room. Breakfast for The Sisters had been fruit salad and an egg dish baked in cupcake pans that, after several attempts in their apartment oven, she had finally gotten to look like little muffins.

"These were delicious, Hope! I love the chives. They made each bite electric."

"Thanks, Carla." She set the tray on the sideboard. "It's so great to have a little space in the garden for herbs.

'Fresh always tastes best.' That's what a chef I used to work with would say."

"Wise woman," Candace said. She drank the rest of the water in her glass. "Or man, I suppose." She refilled the tall glass with water and set the carafe down hard on the table.

Hope noticed Carla watching her sister silently. Candace *was* acting a little strange. Usually, she sipped black coffee with breakfast, and Hope was always amazed at the way she could place her cup on the saucer without a sound.

"Hope?" Candace asked. She seemed totally oblivious to Carla staring at her. "Is there a sandwich shop hereabouts? We didn't notice one here or in Beulah."

Hope thought for a moment. "The grocery store has a deli bar where you can buy premades, but no actual shop."

"That's something that would be really busy here, I would think," Carla said, finally moving her attention away from her sister. "How convenient to leave the beach, pop in for a sandwich, and get back to the water. No big cooler to lug around, or sand in the mayo." She made a face like something gritty was on her tongue.

"True," Candace said. She took another drink of water. "So, what's the timeline on the resort, Hope? Anyone know?"

"They dug a second hole last week," she answered, "but I haven't seen anything else yet. But then, I'm not really watching it, either."

"You do stay pretty busy here at the inn," Candace said.

"And with your little girl," Carla added. "We've seen you two at the beach a couple of times in the evening."

"Oh, that's my roommate's daughter," Hope said. "I watch her when her mom's working."

"That's very nice of you, Hope," Candace said. She finished the water in her glass.

Carla gave Hope a relieved look. "When we were young, all the cousins would come to Gran's house for a few weeks in the summer. We kids used to have so much fun on the beach at night. Maybe even more than during the day when it was so busy. Remember that, Candace?"

Candace's nod was simple and to the point after Carla's gush. Hope looked from one sister to the other, waiting for more from either of them, but this seemed like one of those times they just seemed to know each other's thoughts without talking. "So," she said, "where are you off to today?"

"Today we're going to be tourists!" Carla said.

Candace shot her a kind of "watch yourself" eyebrow raise. "We're going to see the dunes on a trolley out of Empire."

Hope glanced at Carla's sudden smoothing of an invisible wrinkle in the tablecloth. Interesting. "I've heard about that from other guests," she said, turning to Candace. "Sounds like a fun time."

The two women, almost in unison, laid their napkins on the right side of their plates and rose from the table.

"Goodbye, hon." Carla gave her arm a little squeeze as she walked past. "We won't see you at tea today."

"OK. Enjoy."

Candace went ahead of her sister into the foyer. "We'll stop at the grocery store first for supplies."

The other guests had checked out on Sunday morning, which left a lot of time before the Wednesday guests came in. Hope did the little bit of cleaning needed for just those two, trying to prove to herself that she was at least adequate at that. Afterward, she pulled out her laptop to study, but Candace's questions came back to her. There wasn't really a sandwich take-out option in Frankfort. Yet. What if the inn offered a boxed lunch to the guests? With a day's notice, a list of easy menu options, a cute cooler bag...

The details came to her as fast as she could type them in. She checked prices on the food service supplier's website, packaged the whole idea, paused for a moment, and then emailed it to Sylvie. According to the schedule Sylvie sent after her diagnosis, this was a chemo infusion week. It might take some time to hear back from her.

A few minutes later *Love it!* popped up on her phone's notification bar. She opened Sylvie's reply to find links for lettering fonts and a tote. And, bonus, the boxed lunch idea was perfect for her stalled marketing class project, so another win.

Hope started a list of menu options for the box lunches and made some notes to follow up on once she had more time. For now, she wanted to get her ideas down, but her thoughts kept going back to The Sisters. She was getting used to the sharp tone Candace used with almost every conversation, but even so, something was off with both of them. She just couldn't figure out what.

On the clock's twelfth chime for noon, Hope heard voices on the porch. She waited a minute for someone to come in the door and then went to check it out. Candace was slumped in one of the wicker chairs as Carla frantically waved a small notebook in front of her face.

"Is everything OK?"

"Oh, Hope. I don't know what to do." Carla was nearly in tears. "We started off for the trip, but Candace wasn't feeling well, so I drove. She drank all the water we each had, and she's not acting right, so I came back."

Candace had a faraway look in her eyes that Hope had seen before. In the mirror. "Is Candace diabetic?" she asked.

"No. Her doctor has been watching her ABC, but she would have told me if it was worse."

"Her A1C?" This was way above Hope's paygrade, but she asked anyway. "Do you know what it was and when it was checked?"

"Seven," Candace said. Her voice was clear, but weak. "I'm fine. I just need to lie down." She pushed her hand against the arm of the chair and then sat back.

Hope blew out her cheeks. She had to do something. "I'm diabetic," she said. "I think you are having a crisis and should go to the urgent care."

Candace waved her off, but Hope pressed it. The woman would probably refuse an ambulance, but maybe she would agree to a finger poke. "I've got my glucometer inside. Would you at least be OK with me checking your blood sugar?"

"Candace, you've got to let her help you." Carla fanned faster.

"All right, fine." Candace sighed. "Go ahead."

Hope snatched her bag and fumbled for the lancet and strip. As many times as she had done this to herself without thinking, she was suddenly conscious of every step she needed to take.

She knelt in front of Candace, wiped her fingertip with an alcohol pad, and watched the tiny blood droplet seep onto the test strip. Twenty seconds later, they had the answer: Candace's blood sugar was over what the glucometer could measure.

Hope stood up. "I can either drive you or call an ambulance," she said, "but you have to see a doctor, and you need to go right now."

CHAPTER 10

For early evening on a Tuesday, Frankfort was a ghost town. The forecast was for gale force winds and it was like everything and everyone had blown away. Hope held her hair back with a hand and hurried across the street, not even waiting to get to the crosswalk. There was no traffic and The Sisters' car was the only one parked on Main Street. The trees swayed wildly in the wind and she wished there was a garage or something to offer them. After an overnight in urgent care and a few days on insulin, Candace was back "at home" with regulated blood sugar, but Hope was sure another minor disaster was not in the woman's plans.

Hope took the front steps in two and set the security lock on the front door, even though if the power went out, it would be useless. She texted Sylvie about the storm and waited for the reply. When they Facetimed a few days earlier Hope had been shocked to see her boss's thick, glorious hair gone from the chemo and Sylvie's high cheekbones looking more skeletal than glam.

A notification dinged. *Can you stay until it lets up? I don't want them alone if the power goes out.*

Sure, she replied. Hope put away her bag and went to the closet for lanterns. During the last storm, she was alone in the inn, in the dark. The next day, she went to Frank's and probably overbought on the size D batteries, but this time she was prepared.

After setting out the lanterns in the parlor and dining room and flicking the five flashlights on and off, she went to the kitchen to fill water jugs. Her stomach churned like the water that swirled in the plastic container and then overflowed the jug. She shut off the tap and hoisted the big, dripping container out of the sink and thudded it onto the counter.

She debated, then put the second jug in the sink and turned on the tap. The off-key tone sounded from the TV in the parlor, and Hope turned off the water and went to listen to the advisory.

The National Weather Service has issued a severe storm warning until eight o'clock p.m. for the following counties...

The voice added the conditions were favorable for a tornado and instructed them to be ready to take shelter in a lower level. Hope thought of the creepy cellar at the side of the inn. She had peeked in there once when she had to open it up for the pesticide company to spray, and she'd rather chance the tornado than make The Sisters crawl around in there.

"We've been watching the lake from my window," Carla said from the parlor doorway. "It's quite beautiful."

"Do you need any help?" Candace asked.

Hope turned toward them. "I think everything's good. There are some flashlights on the bottom step." She led them into the foyer and pointed out the lanterns she had set out in each room. "And these on the first floor. I've got some water in jugs. I guess all that's left is to wait and see how bad it gets." Wasn't that the story of her life?

"It's a perfect night to pull out the fuzzy blankets and cozy in," Carla said.

"Would you like me to make coffee, or water for tea?" Hope asked them.

"Tea would be nice," Candace said. "We haven't had a storm like this since we were kids. Do you remember that, Carla? We were camping, and Dad woke us up in the middle of the night. We left our tent and everything behind and drove to a twenty-four-hour place like Denny's until it blew over."

"My new sleeping bag was all muddy when we got back," Carla frowned. "The whole tent was flooded. It was a mess."

The Sisters had followed her into the kitchens as they talked. "Did you guys camp a lot?" Hope asked. The closest she had come to that was the summer on the island, if you could count sleeping on a blanket on the beach camping.

"It's one of our favorite memories with our dad," Carla said. "How about you, Hope? What did your family do when you were young? Well, you're still young—when you were younger."

Just stay here so you don't get your dress dirty.

Bring your art bag. You can color in Dad's office during the meeting.

We are the pastor's family. Sometimes you have to do things you don't like.

"We weren't a camping family, I guess you could say," Hope answered. "We had people over to our house a lot, and my father...worked weekends."

"Oh," Carla said brightly. She tore open an Earl Grey packet.

Thunder boomed, and Hope flinched. She had never liked storms. Their house in Grand Rapids had been in a gated community. Super safe against crime, but not safe enough to keep straight line winds, whatever those were, from ripping up the landscaping of the house across the street.

"That sounded like it was just upstairs." Candace's attention shifted to the ceiling like a lightning bolt might come through next.

Hope took a deep breath and smiled. "Anyone want to stress eat?"

"How about some music," Candace said. "Less calories in that."

Carla picked up her teacup and started toward the parlor. "I know just the piece."

Candace settled into the wing chair and Hope stood at the doorway wishing she had gotten the fireplace ready.

"I always have to meet the piano," Carla said, sliding onto the bench. She played a run of notes and pushed the pedals before she seemed properly introduced.

"What will you play?" Candace asked.

Carla winked at her sister. "I think you know."

Thunder cracked even louder, and suddenly, everything went black. Hope shuffled her feet and held her arms out, feeling for the furniture, and feeling stupid for not bringing a flashlight in with her.

Click. Light glimmered from a lantern on the table next to Candace. "I'm glad you set these out, Hope. You thought of everything."

Carla did a flourish on the piano and then started the piece. It was jazzy and sort of familiar, but not quite. Hope paused and then sat on the ottoman near Candace. She took a deep breath and let it out quietly. The music made her feel something she hadn't in so long, like she could let go of her desperate hold on everything.

"*His Eye is on the Sparrow*," Candace said when Carla finished. "Perfect choice."

"I really like that arrangement. Spices it up compared to what we sang in church when we were in children's choir."

That's where she had heard it. Some fuzzy memory surfaced of an equally fuzzy-haired lady playing the piano in her Vermeer grandparents' little church. A six-year-old Hope sitting through the service next to her grandmother, trying not to kick her feet on the hard wooden pew. Hope had liked being there, even if she didn't understand her grandfather's sermon or the big words in the hymns. This one about the sparrow, though, she got.

"Hope." Candace had turned to face her straight on. "I haven't said what I needed to say." She paused. "Thank you for making me see the doctor last week."

"I didn't really—"

"You saved my life. I have no doubt."

"She's right, hon." Carla took a seat in the other chair. "I couldn't even think, but you knew exactly what to do." She looked to her sister and back to Hope. "God's eye may be on the sparrow, but we are so grateful that He made sure yours was on Candace."

CHAPTER 11

As promised, the rain had started just as Hope left the apartment to start breakfast at the inn. The sky was clear all summer, and now, torrential rains twice in one week? Weather, according to the older man at Frank's when she brought it up, was a real thing this close to the lake and not just a way to make conversation.

Whatever. By the time she got this quiche in the oven, both she and the kitchen would be melting in the June humidity. The bakery's delivery that morning was really tempting, but what if the flaky pastries glommed into a big lump of clay before the guests came downstairs? Well, the weather was what it was. She would just have to make everything else as good as it could be.

The rain sheeted against the windows, and thunder cracked overhead like a whip. Hope headed to the foyer to make sure the umbrellas were ready, if anyone actually wanted to go out in that mess. She couldn't imagine how it would be during this kind of storm on one of those big cargo ships she and Lainie had seen on the lake headed for Chicago.

"I am going to regret parking so far away."

Hope turned to the stairway and smiled at Anjelica, another of Sylvie's friends. The woman probably had very few regrets in her life. Her weaves were braided into a complex piece of art, and style wafted from her like perfume.

"I wish I could offer you valet service, but all I've got is coffee," Hope said. "Or tea," she added quickly, in case herbal tea was more Anjelica's vibe.

"I will take that coffee. Straight up."

Hope moved to the sideboard, poured a mug and handed it to Anjelica. "Breakfast will be right out."

"Take your time, I'm in no rush," she answered in her sleek, velvety voice.

"I thought you had an early meeting," Hope said.

"You know, those men can just wait until I get there. I'm the one they answer to."

"Good for you," Candace said from the dining room doorway. "That's exactly what we need more of."

"Settle down, now," Carla said. "This is not one of your lectures." She set a sachet into one of the teacups, poured in water, then turned and carefully set her cup and saucer on the table. "Good morning, Hope."

In the resorts, no one had cared about her name or her family or where she was from. That was the whole point of the service industry—to be invisible, yet pleasing—and Hope had spent her whole life training for just that. "Good morning, ladies," she answered. "Help yourself to the fruit. I'll be back in a few minutes with the hot dishes."

Hope pulled the quiche out of the oven to rest before cutting. She loaded a tray with croissants, butter, and the locally-made strawberry jam. As she brought it to the dining room, she caught a bit of the conversation.

"We grew up during the beginning of women's rights," Candace was saying, "so we didn't have a lot of role models."

"My mother was the first woman in her family to go to college," Anjelica said. "Nobody knew how to even talk to her when she went back home to the neighborhood."

Hope carried their words with her into the kitchen. Her friends' moms and almost every woman she had known from church had all gone to college for at least one year. Her own mother had been a student at Cornerstone for a few semesters before getting married, but Hope had no idea what her life plan had been.

"In our grandmother's day, it was unheard of for a woman to be in business for herself," Carla said.

Hope moved the plates, each one holding the triangle of quiche and a garnish of parsley, onto the sideboard. Just because her degree prepared her to work at a big hospitality company didn't mean she actually had to work for one. Maybe she could work for herself. Women did it all the time now; look at Sylvie. Hope sighed to herself. But she wasn't Sylvie.

"So true," Anjelica said. "No one back then thought women could do much for themselves. What kind of business did your grandmother have?"

Candace laid her silverware across her empty plate. "She owned the general store here in Frankfort, but the building's gone now. I think the fire happened a few years after she sold it. Then she invested in utilities, which you can imagine was pretty forward-thinking when some people didn't even have cars."

"By the time she died, she was a very wealthy woman," Carla added. "And one of the wisest people I've ever met. She used to say, 'Have faith in yourself, and others will, too.'"

"Very good advice." Anjelica laid her napkin next to her empty plate. "Thank you, ladies, for some great conversation. It looks like the rain may let up after all."

"Please drive carefully," Carla urged. She laid her hand across her chest as if Anjelica's driving would somehow endanger her personally.

Anjelica nodded. "You all take care, now. Thank you, Hope."

"You're welcome. Can I help you with your bag?" They walked to the foyer where Anjelica's luggage waited at the bottom of the stairs.

"No, I'll be fine. Please give Sylvie my best." She eased on her full-length raincoat, which made her look even more glam. "Tell her I'm sorry I missed her this time."

Hope nodded. "I will. Goodbye." She closed the door and leaned against it, looking around the foyer where every piece of furniture, every picture, every vase of flowers was hand-picked. Sylvie served her guests, but she was not a servant. Neither was Anjelica, and probably not The Sisters' grandmother either.

She took her mother's letter out of her bag and unfolded it.

Hi, honey:

Sorry I haven't written in a while. Right now, I'm in northern Alaska, and we're having twenty hours of daylight this month, so I'm awake. A lot. Anyway, I've been doing some thinking during all these hours that I'm not sleeping. Thinking about you and how sorry I am for where you ended up. Not where you are physically. I'm glad to hear you're back with Sylvie and loving the inn. I mean, the headspace you ended up in.

There's a difference between caring for people and being consumed by them, and we crossed that line a long time ago. I'm sorry I allowed that to happen to you. I only hope you can get past growing up under the microscope, and all that criticism and judgment, and find a healthy way to use those gifts you have been given.

Living in fear of The Consequences had made her feel like she never did enough, like she never was enough. For Anjelica's mother and The Sisters' gran, it would have been easier to keep their heads down and stay quiet, just like she had. Instead, these women had done the hard things, had written their own stories. So maybe she could, too. There had to be more she could do. More she could be.

CHAPTER 12

After breakfast, Carla announced, "It looks like this will be an inside day, which is all right. We've done a lot of driving."

"You ladies have had a busy schedule by the sounds of it," Hope said. "I hope a day off is OK." She gathered the plates and loaded them onto her tray.

"It's fine," Candace said.

Hope smiled. "I'll make more coffee. It should be ready in a few minutes."

She carried the dirty dishes to the kitchen and put them in the dishwasher while the coffee perked. The stream of coffee stopped and Hope pulled the pot out. She refilled the carafe and started the hot water pot before going back to the dining room.

"Here you go. I've got the water going in case you want tea later."

"Thank you, hon."

Carla had called her that since the second day of their stay. Carla reminded Hope of Ellen, one of the few ladies at her home church she had actually liked. A lot of the others were either too shy around The Pastor's Family, or else Hope felt like they were watching for her to slip up. Ellen had been different; she had been nice.

"Hope, we noticed you studying." Candace sipped her coffee.

"Oh." She had tried to squeeze in as much studying as she could, but had she messed up? "Was there something you needed me to do? Sylvie said it was OK, as long as the guests were settled. But if—"

"No, no," Carla said quickly. "We just wondered what you were studying."

"Oh, good." She put her hands in the pockets of the frilly apron Sylvie had sent. "I'm finishing a hospitality management program."

The Sisters glanced at each other. "We haven't been to this area in a few years. Is there a college near here?" Candace asked.

"No, I've been taking the classes online. I've, um, moved a lot over the last few years, and it was just easier than going in person."

"That would be convenient," Candace agreed. "So, you're finishing up. What will you do next?"

Hope reached out to straighten the caddy that held the little packets of sugar and stevia. "Well, I'm not sure yet. After the season ends in September, Sylvie will close up."

"I meant, what will you do with your degree?"

The image of 408 popped into her head. She could smell the scent of baking cinnamon rolls, hear the hiss of the espresso machine. "I always thought it would be fun to own a café." Oh, God. She had said that out loud.

"Hope, that's a wonderful idea!" Carla leaned forward, her hands folded under her chin like a kid waiting for a surprise.

"Would you stay in Frankfort?" Candace asked.

"Oh. I'm not...I mean...It's really just more of a fantasy? I guess?"

The Sisters looked at each other again. What would it be like to have someone you could talk to without saying anything?

"Hope," Candace said, "would you mind if we talked to you about this later?"

Hope straightened. "Oh, sure. You probably want to get your day started."

"No, hon, we mean when you've done whatever you need to do this morning, would you come get us? We really want to hear your plans." Carla laid a hand on Hope's arm. "Only if it's OK with you."

Hope felt like she was standing at the edge of a cliff, where jumping off was safer than turning back. "OK," she heard herself saying, "I'd like that."

The conversation with The Sisters played on repeat in her head all afternoon. She had told them everything. Her dream of the café. Her obsession with 408, even though from the outside, the walls looked like they were ugly-crying and just inside the big front window, flies had died trying to escape. Still, it was so perfect.

She could fantasize about this all day long, but where would she even start? Where would she get the money for any of it? She was trying to be realistic, but the problem was, the more Hope tried to push away the thought of the café, the stronger it returned. It reminded her of the loons she had seen on her last trip to the beach. The birds dove under the water's surface and stayed down for a long time. Just when she almost forgot about them, they popped up somewhere else.

She had Googled the birds and learned they could dive down more than two hundred feet and stay submerged for almost five minutes, fishing for their dinner. Maybe she should do the same with her idea. Let it swim around for a while, get its belly full. Then see where and when it raised its head above water.

As Hope reached the corner on her way home from the inn, a family loaded down with totes and floats bounced into her.

"Sorry!" the mother said, her hand tugging on the shoulder of the boy in front of her. "Jeremy, walk behind your sister. We're so sorry."

"It's OK," Hope said, her face involuntarily springing into its summer perma-smile. She watched them ooze down the sidewalk like some kind of sun-screened amoeba. Then she glanced at 408, envisioning the mother popping in for an after-beach iced coffee and a muffin to split between the kids. This café idea would not leave her alone. She turned back to face the inn and her real life. "Get it together, Hope."

CHAPTER 13

Hope had given in. All of the café details that had flown around her head like little birds now perched in the boxes of a spreadsheet. She had flinched at the budget when it was small, and now it grew larger with every new entry. She closed out of the program and put away her laptop.

It was time to get things around for tea, something she had done nearly every day all summer long. Today, though, every move she made seemed like it was happening both in the present and in the future, like two parts of her life were exactly overlapping. Hope poured the hot water into a carafe and pushed the brew button on the coffee maker. She went into the dining room, still thinking of more details.

"Hi, Hope." Carla turned from the table. She pointed to a transparent vase-like centerpiece threaded with fine pastel streaks. "Is this new?"

"Yes," Hope said. "Just came today. It's by a glassblower Sylvie met last year at a festival."

"It is stunning," Carla said. "So much motion in this coloring."

Hope couldn't help but smile at the woman. Carla had that effect on not just her; Hope had seen the other guests do the same.

"My sister will be down soon."

"OK." Hope continued laying out the caddy as she and Carla chatted. She went back to the kitchen a few times for teacups, pastries, and the tray of artisanal cheese Sylvie had sent. She was so lucky to work for someone who so carefully prepared for the guests' needs, even including a keto-friendly option. Another little bird to add to the spreadsheet.

Both sisters had chosen tea and settled into their usual seats. "And how are you, Hope?" Candace asked.

"I'm good. Where did you explore this morning?" These ladies had covered some serious real estate during their stay.

"Oh, today was a little business trip," Carla said. "Every so often real life finds you, even on vacation." Hope loved her laugh, like someone running a hand over the tinkly keys of a piano.

"Have you thought any more about the café plans?" Candace asked.

Hope took a deep breath. "I have, but I just don't know. I mean, I don't have any money to put toward it. I'm probably not even the right person to start something like that."

Candace frowned, and the *tink* of her cup hitting its saucer startled both Carla and Hope.

"To be honest," Candace said, "I don't like to hear you talk like that, like you aren't capable or a good fit for this kind of endeavor." She steepled her fingers and leaned forward. "Sure, it takes money, but the energy and the passion are what make a business work. And you bring those."

Hope fiddled with one of her rings.

"Could we pray for you, Hope?" Carla asked.

Here it came: the prayer-lecture. *God, help her to know Your Will is (fill in the blank) and keep her from (fill in another blank). We know You have a plan, blah, blah, blah.* She had heard this a thousand times, either for herself or someone asking her father for guidance. The blanks were always whatever the pray-er wanted the pray-ee to hear but using The Voice of God to say it.

"Sure," Hope answered. Whatever.

The women each laid a hand on Hope's arms and Carla prayed over her for understanding, courage, and peace in the decisions she would be making. So many things could change. They were already changing, but maybe now she would get to choose. Not just cups and napkins, but how her life could go without someone else telling her what was possible.

No one had ever prayed for her like this, not even her mother. For sure not her father. His silence during the trial, and the way he wouldn't even look at her told her he thought she would always be a big disappointment.

Carla gave Hope's arm a little squeeze. "Amen."

Hope took a deep breath and looked at each of them. "Thank you." She had no idea what would happen, or if anything could happen, but with Carla and Candace in her corner, though, it felt like she just might have a chance.

CHAPTER 14

Lainie was finally asleep. With the inn filled up the last few weeks, Hope had had little time to study for the final. She pulled out her laptop and clicked on the portal. There was a soft thud on the landing, and then Maya pushed the door open with two full grocery bags in her arms.

"Hey," Hope said, getting up to help her. OK, so maybe no studying at all. "I thought you were done at eleven."

"Marty found someone else to cover for Therese tonight so he wouldn't have to pay me overtime."

"O-kay." Strange. Usually, Maya would have been irritated about losing the cash from waitressing an extra shift, but tonight she didn't care?

"So anyway," Maya said, closing the refrigerator door.

"Yeah?" When Maya didn't say anything more, Hope turned from the upper cupboard they used as a pantry.

Maya reached up and brushed her hair back. A tiny sparkle caught the light.

"What is that?" Hope grinned at her. "He asked you?"

"He did." She stepped toward Hope. "I was going to text you, but—"

"Let me see that." Hope took Maya's hand and studied the ring. "It's perfect."

"I know, right?" Maya turned her hand to get the light. "He totally surprised me with it."

Hope wasn't shocked, at least not about Marty. He had been crushing on Maya since before Hope started at Boyne. Maya was the real surprise. After the disaster that was Lainie's father, she had sworn off men, and Maya was as strong-willed as she was beautiful. But Marty must have found the way to melt her heart into this puddle.

Hope laughed and put the "fishies," Lainie's faves, on the shelf. "No wonder he didn't want to pay you overtime," she said. "That thing's huge."

"It's not huge," Maya said. She took two cans of soup from the bag and passed them to Hope. "Anyway..." she said again.

Hope waited for Maya to hand her something more, either the groceries or the words.

Maya's mouth twisted on itself. "OK, here's the straight talk. I'm moving in with him when our lease is up."

The landlord had sent them an email a few days before, telling them he had to change his plans for the winter and go south. The house and their apartment would not have heat or utilities while he was gone, which meant they would have to move. Now with Maya and Lainie leaving...

"I'm sorry." Maya flinched.

"What sorry?" Hope said. "It's all good. Go. I can find a roommate. I mean, I'll miss you and Lainie, but I'll be fine."

"Are you sure?"

"Yes. I'm serious." Hope swatted at the thoughts buzzing around her mind. Maybe her mother would move back and they could get a place together. Probably not in Frankfort, but anything was better than nothing, right? Otherwise, how would she afford this by herself? Where would she even work when the inn closed? And, Maya and Lainie had been her little family. How would she do this, all of it, without them?

Her favorite bench was occupied, again, so she wandered out to the water's edge and walked on the firm, wet sand, sometimes letting the water catch her feet. She moved up the shoreline past the moored boats that belonged to the houses on the bluff. They reminded her of the beach day that her summer youth choir had spent at a house like these, owned by someone's grandparents.

Hope reached the driftwood log and sat down. It was technically on private property, but as many times as she had come this far down the beach, she had never seen anyone in the water. The lake spread out before her, its frothy edge reaching for her and then backing away. The words to one of the songs from the choir tour came into her head comparing grace to an ocean and everyone sinking.

Grace was one of those church words you never heard anywhere else. She wasn't even sure what the word actually meant, let alone wanting to sink in it. She guessed the word picture was supposed to mean there was more than enough for everyone, rather than meaning a person could drown to death in grace. Although that was how it felt.

If people only knew that what went on behind the doors of the pastor's house was totally different from the perfect family image her father wanted everyone else to see. Well, there was no hiding anything now, not while he sported a bright orange jumpsuit. But his new suit was nothing compared to the failure and guilt that he had made Hope wear all her life. It was invisible, but it was there.

She picked up a pebble and threw it. She watched the ripples disappear as the next wave crested. The sound of music came from the bluff behind her and Hope turned expecting to see someone. No one was there.

She knew the words to this song, too; had heard them over and over the summer on tour with her youth choir group. It was the money shot, the song played during every love offering, inspiring people to make a donation reflective of their personal faith. The lyrics were to remind them they could feel loved, strong, held, even when they fell short of the ideal. The chorus ended with "and I believe."

Did she? Did she believe there was a God who really thought that of her? Who cared anything about her? As a little girl, she had hoped God would be like her father. Later, she hoped He would be nothing like her father. Eventually she hoped for nothing at all.

The song kept playing behind her, and she thought about the words. What would it be like to totally give up? To take her hands off the wheel and see where her life went. To just walk out there with nothing and say she believed. Candace's scare and Sylvie's unplanned chemotherapy practically shouted what Hope already knew: life was short and nothing was guaranteed. Even though it didn't feel like it now, maybe this whole move to Frankfort was a sign. Maybe God was telling her to go for it, all of it, and that for once, He would handle the consequences.

CHAPTER 15

Hope scanned the balances in her bank accounts. For some reason never entirely clear to Hope, a plaque in the women's bathroom at her home church had reminded everyone as they washed their hands, *Whatever you do, work at it with all your heart, as working for the Lord.* Based on what she saw on her screen, just to simply exist, she had to make some money working for someone human.

With Maya moving out, she couldn't afford an apartment alone, so as far as she could see her only choice until she graduated was another resort job, hopefully one with staff housing. She clicked over to the Crystal Mountain site. Even if there wasn't housing, it was the closest place to Frankfort, so when she got a car, if she got a car, it would not be hard to come back and see Maya and Lainie. A metropolitan hotel or another northern resort wouldn't give her that. She checked the time. Several guests were checking in that afternoon, and she still had the errands to run.

As Hope walked to the post office, she sorted through other scenarios. Maybe if she asked, her grandparents would renew their offer. If her mother would consider coming back to Michigan that would definitely open up some options. She could look for some postings closer to Kalamazoo or even GR if her mom was willing to go back there again. At this point, everything was on the table.

She retrieved the mail for the inn, then unlocked her own box and took out the envelope. Perfect timing. She could scope out her mother's current status and possible future plans. Hope slid it into her bag, and then fished it out again and walked over to one of the post office sorting tables. She had to get traction on this job thing.

Hope unfolded the letter, and a photo fell out onto the counter. She almost didn't recognize her mother, smiling like Hope had not seen for a long time, her arm wrapped around a totally buff dog that was all black except for a jagged hairless streak down the side of his face. She set the pic aside and smoothed out the letter.

Hi from Seward:

To stand at the base of the mountains, or look out onto the ocean—I can't even tell you how beautiful it is and how small it makes my problems seem.

This is Pacino. He's very sweet and a rescue, which seemed appropriate. He got a little chewed up in his pre-vious life, and I felt like we could relate. We're traveling in a rental RV with a group of nomads who have taught me a lot about survival. It feels good to have people around me that have my back.

That was true—it did feel good. If her mother had support from anyone like Maya and Sylvie, she was in a good place. Hope picked up the pic again. This new look for her mother was a good one. Gone was the plastic clip her mother had used to restrain her hair. Instead, the photo captured how the wind lifted her mother's curls, setting them free.

Hope reread the letter. This sounded more like her mom was going off-the-grid on purpose and less like she planned to catch the next flight home. She sighed, refolded the letter, and put it all in her bag. So much for her mom being the answer to her problem.

Like she had so many times, Hope let herself be drawn down the sidewalk to 408. Even just touching the brick had been centering over the past few weeks. But not today. Hope stood in front of the large window and stared at the sign that read *For Sale* in huge red letters. There was a realty company listed and a phone number. For the right price, someone could, and would, buy her dream.

For two weeks, Hope smiled as she served tea, made reservations, and did all the things. Like if she reversed *If You're Happy and You Know it,* and let her face really show it, she would get somewhere close to happy. It wasn't working. She found the most depressing playlist she could and listened to it over and over, just so she knew someone else had things worse.

Honestly, she had asked for this that day at the beach when she basically told God to take the wheel. When everything starts to fall apart, it's pretty clear that the answer from the universe is *Stop. Just. Stop.* Hope took the inn's kitchen laundry out of the dryer and dumped it onto the prep table, suddenly aware of a loud beeping coming from outside. She met The Sisters at the front door.

"There is a big crane in the middle of Main Street," said Carla. "I saw it from Candace's window."

"O-kay." Hope drew out the word.

The three of them went out to the sidewalk, which was now standing room only. The street was closed to traffic, and the giant crane sat at the entrance to the beach parking.

Hope turned to Kendrick from the brew garden. "What's going on?"

"Looks like they're gonna knock something down." He pointed to the wrecking ball hanging from the top of the crane.

Her mouth was instantly cotton. No. No, no, no. "Did you know about this?"

Kendrick nodded. "I mean, kinda. We got an email last night around seven. Street parking closed between one and four p.m. today."

Hope groaned. Email was at the bottom of her long morning chore list and she hadn't read them yet. She couldn't move, like she was in a dream and couldn't wake up. All she could do was watch the big, iron ball swing like a hypnotist's watch. Suddenly the crane turned on its base and crept toward the end building on the block. Creepy music played in her mind like a psychotic version of New Year's Eve as the ball rose and then dropped squarely onto the roof of 408.

She was aware of The Sisters, one on each side, Carla's arm around her waist. Over and over the ball jerked and fell, the sandstone crumbling, until the building poured into the street like a mudslide. The crane retreated toward the beach and a giant yellow machine rolled down the drive from the resort, scooping up brick and glass and dumping it into the waiting truck.

Hope pulled away from Carla and ducked through the door of the inn. She stumbled to the dining room and grabbed at the back of a chair, feeling like she might vomit or scream, or both.

"Oh, Hope." Candace was beside her.

Hope watched the color drain from her own hands as she gripped the chair. She could not let go, squeezing it until her arms shook.

"Maybe you should sit down, hon." Carla's worried face appeared at her other side.

Hope relaxed her hold, closed her eyes, and let out one long, slow breath. "I'm OK," she said. She let her hands fall off the chair. "I'm good."

"We know how much that meant to you," Candace said, her voice soft.

If she had needed a sign, an imploding building would do. Hope shrugged and opened her eyes. "Well," she said to herself as much as to them, "not all dreams come true."

CHAPTER 16

H ope pushed the blue cereal flake under the milk
and watched it float to the surface. She targeted a
green one, then an orange one. Her father was probably
not at this moment eating Fruity Pebbles with a metal
spoon. She doubted what he ate for breakfast would be
the topic of whatever letter he wanted to write to her.

She finished the cereal and then washed the small pile
of dishes. Maya and Lainie had walked to the beach, but
Hope didn't go with them. Even the huge expanses of
water and sky couldn't make her feel less boxed in by
life. This must be how her father felt, except that unlike

Hope, there was no question for him of where to live or what to do for the next few years.

Not that she wanted to go back to that life where someone decided everything for her. Even when there was a script, she still managed to do it wrong, to mess it up. She had spent her whole life trying to make him happy, only to crash it all with her testimony. That was probably what he wanted to write to her about if and when she gave him her address—all the ways Hope had disappointed him.

She settled on the couch and pulled a pillow onto her lap. Then she reached for her bag and got out the letter from her mother she hadn't had time to read the day before. It would probably ooze patchouli oil and her mother's new philosophy of life as a beautiful adventure. She scanned the first section written in big, loopy writing where her mother listed the Alaskan village names she could not pronounce.

Part way down the page, the handwriting tightened up, and Hope slowed her reading. The tone had changed, and so had the subject.

Your father tried so hard for that job. He wanted everything just right, so that nothing would take away from his chances of being hired. Afterward, the church became an extension of himself. If something was amiss, it needed to be handled right away.

When we first came here, the church was average size for the area. The plan was to expand across the area by church plants and home churches. Instead, it spread across the parking lot, and continued to spread, buying out the neighboring houses. Then going to two services, three, five per week. There is energy in a full room, and your father worked to keep the room full. And then build a bigger room.

And that's where the trouble started with her father basically laundering money and taking a cut for the church.

The church had become so big that it was all about itself, and not about the people who made it up. It became more about growth in numbers than depth in faith, and your father's charisma turned into calculation. Not in the way you probably think. He worked so hard to keep up the perfect facade because all he could see were his own flaws.

Hope reread the line. All this time, she thought her father was high on himself, when it was the total opposite. He was trying to be more.

Memories flooded back, but this time, it was like Hope was having some kind of out of body experience where she could see all of it at one time. Her mother herding her into the pew as her father's shoulders relaxed. Her own voice saying the words she knew he wanted to hear as his breathing slowed.

The things she did and said trying to win her father's love had not been so much because he demanded it, but because she sensed it made him more secure. She had fed his obsession because she wanted someone to feed hers. Both of them tried so hard to be perfect, because they each saw themselves as failures.

If she was honest, she still felt that way. Sylvie had basically dropped the inn in her lap, and Hope picked it up and ran with it. It didn't matter that the more she did, the more she felt she needed to prove herself, Hope still expected some tone of disappointment in Sylvie's reply to a text or a question.

But disappointment never came. Just like with her idea for the inn to provide box lunches, it was almost like Sylvie intentionally sat back and waited to see what Hope would do next, just so she could cheer her on.

I know the plans I have for you.

The verse instantly reminded Hope of sitting at the table during the weekly Gems meeting. Miss Christine would say a line, and the group of ten-year-old girls repeated it back to her over and over until they could remember it without her.

Plans to prosper you and not to harm.

If Hope really thought about it, the times she needed help—finding a job, an apartment, a ride to the next town—it came right to her. So many times, she had hit a dead end only to turn and see a way out.

Plans to give you a hope and a future.

During the trial, Hope had been afraid, so afraid. And then afterward, when her father wouldn't even look at her, she had been so angry it melted her insides.

I know the plans I have for him too.

What? No. He did not deserve to have the prosper-hope-future thing. No way.

Now, the image of the Prodigal Son, clothes all torn, sitting in the pig pen, came into her mind. She pictured the older brother of the Prodigal, his arms folded, full-on angry face. Of course, the story always focused on the younger brother and how he made up for his sins by asking to come back. The older brother was always the uptight, spoiled kid who complained because nothing was fair. Now she saw where he was coming from. She got it, 100%.

But then, there was the father. He didn't hammer his loser son for everything he had done wrong. And the consequences she had heard of all her life? In the Prodigal's story, they had already happened. There was nothing more to say. He knew his mistakes, suffered, and then was welcomed back home. That was the point of the story. Not the consequences, but the celebration after the consequences. The restoration. The chance to begin again. To have a future.

Hope wandered around the apartment, touching random things. She could make all the plans she wanted, but she could not move on with her life until she did this thing. Hope pulled out the letter from her mother, and on a new envelope, wrote her father's name and the address of the prison. She tore a page from a notebook and held the pen over it. What would she write? What words would say everything that needed to be said? She closed her eyes and slowed her breathing until everything in her head quieted. And then she wrote.

Tolstoy said this, but I think it applies:

Let us forgive each other—only then will we live in peace.

CHAPTER 17

Life happened, whether she liked it or not. Hope had thought about this for days, and now, she just needed to get on with it. She opened the tab for Crystal Mountain and clicked on the job opening for night manager. As soon as she typed her name, a text notification popped up. Hope minimized the application and opened the text from her mother.

Hope, I did a thing. I think I told you I've been going to a survivor's support group. We are encouraged to record our story. Partly for the healing and the release of saying it out loud, but also so it can help someone else down the line. *Here's a link to part of the video. I thought maybe hearing it from my angle will help you.*

Hope pressed the play arrow. The thumbnail of the support group's logo faded, replaced by footage of her mom sitting near a window that looked out on some big amount of water. The shot panned out to show her petting Pacino. Her mom smiled at the dog, then faced the camera and started talking.

"I don't need to tell you my name because it doesn't really matter. For a long time, I thought I was the only invisible one, but I've learned there are whole rooms of us, all over. The smiling wife at her husband's side. The mother keeping her children clean and quiet. The daughter doing more but never thinking it's enough. All of us lost in the vortex of Another."

She glanced out the window and then continued.

"I always wanted to marry a man of God just like my father. When I met my husband, he was in seminary and couldn't wait to get started in his own church. But the small town was not enough, and he jumped at the chance to join the staff of a bigger church. We had our daughter Hope by then, and I guess I was so busy with her, I didn't notice the change in him.

"Eventually, everything in our lives was replaced by something newer, bigger, better. But in the meantime, I was shrinking. Our lives became focused on how it would reflect on him or the church. Was Hope in the right preschool? Was she on the short list for the elite Christian school? Were her friends from good neighborhoods? Did she excel?

"If my daughter was doing well, then I must be a good mother. If my husband was polished and beloved, then I must be a good wife. I see now that I poured into them because I wanted someone to pour into me, but no one did. No one asked what happened to my art, or if I used the degree I worked so hard for, or if the dreams I had as a young girl were coming true. It didn't really matter; for a long time, not even to me."

Pacino nudged her hand with his head, and she reached to pet him again, rubbing one of his ears between her finger and thumb.

"When something is so wrong for so long, it either causes everything around it to decay or festers within itself. I probably would have let things die if it hadn't been for Hope.

"One day, I watched her fight against herself to get in line with what was expected, and I realized—I did that to her. I gave her the ridiculous bar to get over because it would prove my worth, at least to me. I was creating someone in my daughter that she was not. She was remodeling herself at first to please, then later to be invisible just as I was."

She faced the window again, trying to keep it together, and then turned back to the camera.

"My daughter was also doing it to save me, even if she didn't know it. Her essence is to bring hope, so I did well by naming her that. She gave me hope when I felt alone in my marriage and my life. Now, she gives me hope that I can be healed. There is pushback from my parents about the divorce, and I physically moved so far away I have effectively abandoned my daughter."

She shook her head.

"*But I wasn't what she needed. In fact, she has come so far on her own, I would have held her back.*"

Hope stared at her mother's face, frozen where the video ended. Come so far in what? She had no real job or place to live. She for sure had not "healed." And, yeah, she had felt abandoned.

But being alone had made her do things she never would have done before. Like taking the job with Sylvie, both times she had offered it. Studying for this degree when it would have been easier to save the money for something else. Even thinking about opening a café.

Growing up the way she did had taught her she was going to get hurt in life—guaranteed. But being alone had taught her the rest of the lesson. What she did with that hurt would either eat her alive or make her stronger than she could ever imagine.

Maya cursed. Hope had sensed her standing in the bedroom doorway after putting Lainie down for a nap.

"My God, Hope, you never told me any of that."

Hope pulled a pillow onto her lap and turned her phone over on it. "I never told anyone. I mean, where do you start? 'Hi, my father's a controlling narcissist, what about yours?'" She shrugged and picked at the pillow's fringe. "It was what it was."

Maya sat next to her on the couch. "Yeah."

She had let out her story in little bits over the time Hope had known her. If Lainie was lucky, she would never know anything about her own father.

"So why the video?" Maya asked.

"She's in this victim support group. If people want, when they're ready, they record their stories. Either video or just audio, whatever." Hope tucked a leg under herself and turned toward Maya. "She said in her text that she finally feels free, now that she's told someone."

Maya nodded. "Yeah, it's a lot to keep in for all those years. So what about you? How are you doing?"

Hope shrugged. "All right, I guess. I mean, I get up every day and function." She turned to Maya. "You know how it is."

"Yeah."

"I'm glad she's found someone, though. Hearing it from her perspective, things were crap for a long time. When you're a kid you only know what you're shown, but she..."

Tears gathered in her eyes, and Maya squeezed her hand. Hope took a deep breath. "We're not going back, nobody wants that." She swirled her hand around in front of her face. "So, this is me moving on."

Maya tipped her head, studying her. "I like it. It's a good look."

Chapter 18

W indow washing was on the chore chart for the day, something the cleaning staff could do, but for her mental health, Hope needed a goal she could achieve right away. She got out the bucket, opened the front door of the inn, and her eyes immediately searched across the street for the empty spot at the end of the block. Now that all of the brick and debris was cleared away, the only thing left of 408 was the pipe sticking up out of a small slab of concrete.

Hope set down the bucket and crossed her arms. A bird peeped from the tree at the edge of the yard, then flew across and landed in front of her on the porch railing. It perched there, turning its black head in quick little moves, first looking at her, then away, then back again.

"Hey, chickadee," she said.

The bird hopped once and then flew to the shrubs of the house next door. Hope listened to the sounds around her of the day already happening. She exhaled, then reached into her bucket for the window cleaner. The same thick dust that covered the glass on the front door and the large parlor windows turned her paper towels a dirty tan. Hope felt like she was holding tiny bits of history, like she was the last one to see the past before it went into the trash.

She dropped the used paper towels into the bucket and moved to the end of the front walk, blocking out the flapping windsocks and the sounds of scooters of the present, trying to imagine how the buildings had looked in the past. If she had learned anything in the last three years it was that life was full of changes. Sometimes that meant destroying the whole mess and starting over, but other times it meant being flexible and ready to pivot.

Sylvie was amazing in so many ways. Even during her treatments she had coordinated tours with the local wineries, which would keep the inn open through November. And she had solved Hope's apartment problem, once Hope got over herself and told Sylvie about it.

"Of course, I would love for you to choose a room. I didn't offer earlier because I didn't want to get in the way of you and Maya."

No rent for at least a few months meant Hope had enough to pay her tuition. As for the café idea, she would get to that when the time was right. Maybe she would start small, like with a coffee cart, something she could expand as she could afford it.

The front door of the inn opened, and Hope turned as The Sisters came out onto the porch, side-stepping her cleaning bucket.

"Oh, my gosh. I'm so sorry." Hope hurried up the walk.

Carla sat down on the wicker loveseat and called out, "It's OK, hon."

"We were looking for you, actually," Candace said when Hope reached them.

"Is there a problem?" Hope climbed the steps, ready to go inside.

"No, everything's fine," Candace said. "We just wanted to talk to you." She sat in one of the two chairs that matched the loveseat.

Carla set her tea on the small side table. "Is this a good time?"

Hope paused; there wasn't really anything else she needed to do until the afternoon. She nodded, and Carla waved her into the empty seat.

"You've heard us talk a lot about our grandmother over the last few weeks," Candace said.

Hope mentally swiped through images of the memories The Sisters had shared. "She must have been an amazing woman to leave such a strong impression on you."

Carla nodded. "Gran truly believed a woman has just as much purpose in life as a man, and she empowered the women she knew to explore just what that was."

"Even before empowering women was a 'thing,'" Candace added.

"She also had a strong faith," Carla said, "that the God who led her in would not leave her alone, no matter what, and that He would show her the way through to the other side."

Hope had always imagined God standing with his arms crossed waiting for her to get her crap together. She had grown up so weighed down by the rules and their consequences. But a God who would go through her stuff with her at her pace and with no judging? She could get behind a God like that.

"Our mother passed away a year ago this October," Candace said. "She left us our Gran's inheritance and legacy."

Carla nodded in agreement.

"We've created a foundation with the money," Candace continued, "and Carla and I have spent the last year looking for people and projects that would continue Gran's legacy of faith in God and faith in people."

Carla sat forward and picked up the thread. "We just felt so strongly that we needed to come back here to Frankfort. Where it all started, I guess we could say." She shared a glance with her sister that said so much without using words. "But we didn't know why, exactly."

"We've been praying for wisdom the whole time," Candace said, "and we think now we understand."

Carla fidgeted in her seat.

"In addition to the money," Candace began again, "there is a building in town, just a block from here. It's a small sliver of a thing, not quite big enough for retail, and it doesn't fit the architecture of either of the adjacent buildings so neither business wants to absorb it."

"I'm just going to say it," Carla broke in. "We want to show it to you."

"To see if it would work for your café idea," Candace finished.

Was she really hearing this? "Wow. I mean, the idea of a café itself is a stretch, and I don't have any real business experience to know how to pull it off." Hope paused, ready for the rejection. "I'm not sure when or even if I would make a profit..."

Candace reached out and patted Hope's chair. "We're pretty good judges of character at this point in our lives, and I speak for both of us when I say this: you know more than you think, Hope. Plus, Sylvie vouches for you. That's why she asked you to run the inn when she knew she'd be gone for most of the summer." She paused. "You just need to have faith in yourself."

Hope took a breath. After hearing her mother's story, she had thought a lot about people on journeys they would never have chosen. The café, if she ever opened one, would give back to them. If she told The Sisters her idea, would they trust her intuition?

"There's one more thing I should tell you both."

"Go ahead, hon."

"Well, I know it's against every business plan out there, but what I want to do at the café is to let people pay what they can afford. I know how it feels to have nothing, to not have enough to buy even a cup of coffee. I want people to feel like they still matter to someone, even when they don't think so."

Another Sister glance.

"Our Gran would have loved that," Carla said. "That's exactly what she lived for."

Carla leaned in, her expression more serious than Hope had seen during The Sisters' entire stay.

"And what you've proposed," Carla continued, "while not traditional, is the very definition of faith. Lay everything on the table. Pay what you can, and have hope for the rest."

Chapter 19

The doorknob turned in her hand almost like magic. Hope stepped into the space, and even though the awning over the front window blocked any sun, she felt lighter just being in the room. The floor even creaked like it was taking a long-awaited breath.

"It hasn't been treated well, I'm afraid," Carla said. She ran a hand over a plaster wall that crumbled under her fingers, then wiped her hands together. "We'd have to do something with that."

"I think it's been a few years since the last business was open," Candace said. "What was it? A coin shop, I think." She looked at Carla to verify.

"Yes, you're right. There's a small bathroom in the back. We'll get a plumber in to see how to make the water suitable for a kitchen too." Carla put her hands on her hips as she looked things over. "I don't know if any of this old display counter would work. What do you think, Hope?"

It was too much to take in. Past the aging structures and years of dust, Hope could already see the room laid out with little tables and chairs, vases with stem flowers, the glass case full of tasty treats. "This is amazing. I just...wow."

The Sisters did the glance thing and smiled.

"We should look at the apartment," Candace said. "See if there are any leaks after that rain. It's out back and up the stairs."

Carla, who apparently could be amazingly quick, was already out of sight.

"An apartment?" Hope asked.

"It's very small, not surprising," Candace said, looking around and then up at the ceiling, "but you're welcome to that also."

This was unreal.

Candace nodded toward the back door. "We'd better catch up to her."

She wasn't going to lie, the wooden stairs were scary. Hope followed in Candace's cautious footsteps up to the open door where Carla motioned them into the space.

"Have a look around, hon."

There was a small kitchen to the right, and two doors to the left. The first opened into a tiny bathroom, and the second to a bedroom with a window that over-looked the street. Hope closed her eyes, trying to calm down, before joining The Sisters in the main room.

"We would have it cleaned and painted, of course," Carla said. "It's almost embarrassing to offer this." She did her handclap thing like she was removing dust. "Do you think you would be OK up here?"

"I—love it," Hope said. "I just can't believe you would…" She shook her head, and tears squeezed out of her eyes.

"Oh, hon," Carla moved forward and folded her into a hug.

Candace dug around in her bag and came out with a plastic packet of tissues.

"This is why, right here." Carla made a circling motion with her finger as they all wiped at their eyes.

"I'll admit it, you were right," Candace said. A Glance. "We had a difference of opinion," she said to Hope. "I wanted to sell the building, and Carla didn't agree. She didn't 'feel it.'" Candace rolled her eyes. "And, if she doesn't feel things, she can be really stubborn."

"And really right," Carla reminded her.

"So," Candace went on, "we have traipsed all over this area talking to prospective renters and artists looking for studio space, and Carla gave them all a thumbs-down, even before you told us about your café plans."

"They weren't right. I could—"

"Feel it. I know," Candace said. "So now, apparently she's giving you a thumbs-up."

"Two." Carla smiled and stuck up her thumbs.

Candace put the tissue packet back in her bag. "So. It's a lot," she said, "all of this. My advice is to take a few days, think about it. You can say no, and you won't hurt our feelings."

Carla nodded her head. "All good."

"Then we can sit down and write up an agreement."

"And get you in business," Carla finished.

A business, a building, an apartment? What was happening? They trusted her with their grandmother's legacy. Hope felt like she had not one but two fairy godmothers. "OK," she said, looking around one more time. She had no words. "Thank you doesn't seem like enough."

"It's just fine for now," Candace said, and Carla added, "Amen."

Hope smiled at the readout on her phone and pushed the button. "Hey, Sylvie."

"Hope, Candace just called to tell me the great news." Hope loved the way Sylvie rolled her r's when her Greek accent slipped in. "I am so excited for you, and a little sad, I won't lie."

Hope's stomach jumped. "Why?"

"You have been an amazing employee, and I don't want to lose you," Sylvie said.

Hope breathed out, surprised. "You're not upset?"

"No, of course not." Sylvie laughed. "In fact, I called to offer you some advice on getting approved by the planning committee."

"That would be awesome." She thought of the stack of forms and regulations that had come the day before.

"I'll be there tomorrow, Hope. It will be good to see The Sisters again."

She laughed. "That's what I've been calling them too. Just in my head," she added.

"I think they're used to it. So, OK? Tomorrow?"

"Can't wait."

There was so much to think about: dates, colors, equipment. And it all took money.

"Don't you worry," Carla had said. She had a good feeling.

Candace was more concrete. "We have a good network of people who can help you with most of what you might need."

"You're not, like, part of the mob or something?" Hope laughed, a little nervously, if she was being honest. It was all too good to be true, and a little too close for comfort considering her father was serving time for fraud.

Candace had just raised one eyebrow. "Better. American Business Women's Association."

CHAPTER 20

The tiny storefront had gotten the ultimate makeover. The awning was gone, there was running water upstairs and down, and the fragrance of the day was a mix of sawdust and paint. Hope stood at what would, in just a few more weeks, become the serving counter in the café that she never thought would ever exist. She pushed the color strips together into a pile, then spread them out again; she had to make a choice.

Bella's, the high end bakery a few blocks away, was all pinks and grays. Very elegant. Not that Hope didn't want to be chic. But she wanted people to come in and sit down, even if they were sandy or sweaty or tired. What color scheme spoke to that vibe?

She brought a denim blue and a light green together. Not quite. She pulled out the green and replaced it with one called "Granny's apple." The two colors meshed and would go well with a sandy stripe. The beach was definitely her happy place now after all the time she spent there sorting through her life.

Maya's voice called from the back door. "He-y."

"In the front," Hope said. "You made it. How's Lainie?" The little princess had Maya's fiancé wrapped, and tight.

"She was pumped to hang out with Marty all by herself."

"He has been so good—for both of you."

Maya lifted a big paper bag to the counter. "So, I brought some dinner. And deep-fried pickles, of course." She pulled out a wad of napkins and two foiled packets.

"We don't actually have any furniture yet." Hope scanned the room and shrugged. "Sorry."

"I can eat pickles anywhere." Maya unwrapped the foil. "What's that?"

Hope pushed the strips together again. "I'm going over colors for the café."

"Yeah? And what about upstairs?"

"I'll show you after we eat. They just finished it today."

Maya handed her a fork and one of the Styrofoam containers. "I didn't bring plates."

"We've eaten off worse," Hope reminded her.

"Not going back to that again." Maya shook her head. "So, what are you gonna call this place?"

"I'm as clueless on that as I am on the color scheme. The name of a business is important. You want one memorable but not too weird. Early in the alphabet in case people are scrolling categories. Then there's the logo. If the name is too long, then you can't fit it on the image." Hope blew out her cheeks. "It would have been good to take more marketing classes."

Maya wiped her hands on the paper napkin and closed it up in the empty container. "What have you got so far?"

Hope turned over her phone and clicked open the note where she had collected ideas. She read the first one. "Beach Brews."

Maya scowled. "Sounds like a bikini bar."

"No on that." Hope backspaced and erased the letters. "How about Dune View Café?"

"We have sand, but no dunes." They were both quiet for a minute, Maya frowning in thought. "Do you like...The Cupful?"

Hope tipped her head. "It's a hard word to say. Sounds like 'couple.'"

"Yeah. No good. Hey, did you tell your mom about this yet?"

Hope nodded and took a sip of water. "Yeah, I actually talked to her for the first time in a few months. She was pretty excited about it all. Did I tell you she's training Pacino to be a therapy dog?"

"That's cool."

"Some of the other women asked if they could borrow him when they made their videos."

"What a good boy." Maya spread out the paint chips. "Which ones are you looking at?"

Hope pulled out the blue and green color strips. "I think I like these together. I'm thinking with white accents."

"I can see that in here, pretty caszh," Maya said, looking around the room. "You could use reclaimed chairs, some of each color."

"That's a good idea."

Maya smiled. "I think that's it."

"What's it?"

"You should call it Café Hope."

Hope crossed her arms. "That doesn't sound conceited at all."

"Not, Hope's Café. Café Hope. Check it out: you wanted the café to be a place where people can be themselves, and you plan to donate to the women's shelter." She raised an open palm. "It's just like your mom said in her video, you give people hope."

Isn't that what everyone wanted and needed? Hope. Not her, but the concept, the feeling. The sense that even though they didn't know how or when, things would work out. It might take seeing something in a different way, like a tiny storefront overlooked for years. It might even take seeing *themselves* in a different way.

"Café Hope. I like it," Hope said. "Yeah, I think that's it."

Maya turned her hand over and fist-bumped the air. "Boom."

CHAPTER 21

Hope couldn't believe the café had been fully in business for eight months already. Any time she was open, it was busy, and she had extended the hours when the construction crews from the resort started lining up outside every morning, even before she turned on the lights. She needed help.

The sprinkle turned to hard rain, and Hope dug around in her closet for a coat to wear. She only had to go down the wooden staircase from her apartment to the café's back door, but a lot could happen in fourteen steps. She flipped the hood up over her head and closed the door. At the bottom of the stairs, now a lot less scary thanks to Bryant the Builder's construction awesomeness, she did a quick turn toward the café's back door, and movement caught her eye.

Someone or something was tucked back into the partially enclosed space under the landing. Hope's heart raced. She had her computer bag in one hand and her café key in the other. There was no way she could fight off an attacker.

Not to harm you.

Hope took a deep breath. "OK. Come out of there." In the dim light, all Hope could see was the dark-colored hoodie pulled all the way up, long fingers on a backpack strap, worn-out shoes, and skinny jeans torn, not in a good way.

"I'll move on." It was a girl's voice, quiet but tough.

"No. I'm...You just startled me. Hey, come in out of the rain." Hope unlocked the door and pushed it open. The girl snuck a peek at her and then slipped into the café. Hope set down her bag and took off her dripping coat. The girl stood still, looking at the floor.

"Come on through," Hope said. "I'll turn some lights on."

Once, when the youth group helped at a downtown soup kitchen, Hope manned the drink station, passing out cups of juice or coffee. Some of the people were friendly and said "thank you" a lot. But some were like this girl, guarded, invisible. They waited for Hope to ask them what they wanted to drink and only answered with a word or two. At the time, she thought they were kind of rude. Now, after learning from the women's shelter training about what could happen on the streets, she knew better.

"I'm Hope," she said. "Have a seat, and I'll bring you something." Hope went behind the counter and turned on the machines.

The girl went to the table farthest from the front window and pulled out a chair. The backpack inched off her shoulder onto the floor, and Hope recognized the moment of near-fear when you let go of everything you have in the world.

"Do you want coffee? I'm making some for myself," Hope called.

"Just water."

OK, so she had no money. Hope filled up a cup and put it on a tray with a muffin. "Help yourself." She waved to the muffin. "We're going to get a new box in about half an hour. This is from yesterday, so it might be a little dry."

The girl nodded and kept her hands in her lap.

"OK. Well, I'm going to do some stuff. We open in a little while." Hope saw the first pickup pull into its spot. On such a rainy day, the on-street parking would fill with work trucks in just a few minutes. She noticed the girl kept her hood up, but the muffin disappeared into it in four bites. So, also starving.

Hope went to the storage room to think and throw out a quick prayer. *Help me to not screw this up.* The boxes of T-shirts caught her eye, and she sorted through until she found some of the right size. Then she grabbed an apron from the hook, a page of wide labels, and a blue Sharpie from her computer bag.

Hope laid her armful down on the counter just as one of the guys pushed on the locked door and then peered through the window when it didn't open. She held up a hand and mouthed "five minutes." He nodded. She saw the doors of the other trucks swing open.

"I am going to be swamped in just a little bit," Hope said.

The girl grabbed her bag and stood up. Crap.

"I mean, my helper's...not starting until later. So—would you like a job? If you could just get me through this morning rush..." Hope gestured to the line forming outside the front window.

"I've never done that," the girl said.

"That's OK. These guys have been in before. They'll tell you what they want for a sweet, and they all drink only black coffee."

The girl looked down at her clothes.

"Oh. Here, I've got some shirts. Do you want long-sleeve or short?" Hope held up the two shirts with the Café Hope logo.

"Long." She came to the counter, and Hope handed her the shirt.

"The bathroom's that door there. You'll probably get hot with the hoodie on once everyone starts coming in."

The girl studied the shirt and then the matching framed prints across the room. "Dickinson. Nice." Then she went into the bathroom.

"The thing with feathers," Hope said to herself.

A few minutes later, the girl slipped out of the bathroom, her bleached hair tucked back behind her ears, her bag puffed out from the addition of the hoodie.

"That color looks good on you," Hope said. "You can put your bag in the storeroom there—it will be safe. I'll make you a name tag." She held up the Sharpie. "What do you want to be called?"

The girl pressed her lips together and then, "Andi."

"A-n-d-i?" Hope asked, and the girl nodded. "OK. Here we go." Hope laid out the apron and nametag and went to open the door.

For the first wave of customers, Hope did the greeting and had Andi slip the muffins or cookies into bags. Hope took the money and handed out the coffee. Once the last guy was out the door, Andi turned to her. "How do they know what to pay? Everybody gave you something different."

Look at you, being all observant. "We don't have prices. Everyone just pays what they can afford. They don't usually want change back," Hope said.

"What if someone can't—"

"It all works out." Hope smiled. "Let's get these cookies on a tray before the next group comes."

Hope glanced at the window. If it stayed this busy, she might have to call the bakery for more muffins. Months earlier she had given up on trying to bake all the sweets herself and contracted with Bella's and their industrial scale ovens. Carla waved at her from the sidewalk. Something was up.

"Grab a cookie if you want," Hope said to the girl, moving around to the front of the room. "Just eat it at a table and not behind the counter." She turned to The Sisters. "Good morning!"

"Hi, hon." Carla gave her a hug.

"Good morning, Hope," Candace said. "We saw the crowd earlier and thought we'd better let you take a breather before we came over."

"I think they're trying to hit a deadline at the resort. They called everyone in, I guess." She moved around behind the counter. "What can I get for you?"

"I'll take the lemon herbal tea," Carla said.

"I'd like chai, and we'll split..." Candace peeked into the case, "a banana nut."

"Great."

Andi finished the cookie and went to wash her hands. The Sisters looked from her to Hope.

"I'll bring that right over," Hope said. She turned so Andi couldn't see her and raised her eyebrows at The Sisters.

"Here you go." Candace handed her the cash.

Andi came back to the counter and waited. Hope really wanted to talk to The Sisters, but in the small room, the girl would hear everything. "Andi, could you take this towel and wipe off the table and chairs on the sidewalk? I don't know if anyone will want to sit there, but if they do, we'll be ready."

"Sure." Andi crossed the room in silence.

As soon as the door closed, Carla pounced. "We could hardly keep away! Remember how we said we would pray for an assistant? Just this morning we both, separately, had this strong urge to come talk to you."

Candace nodded. "It's only happened to me a few times, but it's powerful. Who is this girl?"

"She was under the landing out back this morning staying dry. She kind of scared me; I thought it was a bird." Hope exhaled. "We haven't talked much yet, but I'm pretty sure she's homeless."

"You don't know anything about her?" Candace asked.

"Just her name."

Candace nodded but said nothing.

Hope glanced out the window, watching Andi's methodical motions. Hope couldn't get a read on Candace, or on the situation, but something was going on here, something bigger than just letting a girl come in out of the rain.

The new prints of a finch, each captioned with a line from the Dickinson poem, caught Hope's eye and gave her the words. She turned to the women who had believed in her before she had believed in herself. "Almost a year ago, I met a couple of guests who took my partially hatched dream and helped it fly." Hope tipped her head. "I've been given so much. I think it's my turn to pay what I can..."

"And have hope for the rest," Candace finished.

"Exactly." She held her breath and then exhaled. This was definitely some kind of step of faith, and until she took it, she wouldn't know what was possible. She turned her wrist slightly and read the words inked there. *I am enough.* She brightened.

"I'm going to hire her," Hope said.

"Well, then." Candace held up her teacup. Carla smiled and touched cups with her sister. "To the next chapter of Café Hope."

Andi

CHAPTER 1

A ndi wiped down the table and chairs. How had
she gotten here? It was like she had stepped
out of the motel room right into another world, and
trying to find the door that would take her back was
impossible.

*You got to go, chica. If that motel lady find you stayin'
with us, she throw us all out. Why you wanna be seen
with us anyway?*

You're all I have.

No, chica. You got the key.

I know, the key to the truck.

To the future, mija. You got papers and the key. You belong here.

Torres, yo man, we don't go now, we get fired.

We park the truck for you, Andi. You look around. Get a job. Todo será bien.

Everything *would* be OK, when she and the crew were back together again. OK, but never like it was before. Before her father collapsed in their motel room. Before either of them knew what a pancreas was. Before the doctor told them there was nothing anyone could do about the cancer that had burned through both their lives like a wildfire. She sighed and went back inside the café.

Hope called to her. "Andi, could you come over? I want you to meet some friends of mine."

She crossed the space, not much bigger than some of the motel rooms she and her father had stayed in over the years. A raised shelf with bar stools stood against the wall to her right. Her temporary boss and two older women sat by the window at one of the eight small tables set with a mix of sky blue and bright green chairs.

"These ladies are—well, they're a lot of things, but I want you to meet them. Candace and Carla." Hope pointed to each woman in turn. "You'll probably see them here a lot."

"Hi." Andi flashed a small smile at the women. She reached back for her hood but found instead a handful of hair. Her hoodie was zipped away in her bag with everything else of the life she used to know.

"Are you from Frankfort?" one asked.

"No, I came here...a little while ago." Had it just been a week ago she was riding with her father, pointing out farms and cows and trees and the sunrise that he would never see again?

"Well, we hope you like it and want to stay," said the smiley lady.

"Thank you." Andi looked down, around, anywhere but at the women who seemed to be having a "moment" with Hope.

"Andi," Hope said, "the bakery sent more cookies. Could you put them into the case?"

"OK." Andi put away the towel and washed her hands. The room was tiny, so while she worked, she heard everything the older women said about their search for a small cottage. They wanted a *second* house, and *she* didn't know where she would sleep that night.

From her spot behind the counter, Andi studied the prints hanging above the coffee bar–shelf thing. Each poster was a different view of a yellow bird on a flower stem. When she moved her focus quickly from the first to the last, it was like the bird moved its head, listening and looking around. A line from the Dickinson poem was printed under each image of the bird.

Hope is the thing with feathers
That perches in the soul
And sings the tune without the words
And never stops at all

Just then, the door burst open, and a large man in a sweatshirt and swim trunks came in, followed by two girls about her own age and a jittery woman Andi pegged as the mother. "Let's just see if those clouds pass over," he said. "Go ahead, pick out something." He waved the girls forward.

"Andi, do you mind helping them with their order?" Hope asked. "I'll just be a minute."

"Sure." Andi moved to the "Order Here" part of the counter. "Hi," she said. "Welcome to Café Hope. Go ahead when you're ready."

The family studied the large board above Andi's head, their faces moving into the frown of indecision. From the corner of her eye, she saw Hope reach across the table and squeeze a hand of each of the women.

"You don't have any prices," the wife said.

Andi gave her a small smile. "At Café Hope, you pay what you can."

"Well, how does a business survive that way?" the man asked.

"I don't know," Andi said, glancing Hope's way. She turned back to the man and shrugged. "It just all works out."

The family made their choices and found seats, the daughters at the coffee bar and the parents at a table. Andi wasn't so sure the tiny, green, wooden chair was a good choice for the man. As soon as she finished their order, two more people came in, and the whole ordering thing repeated. A woman and two kids chose cookies. A man picked up a coffee, black. Over and over and over.

Andi knew she had to get a job and that it might take weeks to make enough money to get back the tools.

Maybe even weeks after that before she could be good enough using them to join up with the crew before they moved on. But right now, she just had a few hours to figure out what to do when the café closed and she was alone.

CHAPTER 2

When the cutesy coffee cup clock showed four o'clock, Hope locked the front door and turned over the sign. "You're, like, amazing, Andi. You never quit." She exhaled a big breath. "It was busier than I thought it would be, even with the rain this morning. Thank you so much for helping me out."

"You're welcome." Andi sized up the café. She had wiped down everything she could think of, emptied the trash a few times, and washed the dishes. "What else do you need me to do?"

"If you could sweep and mop while I get the deposit ready, that would be great. I'll show you where everything is."

Hope led her to the storeroom and pointed out the mop bucket and the floor sink. She explained how much of what to add to the water, and then froze mid-sentence. "I totally forgot about any kind of paperwork or time card." She turned to Andi. "Full disclosure—you are my first employee."

She looked at her watch. "So, you started early, like seven, and now it's four. Let's say four thirty by the time we're done. So, nine and a half hours at nine sixty-five an hour. I can either give you cash, or...if you're willing to go the long haul, I'd love to offer you a job."

A job. All Andi had meant to do that morning was walk along Main Street to the beach. Then it started pouring rain, and she had only made it as far as the café's back door. Nine hours later, Hope offers her a job.

Hope held up a hand. "You don't have to answer me now. I mean, if you don't have plans, we could get some dinner. The Logslide has amazing wet burritos, and I can't eat a whole one by myself. We could split one, or you could order something else. Whatever you want." She waved her hands. "Anyway, we could talk about the job at dinner."

Andi took a breath. "OK."

"But let's get this done before the bank closes."

Andi considered the idea as she stacked the chairs onto their tables. The day hadn't been so bad. Hope was nice. The café was small, and small was all she could handle right now. The big picture was too big.

The truck was still in her father's name. All she really had in the world fit into her backpack, the tiny box of her father's ashes hidden at the very bottom. Tomorrow was the first birthday she would have without him. Legally, she would be an adult then—eighteen years old. Technically, she had become an adult five days ago at 3:19 in the morning when her father stopped breathing.

The tangy scent of the mop bucket was the same smell as in the hospital where she had crawled onto the bed next to her father and sobbed, pulling his lifeless arm over her like a blanket. He had the sour smell of death on him then, so different from the cologne of sawdust and sweat that he usually wore back from the job site each night.

Andi took a breath and pushed the mop bucket toward the drain. If she could focus on just the next thing, if that was all anyone asked of her, she might be able to handle it. But no questions, like where she would live now that the motel closed the door to her. And what she would do with a truck she didn't have a license to drive. Even the paperwork Hope talked about. Would she have to tell Hope her story? The story she could not even tell herself yet—that whatever happened next, she was on her own.

"Was that a yes for dinner?" Hope asked her after she turned the bucket over to let it drain.

"Oh, yeah," Andi said, "that would be great."

"All right." Hope pointed to the hooks on the wall. "Your apron can go here. You can keep the shirt and wear it to dinner even. Free advertising." She raised her eyebrows and then winked.

Andi moved her face in what she hoped passed for a smile and picked up her bag.

"We're just going a few blocks, so if you want, we can lock up your bag here. Dinner's on me."

Andi thought about her father in the little box, sitting in the dark storeroom while she went out for dinner. "That's OK. I'll bring it."

"Gotcha. Ready?"

Andi had never just walked down a main street before. Either the city was so big there wasn't one, or so new the area wasn't developed. Goodwill was really the only place they had shopped, or if the grocery store was big enough, they bought clothes there. An entire store for just T-shirts, or candy, or flowers amazed her. Even the air smelled different, like sun and caramel corn, not the dust and diesel fumes she was used to.

"Here it is," Hope said. She stopped outside a building covered in logs stripped of their bark. Where windows would have been, there were black and white photos of men balancing on floating logs, prodding them along the river with long iron poles. Inside the dining room, though, The Logslide was not much different than the sports bars Andi had eaten in over the years with the crew.

She scanned the room expecting to see Torres and the guys at a high top table, but then remembered it was only Monday. Paychecks came out on Fridays, and on Saturdays, the guys would eat out. They always hoped to get the right bartender who would change the station to a soccer match so they could cheer Mexico over anybody else.

"Hey, girl." The waitress reached down and one-arm hugged Hope, her thick, dark hair pushed back by a bright pink bandana. "Who's your friend?"

"Hey." Hope leaned into her. "This is Andi. Andi, this is Maya. We've been roommates for two years. Well, we *were* roommates until she got engaged, and I moved to the apartment over the café."

"Hi," Andi said.

Maya straightened. "Nice to meet you. You guys want menus?"

"Do you want to see what they have," Hope asked, "or split the burrito?"

Andi thought how, even after they had pooled their paychecks for the cremation, the guys on her father's crew had slipped her folded tens and twenties as they told her *adios* that morning. She would have to make the money last. "I'll share," she said.

"One full to split. Two cokes. Is that OK?"

Andi nodded.

"Two cokes, got it."

Maya moved away, her hair bouncing along behind her like a happy puppy. Andi pulled at the ends of her own hair, wishing she hadn't hacked it off herself.

"We worked in Boyne together," Hope said. "Now here in Frankfort. Are you from Frankfort?"

"No. I've just been here a little while." Please don't ask anything else.

"Me, too, actually. I came at the beginning of the season last year to work at one of the B&Bs. That's where I met The Sisters, the women from this morning. They were huge in getting the café up and running."

"Is it theirs?" Andi asked. "I mean, it's called Café Hope."

"They run a foundation. Grants from there were my seed money to start the business." She tipped her head. "So, kind of?"

Andi nodded. She had no idea what Hope was saying. Maya set two drinks on the table and pushed one in front of Andi. "Here you go."

"How's Lainie?" Hope pulled the paper cap off her own straw and took a sip of the soda.

"She no longer wants to be queen." Maya waggled her head. "Now she wants to be a pet doctor."

Hope nodded. "Probably easier to find a job in that field."

"Give her time. She'll find a way to do both." Maya tucked the tray under arm. "I'll check on your plate."

Andi recognized the purposeful movement of a busy waitress. If the crew was here, they would have left a big tip.

"Lainie is Maya's daughter," Hope said. "She's four."

Andi nodded and played with the straw. She never remembered wanting to be a princess. These women with their nail polish and styled hair were so far from what she knew. She so wanted to go back to the motel, pull her hoodie up over her head, and crawl under the covers for ten years.

"We should talk about the job." Hope stirred her drink with the straw. "I really do need someone, probably three days a week. Mornings at least. And all day on Saturday, at least for the next few weeks." She exhaled. "The season is usually winding down by the end of

September, except for the color tours and the ones that spin off to the winery even into the winter. I can do only minimum wage, but for—" she counted on her fingers. "Fifteen hours and eight each Saturday you work. As many as you want to commit to. How does that sound?" She smiled at Andi, waiting.

What was minimum wage? She would have to look that up. If it was nine dollars and something an hour she could still make almost two hundred dollars a week. "It sounds good," Andi said.

"Great." Hope looked up. "Oh, here's the food."

Two hundred dollars a week. If she took the job, then all she would need to do was find a pawn shop that had the right tools, practice using them, and she could go back on the site. Andi let out her breath. It seemed like what Hope had said that morning was true, that everything just kind of works itself out.

CHAPTER 3

T uesdays were as busy as Mondays, apparently, and it was almost eleven before the café was empty.

"Wow," Hope said to her. "That was intense. Now I'm *really* glad you're here."

Where is *here*? Whenever they went to a new place, Andi had waited in the truck with the doors locked while her father checked into the motel. She always tried to guess the room number, and she liked to look at the keychain to see how worn it was.

A new keychain could mean a new room, but more likely, someone had just lost the key, and the lock was changed. Which was also good. A worn keychain could mean a lot of drama—that's what she called the yelling and slamming doors she heard some nights at the motels.

Screeching seagulls and clanging dumpster lids woke her up this morning, not that she had slept very much. The guys had fixed the passenger window as well as they could with some clear plastic, but it wouldn't take much to punch it out again. Had it been just three days since her father's tools were stolen in a smash and grab?

Andi shook away the memory. "And now we're out of cookies," she said to Hope.

"I'll call and see if they'll send a few more dozen. Hey, now that it's quiet, let's get that paperwork out of the way. I'll bring it out when I'm off the phone."

"OK."

"Why don't you take a break while you can?" Hope said. "Have a cinnamon roll. They are amazing."

Andi pulled a square of wax paper from the box and snagged the pastry. She hadn't eaten since the burrito and wondered if Hope heard her stomach growling. She poured a cup of water and took everything out to the sidewalk table. Except for going to The Logslide with Hope, she hadn't been away from the café, or the truck. She'd have to figure something out for food later. Maybe take it down to the beach and eat her dinner there.

She wondered how the crew was doing. Torres had told her the condos were just three blocks from the café. It would be so easy to go see the guys—and a good way to get somebody fired. Her father had told her that one day when she complained about staying behind in the motel room. "You can't come on the jobsite. If OSHA found a kid on premises, we'd all be fired. Either wait in the truck or go to the library. OK?"

If it was a bigger town, the library was open every day. Township and village libraries were only open a few hours a week, but if she was lucky, they had at least a computer. The library was the first thing she wanted to find every new place they went, but she hadn't searched for the library in Frankfort. Everything had happened so fast.

"What a great day." Hope sank into the chair across from her. "A perfect beach day. A little bit hot, not much wind off the water." She smiled up at someone passing on the sidewalk. Every few minutes all morning long, Andi had noticed people with tote bags and coolers wander past the café window at flip-flop pace.

"I haven't been to the beach much this summer." Hope sighed. "Last year, I went almost every day, sometimes at night if I worked an afternoon shift at the inn. There's never a wrong time to go, right?"

Andi nodded and took a quick sip of water. She could think of a lot of wrong times, like when your father was being eaten alive by a cancer he didn't know he had.

"I left everything on the table in there for you."

"OK." Andi stood up and gathered her trash.

"Let me know if you need any help," Hope said.

"OK."

Andi went inside, tossed her things into the garbage, and washed the sticky icing off her hands. Then she went back to the table and picked up the top paper from the stack. The form wanted her name and birthdate, which she filled in. The next line was for her address, and Andi's stomach rolled. Phone number. Social security number. Bank account number. She set the pen down and grabbed at her hood. All she got was the strap from her apron; the hoodie was in her bag. She stood there, making herself breathe in and out, in and out.

The bell on the door jangled as Hope came in. "Did the cookies come yet? I see people heading back from the water. Andi? Are you OK?"

In and out. In and out.

Hope was at her side, pulling out a chair. "Hey, why don't you sit down?"

Andi lowered herself, blinking back the tears that blurred the paper in front of her.

"It's OK." Hope's hand was gentle on Andi's arm. "It will be OK."

She heard the delivery guy from the bakery come through the door from the storeroom. "Got your cookies. Two dozen chocolate and one dozen monster. "

"Thanks, Charlie," Hope said. "You can leave them there on the counter." She sat down next to Andi and waited for him to leave. Then she pulled the paper across the table toward her and looked at it. "Today's your birthday."

Andi nodded.

"Are you here alone? Without your...family?"

Andi hesitated. In a group like the crew, everybody had a story they weren't telling, and the fewer people who knew it the better.

Hope put the paper back on the stack. "Can I tell you something?" She paused. "I started working at resorts when I was nineteen. My first job was six hours from home, on an island. I knew no one. It was really rough, but it got better." She smiled. "What I found is, people want to help where they can. You just have to let them."

Andi nodded but didn't make eye contact with Hope.

"We should probably get ready for the after-beach munchy crowd. Why don't you just get these back to me tomorrow?"

The guys always went to the check-cashing places and then Western Union to send money home to their families. Whatever was left went into their pockets, at least for a few days. No one ever went to the bank or used a checking account.

Andi stood and took the papers to her bag. How would she be able to fill them out? How had her father done that all these years without an address? She remembered going to a mailbox store a few times a year, but she never knew why. Maybe now she did.

Andi reached again for her hood but stopped. She had to do this. *Think, think, think.* The blue bag. Her father had told her to look for the blue bag. She hadn't known then what he was talking about in the hospital with him making no sense from all the painkillers.

She hadn't found anything like a blue bag in the motel room or in her father's duffle. Most of his clothes she gave to the guys, saving just a faded denim shirt that still held his scent. The bag had to be somewhere in the truck. Well, that would be her work for the night, taking inventory of her little bit of life.

CHAPTER 4

Andi jerked awake. The hum of boat motors had replaced the usual weekday noises of big trucks. She squinted in the dim light at the travel clock she had found in her father's things. Seven. Hope had let her keep working full days the rest of the week even though she hadn't turned in her papers, but today, Sunday, the café wouldn't open til nine.

Andi folded up the blanket and pulled out the last of her clean clothes. She changed in the port-a-potty across the parking lot, and then checked the clock again. That had not used up much time, just twenty minutes. She pulled out her dictionary, its red cover crumbling at the edges, and randomly opened it to a page.

Every time she learned a new word, she underlined it, and the page was almost all lined. The one word that stood out to her for that day was "busy," having a great deal to do. The night of her birthday, she had walked down to the lake, but there were people everywhere, so she had gone back to the truck instead. Maybe now, she could go see the beach when it wasn't so busy.

The seagulls that lined up in the beach lot's parking spaces ignored her as she passed by. More birds marched around at the edge of the water, and Andi sat down on a bench to watch. Whenever two got too close, there would be a fight. One would squawk and chatter until the other bird moved away, and Andi didn't blame him. The motel rooms had not seemed small to her, even when her father was off work at night, but when the café was busy, Andi felt almost trapped by all the noise. And the talking. It was a lot.

The water was calm, brushing the shore and then gliding back out. Andi liked that. She dug through her pack until she found the plastic bag full of colored squares of paper. She took out a light blue one, her father's favorite color. She spread it out on the bench and folded it in half to make a triangle, then opened it and folded it the other way to make another one. Over and over, she folded and smoothed the creases until she had a bird.

She had read in the origami book that cranes were a symbol of success, luck, and dreams come true. Well, none of that applied now. Her father had been dead for eight days. Andi stood and walked down the side-walk to the pier, hesitated, and then walked all the way out to the little lighthouse.

This light, according to the sign, marked the chan-nel opening for boats coming off the lake so they could find the way when it was dark or bad weather. She could see the real lighthouse if she turned and looked up the shoreline. Andi lay down on her belly at the edge of the pier and stretched her hand toward the lake. She dropped the crane onto the water and watched it bob with the waves. A minute later, it moved away from her and out into the lake. She stood up and watched until her eyes hurt from straining to see the bird.

It was time to go, anyway. The guys had told her to move the truck every day to keep the police from marking it abandoned. Manny and Torres had dropped her off Monday before going to the job site, and then every morning, she reparked the truck before any other cars came so that she didn't risk hitting them. Her father had been teaching her to drive, but they hadn't finished. Now, here she was.

Hope's light was on when Andi started the truck. There were more empty spaces than earlier in the week, so Andi practiced going down one aisle and around to another before choosing the new spot. Soon, she would have to try parking on the street.

Andi turned off the motor, grabbed her pack, and carefully locked the door. When she reached the alley that separated the public parking from the businesses,

Hope waved to her from the top of her steps. "Hey, good morning," she called.

"Hi."

"I thought that might be you. Ready to work?"

"Good to go," Andi said.

Hope came down the stairs and unlocked the café door. "Sunday morning is all about the pastries," she said. "Even Bella's can't keep up." Hope laid her computer bag on the desk. "Let me know how we're doing on all the paper products so I can get an order started. I don't want to run out in the middle of next week, but that's what happens when you use a little here, then a little more, and a little more..."

"OK." Andi tied her apron over a blue Café Hope t-shirt. She washed her hands and loaded the case with muffins and cinnamon rolls, leaving one shelf open for afternoon cookies.

Andi flipped on the espresso machine and then squatted down in front of the stacks of plates and paper bags, trying to guess how many were in each, when the thought gut-punched her. How much gas was in the truck? She had never checked the gauge. She remembered her father talking about how he watched mileage, but what was the magic number? She clutched the shelf in front of her. *Breathe. Breathe.*

"Andi?"

"Down here." *Breathe.*

"Hey, I didn't tell you any reorder points. I'm so used to you being here, I forgot you don't already know these things."

Hope chattered about bags and boxes. Andi nodded, but her mind was still on the truck.

"Well, let's unlock the door and let these people in."

Andi stood up and went to her spot. There were so many things to keep track of, and she would have to do it. There wasn't anyone else.

"So goes another week at Café Hope." Hope locked the door and flipped the sign. "I'm still so amazed at how this is happening," she said.

Andi nodded. She untied her apron and pulled it over her head.

"So, I have stuff to talk over," Hope said. "Why don't you grab your forms and come to the table. I'll get some cookies for us."

A new song from Hope's playlist started as Andi went into the storeroom. Hope had stuck a name tag that said "Andi," with a flower dotting the i, over a hook on the storeroom wall. Andi hung up her apron, grabbed her whole pack, and brought it to the front. The song was talking about not being forgotten or hopeless.

"Here you go." Hope pushed the plate toward her. "Remember when I told you I worked the resort circuit? Well, I met a lot of people with a lot of different stories. So, whatever you say next, I've probably heard it." She paused. "Andi, do you have a place to live?"

Andi pulled her hands into her lap, fighting the urge to reach for her hood. She nodded her head yes.

"Are you in danger?"

"No." Her ears picked up on the words *shelter* and *darkest night* as the song continued. Andi didn't want to think about what could be dangerous about living out of a truck with one punched-out window.

"Good." Hope exhaled. "I don't want anything to happen to you."

Andi looked up at her. No, not going there.

"Do you want to tell me what happened?"

Andi swallowed. "My dad died last week." Tears pricked her eyes.

Hope shook her head. "I am so sorry. Was it just...the two of you?"

Andi nodded. "And the rest of the crew. They traveled around doing construction."

Hope wrinkled her forehead. "How long have you been on the move?"

"As long as I can remember."

"Did you ever know any other family? Your mother?"

"No."

Hope looked at the ceiling and blew out her breath. "Wow. So, losing him was...everything."

Andi nodded.

"How old are you? Really."

"Eighteen."

"OK." Hope exhaled again. "So, you are an adult. That means you have the say for some things like where you live. At least in theory. I'm twenty-three and have my own business, but I can't rent a campsite without my mother cosigning. Anyway." She pushed some hair behind her ear. "Wow. I have to tell you, I don't know exactly what to do, but I'll help you in any way I can. And we can contact the state social services and see what they have."

The buzzing from Andi's stomach was pushing up fast, and she reached for her bag.

"Andi, hey. I'm sorry. Probably too much there." Hope blew out her cheeks. "Why don't we just start with this: what do *you* want to do?"

Besides going back in time, talking to my dad, and moving on when the crew leaves for a new job in a few months? Besides all that? "I want to keep the truck. It was my dad's."

"OK. First, you're going to need insurance and plates." She stopped. "When was your dad's birthday? What month?"

"November."

"We've got a few weeks then." Hope rubbed her lips together. "Well, why don't we look into how to get everything transferred over to your name. OK with that?"

"Yes."

"You can do this, Andi," Hope said. "I know you can."

CHAPTER 5

"It's going to be slow today, I think. Thursdays are sometimes like that." Hope studied her watch. "You've been here a lot these last few days. Why don't you punch out and have some time to yourself?"

"OK." Andi went to the storeroom, took off her apron, and hung it up. She wrote the time on the tan card and slipped it under the keyboard of Hope's computer. She put her backpack on her shoulder, went out the back door, and sat down on the bottom step of Hope's stairway. Where would she go?

A city worker used a leaf blower to clear the flower beds near the big anchor sculpture in front of the marina. A boat idled in the water. Two cyclists rode by on the trail that ran beside the channel, so Andi stood up and followed them.

After walking five blocks, she saw something that finally felt like home: the library. A woman pushed a stroller up the walk from the parking lot, a little kid walking beside her. A man came out of the square brick building and then waited to hold the door for them. Andi cut across the lawn and followed them in.

Like most of the libraries she had been in, this one smelled of old books and dust, but Andi breathed the scent in as if it was life itself. The stroller lady veered off to the children's area. Based on the number of kids sitting on the colorful rubber floor squares, story time would start soon. Andi found a table on the other side of the shelf from them, set her bag down, and looked around.

The large print books to her right were divided into categories, each shelf labeled: adventure, mystery, thriller, western. Across the room was the YA section, with some of the books propped up to show off their covers. Sci-Fi was behind her. Around the corner, she saw just what she needed: the bank of public computers.

Andi slung the bag's strap over her shoulder and snaked through the shelves to one of the open seats. She wiggled the mouse to wake up the computer, and a screen popped up asking for her patron number. She sighed. More empty spaces that wanted her to fill them in with information she didn't have.

She picked up her bag again and went to the YA titles. She read the descriptions on the back covers of the displayed books. A few months ago, she might have liked to read about kids her age escaping werewolves, casting spells, or having summer flings. None of it really worked for her now, so she put the books back in their places.

"Can I help you find something?"

Andi turned to the familiar voice.

"Oh, I know you," the woman said, "from the café." She put a finger to her forehead, thinking. "Andi." She pronounced it *Ahn-dee*.

"Yes."

"I am Birgit. Are you new to Frankfort?"

"Yes."

"I hope you like it. It's a *wahn-da-fall* little town."

Maybe she was German?

"Now, did you need help?"

Andi took a deep breath. "I want to use the computer, but I don't have a patron number."

"We can get you a card." Birgit smiled like it was a personal victory, her helping Andi. "Do you have something with your address? A bill?"

"No."

"A paycheck?" Andi shook her head.

"We can do a temporary card, and when you have one of those things, you can bring it back."

Andi rubbed her thumb along the strap of her backpack. "OK."

Birgit hustled off much quicker than any other librarian she had ever seen. Andi followed her to the desk and waited while the librarian scanned the barcode sticker and typed something into her computer.

Birgit smiled and handed the card across the counter. "Here you are. Please let me know if you have trouble."

"OK. Thank you."

Andi went back to the open terminal, typed in the number, and the internet opened for her like magic. She typed in "Michigan Driver License." At the top of the list, there were posts for drivers under eighteen, but Andi scrolled down until she found one that gave instructions for adults. Her father had given her the booklet of rules, and she could handle the twenty-five-dollar fee. The problem was the requirement to drive with a licensed adult for thirty days.

Maybe she could just read the manual and see if they would just waive the rule if she had a good driving test. Andi clicked on the link and flipped through the pages. From the time she could remember, she had been able to see something once and then recall it again later, something her dad had called photographic memory. It had been helpful in fixing the truck. She could read through the Chilton manual once and not have to keep looking at it while they worked on it together.

Thinking of him doing carpentry, fitting the wood pieces perfectly, made it feel like old times, like he was at the jobsite and would come afterward to pick her up. He always came in looking for just her. No one else had mattered. She sighed and pulled on her hair, as if that would make it long enough for her to hide behind. It was so hard to get up every day and know she would never see him again. And then the next day, wake up and do it again.

Andi took a piece of yellow recycled paper from the tray in front of her. She tore a perfect square and then began to fold first the cat's head and then his body in a sassy lounging pose. She used the tiny pencil from the holder next to the tray to give him eyes. She brushed the figure with her fingertips as if she had a real cat to pet. Folded animals were all she could have in the motels. "Hola, Gato," she said quietly. "¿Qué pasa?"

"The library will be closing in fifteen minutes."

Little kids from story time mobbed the area of the big picture books, and Andi logged off the computer. She should get back in case Hope needed her.

She walked back along the paved trail, thinking about the driver's license. It would have been so easy for her father to show her, in any of their hours together, how to do all the things that adults needed to do. She hadn't asked to be here by herself, trying to figure all this out. She might as well have been on another planet for all that she knew about living on this one.

She was confused by this new world. Would her father's rules apply here? Rules like: keep to yourself. The crew was so careful about letting anyone in for fear they would be reported and deported. She cut through the parking lot toward the café and saw the note on the windshield of her truck.

Andi, we're going to have to get you a phone. I ran to the bank, but I wanted to go to the new sushi place for dinner. Do you want to come with? Back soon. H

Or, her father's second rule: don't take what you can't pay for.

CHAPTER 6

Hope waved to her from the pocket park, and Andi waited for her to come around the paved pathway. "Hey," Hope said. "Did you see my note about dinner?"

"Yeah. Sounds good."

"Change of plans. Do you remember Maya from The Logslide? She has the little girl, Lainie? She needs me to babysit tonight. You can come with me, though. Lainie's super smart and fun."

Andi nodded. "OK." She had never been around kids except for those she saw from a distance at story time.

"Maya's got an appointment, so we should go now. Hang on a sec, I'll be right back." She ran up the steps to her apartment and came back with some keys. "Let's drive so we're not late."

While Andi watched Hope drive, she thought about her father and all the hours they had spent in the truck. So many things she could have learned from him if she had known. Why had they not talked about a future, for either of them?

A few minutes later, Hope pulled into the driveway of a duplex that sported a couple of plastic kid toys in the front yard. A little girl waited on the steps, and Maya held her back until Hope turned off the motor.

"Come here, Lainie-licious," Hope called to her.

Andi got out her side and waited at the front of the Jeep for Hope to catch up.

"I'm Lainie. What's your name?" the little girl asked as she tugged Hope along.

"I'm Andi."

"OK. We're going to have a princess night."

Andi glanced at Hope.

"We put on nail polish and watch something from Lainie's stash of movies," Hope explained.

"Oh. Sounds fun." Or not.

"So," Maya said, standing up. "I've already fed the pretty princess, but help yourself to whatever. I really appreciate you doing this. The neighbor's kid is sick, and it just seemed better this way."

"It's all good," Hope said. "You remember Andi."

"Hi, good to see you," Maya said. "OK. Well, have fun. I'll be back in a few hours. Be good, muffin."

Lainie grabbed Andi's hand and then Hope's again and practically dragged them inside. She chattered like a cartoon squirrel at Hope about a friend at preschool and the snack they got every day, pretty serious about all of it.

Andi perched on one of the barstools at the kitchen's small island watching Hope get out food and cooking pans. There was nothing like this in Andi's memory. No Disney or snacks or preschool. No refrigerator or frozen foods. No front yard and toys. She didn't belong here. She wasn't one of them.

Lainie went down the hall and came back with a bright pink tackle box that she handed up to Andi. "You can pick first, 'cause you're company."

"OK." Andi took the box and set it on the counter.

Lainie waited a second and then said, "Open it up."

Andi undid the latch and lifted the lid. Approximately one hundred different bottles of nail polish filled every compartment. Sparkly, solid, pinks, oranges, purples, greens, blues, neon versions of colors—it was too much to take in.

"Do you like this one?" Lainie had climbed onto the stool next to her and picked a bottle of fire engine-colored polish out of the mix.

"Um, I don't think red is my color."

"What about pink?"

As Lainie stirred the bottles, Andi spied a flash of black polish. "I'll take that one."

"OK." Lainie set the bottle aside. "Hope, what color do you want?"

"You can surprise me."

"Aw-right." Lainie studied the box and chose lime green, sparkly purple, and light blue. She studied them all from different angles before holding up the green. "This one."

Hope looked over from the stove and smiled. "I love it. Why don't you pick your movie? This is almost ready."

After eating half of Hope's grilled cheese and making sure everyone had painted nails, Lainie curled up in her blanket next to Hope on the couch. A half hour later, she was out cold. Hope handed Andi the remote and carried Lainie to her room.

Andi let the video play while Hope was gone. The Chinese girl in the movie had skills. She had skills too. The big question asked in the movie was whether the girl using her skills alongside the men would honor or shame her family, but for Andi, it was not a question, it was life. She had never known anything else.

"She must have played hard today." Hope plopped down. "She doesn't normally conk out that fast."

"She's cute," Andi said.

"Oh, Lainie knows it. So, you're welcome to hang out here or take my car back to the apartment. Whatever."

"I'll stay," Andi blurted out.

Hope nodded. "Oh, hey. I was thinking of doing some shopping online. I could order something for you too. If you want. There's not really any place in this area to buy clothes unless you want a souvenir shirt."

"OK, I guess. I mean, I don't really know what I would look for."

"I think this would be really cute on you." Hope swiped a finger across her phone a few times and handed it to Andi. On it was a photo of a model wearing a thick sweater over leggings.

"Which?"

"All of it," Hope said. "Or you could go with tall boots instead of short."

Andi handed back the phone. "I don't think I want to spend any money right now." She couldn't think of anything else to say. No way could she see herself in any of the clothes Hope showed her. Her fingers felt trapped under the nail polish. The hairstyle Hope pointed out in a commercial would make her look like a pixie.

None of it was her. Maybe it was a mistake, moving into this world. She liked it better when she was invisible and could be who she was, not who someone else thought she could be.

"I shouldn't spend any money either," Hope said, laying the phone aside. "It's just—well, sometimes I miss how things were. When I was living at home, I had a really generous allowance and my own credit card. I would buy whatever, whenever. I didn't have too many worries, at least not about money."

Andi felt like there was a "but" coming up.

"But it was all fake. My dad was arrested for fraud, and that was the end of the allowance. I'm glad, but sometimes I want to go back to the not knowing. Not knowing that life could get really messed up really fast."

"Yeah, I get that," Andi said.

"So here we are." Hope shrugged and pointed to the TV. "We're just like her. We can either wish away the future, or go out and make it happen."

CHAPTER 7

Andi closed her eyes, focused on the room in her mind, and saw her father sitting on the bed across from her with the phone to his cheek, but no matter how hard she strained her ears, she could not hear him. Andi sighed. The dream had been so real.

She sat up, careful first to peek out the truck window and make sure no one was watching. She slid her legs around to face forward and felt something under her foot. The blue zipper pouch was on the rubber floor mat. Weird. She remembered tucking it back behind the seat last time.

She laid it aside and pulled her duffel across the seat to her. The plastic bag full of dirty clothes took up most of the bag's space, and underneath were two shirts and her last pair of clean jeans. She ran her hand over the bulge of the inside pocket of the bag where her father's wallet was hidden, and bumped something hard. Andi unzipped the compartment and pulled out a plug box attached to a thin cord.

She could feel her heart rush as she got the phone out of the blue bag, attached the cord to it, and pushed the power button. Andi stared hard at the blank screen, but, no surprise, the phone was still dead. Like it would magically work without plugging it in. She got dressed and waited in her usual spot on the bottom step of the wooden stairway.

"Hey, look at you all early bird." Hope pulled her apartment door closed.

Andi stood and dusted off her jeans. She patted the phone in the pocket of her hoodie. "I woke up before my alarm."

Hope unlocked the café's back door and they started their morning ritual: Hope turning on the machines, Andi taking down the chairs. Before she went out to the front, Andi had plugged in the cord and set the phone out of the way. She glanced at the clock and wondered if the phone would be working by lunchtime. Maybe she would wait until after work instead. The dream had told her to find the phone, and she wanted to be alone when she turned it on. Which was stupid. What did she think? That he would call her on it?

"Go ahead and open the door," Hope called to her. "Let's get this party started."

The Sunday crowd was light. Every fifteen minutes, one person at a time had come in for a coffee, maybe two. The last hour had dragged.

"I think we're done," Hope said. "I can handle the cleanup today."

"OK."

"I saw you got a phone. Can I get the number?"

Andi had no idea how to find the number. "I don't actually know what it is."

"That's weird they didn't tell you. If you look in Settings, you should be able to find it. Is it a contract phone?"

Andi didn't know that either. She tugged on her hair trying to think what to say.

"I don't want to get all up in your business," Hope said, "but I can look at it for you, if you want."

Andi nodded. "I've never had a phone before."

They went to the storeroom, and Andi unplugged the phone and handed it over. Hope studied it, pushed the small button on the top and ran her finger down the screen.

"So right here, this little flower-looking thing, or I guess it's probably a gear, is the icon for Settings." Hope pushed the picture and ran her finger over the screen. "You just swipe it like this to move up and down the list. Here it is—phone information." She pointed to the phone number. "That's what we wanted, there. I'm going to send myself a text so I have your number, and you have mine. Do you know how to send a text?"

Andi shook her head.

"That's OK. So, it looks like this little thing is the text icon."

Hope went on explaining the process, creating a contact, and looking for the carrier. Then she typed in the password for the café's Wi-Fi. Andi's stomach sank with every word. This was just supposed to be a phone, but there was so much to know about it.

"Let me look up how to find out how much service time you have left," Hope said.

Time would run out? "OK."

Hope tapped something into her own phone and swiped with her finger. "Looks like we can just text to this number and see what you have. When you get to the end of your minutes or days, you'll have to buy a new card." She tapped into Andi's phone, and a moment later, there was a ding. "So, you have ten days left."

"Where do I buy a card?" Andi asked.

"I've never had this kind of service, but I think any of the dollar stores would have them."

"How much do you think they cost?"

"Let's find out." Hope typed on her phone and then turned it around to Andi. "Here are some options."

She could handle that.

"Let me just show you how to find your contacts, and then I should lock up the café." Hope swiped a couple of times and pointed to an icon. "If you press that, you can see everyone you've got. When I put my name in, I saw you already had some others. Was this your dad's phone?"

Andi nodded.

Hope smiled and handed the phone to her. "Let me know if you need any more help." She winked. "You've got my number."

After Hope closed the café, Andi went to the bench by the marina and took the phone from her bag. She pressed the power button and swiped at some things and pressed on others until she found the Contacts icon. A list of names filled the screen, and she traced the screen with her finger to show the rest of them. "Torres" made her breath catch.

She could call him. She hadn't seen any of the crew since they dropped her off weeks earlier. She pushed the little picture of the telephone and held the phone to her ear.

"Hello?"

"Torres, it's Andi."

A rush of breath, then Torres speaking rapid-fire. "*Dios*, Andi. Nate's name on the screen. You scared me."

"I'm sorry." Her heart squeezed in her chest just hearing his voice. She could hardly remember a time when Torres hadn't been on her father's crew. He was as close to family as anyone could be, besides her own father.

"It's OK. How are you?"

Tears gathered and then streamed down her face.

"Andi?"

"I'm OK." She swiped at her eyes with her sleeve. "I, um, got a job."

"*Bueno*. Where?"

"At the café by where you parked the truck."

"You doin' good?"

"I guess so. Well, no, not really." She sniffed. "I don't know what to do. I don't have a bank or a room. I'm so afraid they'll take away the truck and then I won't have anything. I don't know how to drive. I miss my dad." She paused. "I miss you."

"Sí."

"Torres, I want to come with you. When you go to the next job. I don't want to stay here."

There was a long silence. Andi looked at the phone, wondering if she had hung up accidentally.

"Andi."

"Yes?"

"You know you can't come with us, right?"

"I could get a job wherever you are. Someone could drive the truck, just until I get my license."

"No, *mija*."

"Torres, I can't do this. I mean I don't have *anything*."

"You got a lot, *chica*. You can go anywhere, do anything you want, no questions. You gonna throw that away? You know how many people want what you got?"

He was angry. She had never heard him angry, and it made her cry all over again.

"*Mija*, I'm sorry. I'm sorry. It's OK. You OK."

She wiped at her eyes.

"Look, you can't come with us. Before, you had Nate. People saw you with him, and that was OK. But people see a young, white girl with us, they start asking questions. You know?"

"They'll want your papers," she said.

"Sí." He sighed.

"It's never going to be like it was."

"No, *mija*. I'm sorry."

"I just thought, maybe…"

"I know.

She puffed out her cheeks and blew out the air. "Will you at least let me know when you leave?"

"Sí."

It was something, anyway. More than she'd gotten when her dad left. "OK." She nodded. "OK, bye."

But it couldn't be goodbye. She had known Torres it seemed like all her life. Most of the others had been on the crew for years. Maybe she couldn't go with them right away, but she would go later, after she got her license and learned the trade. So, then, it wasn't goodbye forever, just bye for now.

CHAPTER 8

A ndi unlocked the café's front door, took down the chairs, and reset the inside tables. Both beach and color tour seasons had passed, and the café was still busy. Seasons—a new word for her. According to the display at Frank's hardware store, for the next season, she would need gloves. Thick, puffy ones, not the work gloves her father had worn. She wondered if he had ever lived in a place where he would need one of the bright, plastic shovels Frank's had in the window.

A pickup truck rumbled by on Main Street, and her heart jumped at the sound, but it was not any of the crew. Andi sighed and turned from the window. As soon as she got back to the counter, the bell on the door jangled, and three guys came in.

"Hi," she said. "Welcome to Café Hope."

"Yeah, we'll need three coffees, black, and...gimme one each of the muffins."

"OK."

"What'll I owe ya?"

Andi went through the spiel, and the guy did the usual, "Huh. OK," before putting a twenty-dollar bill on the counter.

"No change," he said.

"Thank you." Andi slid the money into the drawer and put on the plastic serving gloves. She got everything ready and set it on the pick-up counter. "Enjoy." Hope's word.

The guys reminded her of some of the crew—rough hands, flannel jackets, farmer's caps. She cleaned off the coffee station for an excuse to stand there and hear them talk.

"One crew I worked on, everybody brought a lunch and set it by the furnace to keep warm. Whole place smelled like Mickey D's. Homeowner wadn't too hot on their four hundred K house smelling like drive-thru."

A different voice picked up the thread. "I worked with one guy, brought his kid to the jobsite. Guess the girlfriend was flighty and would *forget* to be home on time."

"Did she come over and get the kid?" the order guy asked.

"Not usually. He'd be covered in drywall dust from crawlin' round on the floor, but what could the guy do?"

Andi had not thought about her mother in a long time. She had no memories of her, and couldn't remember her father ever really talking about why she was not with them. It was always just the two of them, and Andi never got the idea her father thought it was unusual or hard that way. Did *she* crawl around in sawdust or play in dirt piled up next to the foundation? How had he worked and kept her safe at the same time?

Her dictionary word that morning was "nomad." Had her father wanted this kind of life, traveling like a nomad? Or had *she* been the reason he didn't do something else? Was he running to, or running from life? What would he have done differently if she hadn't been his kid?

As soon as the shift was finished, she found the blue plastic zipper bag, pulled everything out, and sorted through it. She set aside the papers for the truck, the strange key with a number on it, and the social security card Hope had found for her when she filled out the tax forms. What Andi wanted was the envelope with her name, "Cassandra," printed neatly on the front. A few years earlier, she had found the same envelope on the table in one of the motel rooms when her father was outside. In her mind, anything already open was fair game, but, just in case, she had read the form quickly and put it back before he could catch her.

She opened the envelope, unfolded the document inside and read the lines. Mother: Danielle Collins. This she had remembered and secretly called her Dani to be like her own name, just with the letters in a different order. There was the mother's age, nineteen, and place of birth, Detroit, but no current address listed. She moved down the page to the line she wanted. Father: Unknown. Andi sat back. Was her father really her father?

She folded the paper and slid it back into the envelope. Then she went where she always did when life got strange and found a table in the nonfiction section. The books on the shelf with their pages and pages of facts made the crazy of her own world settle down. These things were known, were true. She could count on them, even if everything else was sliding away like a pile of sand.

She pulled some paper from her bag and began to fold triangles, letting her hands lead her. Soon she had a row of cranes lined up in front of her on the table. The crisp paper, the straight lines, the finished product, all of it untangled her inside.

"Andi?"

Birgit stood in front of her.

"Oh, hi."

"I wondered if the cat was your handiwork," Birgit said. "I see you have other skills."

Andi put out a hand to gather up the birds.

"No, no. Please. I wanted to ask you to help me with a display. I want to have books on origami, on Asian cultures, and the symbolism of the thousand cranes. Would you be willing to help me? Even if you could just fold, that would be perfect. I am not very good. My birds fall over, or one wing is too short."

Andi fingered a crane so dark blue it looked black. "I can do that."

"Oh, that is wonderful." Birgit smiled. "I would like to start hanging up some birds over the weekend. Will that be enough time?"

As Birgit talked, Andi nodded at the right times. She imagined the paper cranes on the table in front of her shaking out their feathers and settling in. Had she ever felt that content? That sense of staying instead of going?

"And we have the six-by-six paper. Unless you want a different size, and then I can order more."

"That's a good size."

Birgit did some small silent hand claps in celebration. "Do you want to start now? You can come back to the prep room."

"OK."

Andi followed her to the windowed room behind the desk. Birgit cleared away some stacks of books from the work counter and took a packet of folding paper from a drawer. "How did you learn origami?"

"I read some books on it," Andi said.

Birgit stopped and placed a palm on her own chest like she was in love.

"My heart. Have you always been a reader?"

How should she answer that question? Besides watching TV, the only thing to do in the motel room was to read. Everything she knew, outside of what she learned from her father and the guys, had come from books, as many as she could stuff into a bag for one dollar at a library book sale. "Yes. I kind of...grew up in the library."

"I love it when parents show their kids the wonder of books." Birgit emptied a basket and brought it to Andi. "And schools—so important to have a strong library. Did you go to school in the area?"

"No," Andi said. "I was...homeschooled."

How else to explain the hours she spent in the libraries while her father worked? She had first gone when she saw kids through the library window, sitting in a circle, totally into whatever was being read to them. She wanted to know what they were learning, wanted to read more than the books her father had bought at Goodwill to keep her busy.

"Your parents must have been so committed to take on that responsibility. And so proud of you, too, when you graduated. Did they have a party?"

Andi pulled another paper from the packet and folded it in two. "It was just my dad and me. He...well, I didn't actually graduate. Yet." She could feel Birgit watching her. *Don't ask. Don't ask.*

"Well, if I can help, I would be happy to do that."

She smiled a little smile and looked back down at the paper that was becoming a white crane dotted with tiny orange flowers. "Thank you."

"Good. Well, I have some things to do. Please let me know if you need anything, and, Andi, thank you for doing this."

"Sure," she said.

Fold. Press. Breathe. Fold. Press. Breathe.

She had never thought of graduation. Or a diploma. Or a job. Or any of the things that had blown apart her world. Now, she needed to think of all of that at once. There was more to know about Nate Collins too. Whatever happened, whatever she found out, he would always be her father.

Andi sighed and set the bird on the desk. Maybe she kind of understood now why they moved around. She examined the birds again, wishing she had wings of her own. But where would she go if she did?

CHAPTER 9

Andi pulled the last shirt out of the dryer and folded it on the Laundromat table. She put the small stacks of her clothes in the duffle bag and zipped it closed. She had taken her time, waiting for the parking lot to clear more.

She had been taking small trips in the truck—to the beach parking lot or through the marina boat trailer storage, but this was her first time out onto the street. She had studied the booklet and knew the signs, lane markers, and rules. Eventually, she would drive over to the state highway and then call about scheduling the driving test.

She put her bag on the seat and then walked around the back of the truck. The little orange tag that said NOV caught her eye. The license plates would expire in two weeks. To relicense it, which she found out with Hope's help, she would need insurance and plate renewal fees that cost more than she had made at the café.

Andi wondered how long Hope could pay her, because at some point, the weather would be too cold for anyone to want to go downtown. Even that morning, the lawn around the parking lot had been covered with frost. Andi wondered, too, how much longer she could stay in the truck.

She started the engine and checked around her before putting it into reverse and edging out of the lot. If she followed the residential streets, she could make it to the back alley behind the café without going onto a major road.

She pulled into a new parking space and turned off the motor. Another secret the guys had shared with her: steamed up windows would draw cops. The night before, she had had to roll down the window an inch to keep the glass clear. She had bought a sleeping bag on clearance at Frank's, but even with that, it would soon be too cold to sleep in the truck.

Movement on the tugboat tied up at the dock caught her eye. A man walked back and forth across the deck, holding a big wrench one time, then a tarp, then the wrench again. It reminded her of the mechanic working on a bobcat at one of the jobsites. After watching him, she had checked the library for the Chilton manual for the truck. Andi had studied it and then explored under the truck's hood. The motor compartment wasn't laid out exactly as shown in the picture, but she had gone through all the things she recognized and figured out the rest.

She liked understanding how things worked. She even asked her father for money to buy things at Goodwill just to take them apart. Her first attempts, clocks mostly, didn't work afterward, but she got better the more she practiced. The idea of working on something big like a car was cool.

Andi opened the browser on her phone. Hope was right about the fact that she could use it like a computer. She typed in "Garage Benzie County" and found three mechanics. Andi frowned. She had hoped there was somewhere close enough to walk, but there was nothing in Frankfort, and the closest one was in the next town up the state highway.

The one good thing about driving so far was she could also check out the pawnshop that the map showed was just down the road from the garage. Maybe they would have what she needed there to replace her father's tools. Andi expanded the map to see if there were back roads she could take, but none of them went all the way from Frankfort to Benzie. They either ended at water, or just ended. She would have to go the state highway, but maybe if she waited until after the morning drivers got to their jobs, she could make it work.

Andi drove onto Forest Avenue under the big archway that normally welcomed people to Frankfort and
watched it get smaller and smaller in the rearview mirror. She was *doing* this. A few miles later, she turned
onto the state highway going north. Like every other
image she'd ever studied, she had the map memorized.
Not because she was worried about getting lost—it was
a straight shot, and Benzie was a small place. How hard
could it be to find her way?

The garage opened at seven, and she would be there
at nine, hopefully early enough that the owner would
not be elbows deep in a project. Andi replayed the
things she wanted to say: how she had experience with
changing oil on several makes and models. This was
true. Once the crew knew she was serious, they had
asked her to do their oil changes and replace their
batteries. She even figured out how to fix an exhaust
system on one of the trucks. She knew she could learn
more if she had the right tools and a lift.

Andi pulled into the lot and parked away from the
cars waiting for service. The truck was old enough
it could be mistaken for a tow job. She got out and
checked her appearance in the truck's window. She had
gone through her clothes a few times trying to decide
what looked right before landing on a plaid shirt over a
T-shirt. The bleached blonde color she had used on her
hair on a bored Wednesday had half grown out, but she
took a deep breath and tucked her hair behind her ears.
It was what it was.

The garage lobby door had a bell like the one at the café, and her stomach jumped a little out of guilt. Hope thought Andi was meeting a friend, who had somehow known the number of the phone she'd only had for a few weeks. Anyway.

No one was at the desk, so she waited a minute and then moved to the doorway that led from the waiting area into the garage. On the nearest lift, one of the guys was removing the lug nuts from a front tire, the *vvt vvt* sound of the air wrench ratcheting over all the other noise. He set down the tool and pulled off the wheel. When he looked in her direction, Andi raised a hand. He leaned the tire against a bench, walked away, and came back a minute later with an older man.

The white patch on his blue shirt pocket read "Duffy." She liked that—it sounded friendly. He motioned her back into the waiting area before speaking. "Can I help you?"

"Yeah." She cleared away the squeak and tried again. "Yes. I'd like to see about a job."

Duffy crossed his arms over his chest. "What kinda car?"

"No. I mean, I'd like to apply for a job."

"I gotta woman comes in at lunch to cover the phones and then take payments. Otherwise, I do it," he said.

"I meant a mechanic job."

The man tipped his head to one side and then raised his eyebrows like he'd just taken a bite of a sour pickle.

"How old're you?"

"Eighteen."

"You go to school?"

"I'm, I was, homeschooled."

He sighed. "You go to *mechanic* school?"

"Oh, uh, no. But I know how to change oil, and..."

He held up his hand to stop her words. "You go to school. You get certified. Then you ask for the job." He made a chopping motion after every sentence.

"OK."

Duffy fisted his hands on his hips and shook his head. "No shortcuts."

"Well, thank you, anyway," Andi said.

"You betcha." He touched two fingers to the bill of his ballcap and saluted her. Then he went back through the door into the garage.

Maybe she had just been too excited earlier to notice, but it suddenly seemed a lot colder now than when she had left Frankfort. Andi plodded to the truck, pulled her jacket out of the duffle, and put it on. She sat in the cab, keys in hand, watching the cars on the road go past. Everybody had somewhere to be, something to do, but not her. She felt like she was fourteen again, invisible to the crew, no more noticed or needed than scrap lumber.

Snow started falling, thick enough to need the windshield wipers. Andi studied the levers and then twisted the correct knob. She crept backward out of the spot, shifted into drive, and pulled up to the road. Her hand rested on the turn signal. Everything she owned was right there in the truck. She could go anywhere she wanted. She looked one way and then the other, clicked on her signal, and turned onto the road back toward Frankfort.

What would she do? She'd have to look for a place to live, for sure. Maybe she could park the truck there until she had enough money for the plates and insurance. After that, she could look into mechanic schools like Duffy said.

Without any warning, the truck slid across the pavement. She turned the wheel left and right trying to get straight in the lane. She pressed hard on the brake and the truck spun rear end first once, twice. She was falling backward, down a hill, the sky in her windshield. The sudden stop threw her against the door, and her head slammed into the window.

CHAPTER 10

V oices. Knocking. Her head throbbing. She reached up to push against her forehead to stop the pain.

"She's moving! Hey, stay still in there."

Andi opened her eyes. She could see mud and grass out the window. The seatbelt felt too tight, and she pulled on it, trying to figure out how to get loose.

"The fire department's here. Stay still, OK?"

Andi turned her head toward the voice. A guy outside the passenger window had his hands on the glass.

"I'm going up to them," he said, pointing a thumb over his shoulder. "We're not going to leave you, OK?"

Andi nodded her head, and pain shot through it like a lightning strike. She leaned against the glass and closed her eyes. What was going on? The passenger door opened, and Andi turned her head toward it again.

"Don't try to move. I'm with Benzie County Fire. We've got our first responders coming."

She groaned. "OK."

"What's your name?" he asked.

"Andi." Even her own voice was so loud, adding to the pounding in her head.

"Andi, I'm Doug. I'm going to come in and shut off the motor, OK? You stay still."

She pushed against her head again. "All right." He leaned across the seat and turned the key in the ignition. Andi heard other voices outside the truck. "What happened?" she asked.

"Looks like you hit black ice and spun out. Do you remember that?"

"A little."

A man's voice outside the truck. "Whatcha got, Doug?"

Doug turned his head to talk to whoever was behind him. "Single female, head trauma. Coherent."

"OK, we're ready to extract," the voice said.

Doug faced her again. "Andi, can you put your left hand on the steering wheel?"

She followed Doug's instructions for moving each hand and each leg. Then to reach down and unbuckle the seat belt. Finally, to move her legs over to the passenger side and slide over.

Her duffle was in the windshield, and some shirts had fallen out of it onto the sleeping bag on the floor. She looked back toward the steering wheel. "Where's my backpack?"

"We'll get your stuff later," Doug said. "You first."

Panic strangled her. "I need my backpack."

"It'll be all right; we'll get it. Andi, I need you to keep sliding over. I'm going to help you stand up, OK? It's pretty slick in the grass here."

He helped her out, and other hands took her arms, supporting her as she climbed up to the roadway. Her shoes slipped on the snow, and she shivered against the cold. Emergency lights flashed, and she closed her eyes to block out their accusations.

A couple of people in fire gear steered her to the right. "Let's get her in the back."

Andi saw the ambulance and tried to get loose of the hands on her arms. "I don't want to go to the hospital."

"We're just going to check you out right here." A woman in a white uniform shirt moved to her side. "You took a big hit."

Andi let them help her sit down in the open doorway of the ambulance.

"My name's Carrie. I'm going to look at this head wound, OK?"

"Yeah."

Carrie pressed a cloth to her head, and Andi leaned back away from the pain.

"I don't blame you," Carrie said. "You've got a pretty big goose egg. The cut's not as big as it seemed, so that's good. Can you tell me where you were going?"

"To Frankfort."

"Is that where you live?"

"Yes."

"Besides a headache, does anything else hurt?"

Andi closed her eyes.

"Andi?"

"My neck." She wiped at her neck with her left hand.

"I see it." Carrie pulled back the collar of Andi's jacket. "You've got a lot of burn from the seat belt. Tomorrow, you'll have a bruise across your chest, too." She settled the collar back in place. "Andi, can you read the letters on my nametag?"

She opened her eyes. "C-a-r-r-i-e."

"Good. OK, well, the best thing is to let me take you to the hospital and get your head checked out. You have a concussion at the very least. Doc'll want to run a CT or MRI to be sure everything is OK."

"I'm all right. I just need my backpack," she said. "I can't go to the hospital."

"Well, you can't stay here either." Carrie turned to the other ambulance white shirt. "Patient is refusing transport. Andi, is there a number we can call? If you don't go with us, you'll have to have someone pick you up."

"I'll just wait in the truck."

"Nope." Doug was back. "That truck is totaled. The left front wheel is broken off, and the whole left side is smashed. We've got a tow truck on the way." He put out his hand. "Here's your backpack, and we got the duffle and sleeping bag out too. Is there anything else you need from the vehicle?"

"No," she said.

Andi put her hands to her head and pressed. So much pain. She had to think. She couldn't call Torres or the crew. What would they do with her anyway? The last thing they would want is the police asking them why she was driving illegally. "Can you call Café Hope in Frankfort?"

"OK," Carrie said. "Who do you need?"

Andi looked over at her truck, tipped on its side in the ditch. She closed her eyes, squeezing back the tears. She did this. She had messed up the last thing she had left, and now, there was nothing.

"Hope," she said. "I need Hope."

CHAPTER 11

"The tow service is going to need a place to take this," Doug said, "and a card number."

Andi looked at him and then at Carrie. "Card?" she asked.

"Credit or debit number," Carrie said. "Do you have one?"

Andi closed her eyes and thought of the envelope of checks from the café she had not cashed. There were six dollars in her bag. "No."

Carrie held the phone to her ear. "Hello, this is Carrie Muldoon from Benzie Ambulance service. I'm calling for Hope on behalf of Andi Collins." There was a pause. "She's OK, shaken up. We did recommend transport to the hospital, but she is declining treatment. Would you like to speak to Andi?" Carrie handed her the phone.

"Hello?"

"Andi! Are you all right?"

"I think so. I don't know what to do." The words tumbled out of her mouth right onto the ground. She wrapped her arms around herself and rocked back and forth.

"It's OK, Andi. Tell me what's happening now."

"They said they'll need a place to take the truck—it's totaled. And a card number. I don't have a credit card."

"It's OK," Hope said. "They can use mine for now. Do you have roadside assistance through your insurance?"

What was roadside assistance? "I don't know."

"It's all right. Um, tell them to use the yard outside Frankfort. They'll know it, it's huge. Let me get someone to cover the café, and I'll come get you there. Just have them call me back for the card, OK?"

"OK."

A sheriff's car pulled up behind the truck and Andi's stomach sank deeper. She handed the phone back to Carrie. Would they arrest her for not having a license? She couldn't even afford a fine. She put her hands to her head again and wished it would just go ahead and explode.

"I'm Officer Baer. Are you the driver of the truck?"

Andi looked at the feet in front of her and then up at the man. "Yes."

"I'll need your license and registration," he said.

"I don't have my license...with me," she added. "The registration is in there." She pointed to the still-ditched truck.

"I'll look it up by plate, then."

He put his hands on his hips, just like Duffy had.

"How fast were you going?"

"Fifty-five, like it says," Andi said.

He was silent for what seemed like hours.

"How old are you?"

"Eighteen."

"Have you driven through snow before?"

"No."

"Straight up?" He turned to Carrie, and she nodded.

What was straight up?

He rested his right hand on his equipment belt and motioned at the road with his left. "Looks like you hit some black ice. That first cold day always takes kids by surprise." He nodded. "I'll run the plates. Did you call someone to come get you?"

Andi nodded and instantly regretted it. "Yes, my friend," she said.

"All right. How's the head?"

"It hurts."

"Well, sit tight."

He was back after a few minutes. "Who's Nate Collins? Your father?"

Andi moved her head, more carefully this time.

"He know you got his truck?"

Andi shook her head and then pressed a hand to her forehead. "He's dead."

"I see that."

He raised his eyebrows in a way that said he wouldn't accept any BS she might shovel at him.

"Do you have a license to drive?"

Andi scowled at the ground. "No."

He nodded and took inventory of her bags and sleeping bag on the ground by her feet. "This all your stuff? Everything you got?"

Andi hesitated. What answer should she give? She hurt so much. "Yes."

He rubbed his chin and thought for a moment. "Well, here's what's going to happen. Normally, this would be a ninety-day misdemeanor." He held up a hand when she startled. "Now let me finish. OK. You're not going to jail, all right? There *will* be a fine. Later, you can apply for a temporary license, but it will be suspended and have two points on it. After the suspension is lifted, and *after* a driving class, and *after* the road test, you will be able to drive. But not before then. Is that clear?"

"Yes."

"All right. I'm going to release you to your friend. I hear she's meeting you at the tow yard."

"Yes."

"OK, then, Andi." He nodded and pressed his lips into a line. "You take care of yourself."

The ride to the junkyard was one of the worst she had ever been on. Every bump and bounce split her head wide open. At least, that's how it felt. She had no other obvious injuries besides what was under the small square bandage.

"Rough day, huh?" The tow driver shouted over the noise.

Andi nodded, which killed her head. She put her hands to it again.

"You might wanna rethink going to the doctor. A concussion's a b—well, it's not good. Hurts, too, don't it?"

"Yeah."

He looked across the cab at her. "Anything in the truck I should know about?"

"Like what?"

"Pot, drugs, anything like that?"

"No." Andi scowled at him.

"Just askin'. I gotta stay clean." He was quiet for a minute. "Cop let you off easy. Prob'ly figured your dad would be enough law."

"Yeah." Her dad. A video played in her head of all the times they had ridden together in the truck. Every motel stop, every fast-food window, every trip to do laundry, everything. The truck was the last thing she had of him. She hugged her backpack to herself, her fingers feeling for the edges of the wooden box buried at the bottom. The part of him she couldn't bear to look at, but couldn't live without.

Hope's Jeep was at the tow yard entrance, and as soon as the truck stopped, she climbed out and hurried to Andi's door.

"Hang on a minute," the driver said. He punched buttons on a tablet. "What's the email?"

"I don't have email."

"Does *she*?" He waved the tablet toward Hope. "It's for the receipt and instructions."

"Oh," Andi said to him and opened the door to see Hope better. "Hi."

"Andi, are you OK?"

"Yeah. He wants to have an email."

Hope looked past Andi and spelled out the address.

"All right, you're free," the driver said. "Take care of yourself."

Well, yeah, she was doing a great job of that so far. Andi gave him a small smile and pulled the duffle across the seat to her.

"Hand me your bags," Hope said. "It's a big step."

CHAPTER 12

"I'll take you back to my apartment," Hope said as she drove out of the lot. "You probably have a concussion, and I think you're supposed to keep someone awake after that."

"OK."

"We should call your insurance company. Let them know right away."

"That's a good idea." Andi waited for the lecture, the disappointment, something.

Hope stopped at the crossroad until traffic cleared and then made a left turn. Andi squinted, trying to block out the bright sun that screamed at her through the windshield.

"Are you sure you don't want to go get checked out?" Hope asked. "We could go to urgent care. You look miserable."

"I'll be OK."

Hope pulled into the spot behind the café and turned off the motor. She sighed. "We have to talk about this."

Here it came. "OK."

"Were you living in the truck all this time?"

The scene replayed itself. The motel woman at her door, gasping and panting her smoky breath in Andi's face. *I can't have that truck out front—the smashed window is bad for business. Tell Nate he's got to move it around back. You his kid? He didn't say nothin' about having a kid. How old are you?*

"Why didn't you say something?" Hope shook her head. "No, it was my bad. I should have done...I don't know." She turned toward Andi. "Do you *want* help?"

I can let you have the room one more day, then you gotta go. You hear me? I'm sorry about Nate, but I can't have CPS pokin' around here.

Andi fingered the zipper on her pack. Torres and the guys had done all they could for her, but she still needed help—that was obvious. There was so much she didn't know, couldn't have known. Why was she so afraid to let Hope in?

"Yes." She turned to Hope. "I want help."

"OK. I can do that." Hope smiled and unbuckled her seat belt. "My apartment's pretty small, but you're welcome to stay as long as you like. I'll get your stuff."

Andi followed Hope up the stairs she had hidden behind so many weeks ago when her world had collapsed the first time. Hope stepped inside the apartment and set the bag on the floor by the bathroom and then turned back to Andi. "Come on in."

As Andi moved inside and closed the door, Hope evaluated the apartment. "I think if we move things around a little, you'll have some space of your own," she said. She turned back to Andi and waved toward the couch. "So, get comfortable. Did they give you anything for the pain?"

"No."

"Well, let's start with that."

"Thanks. That would be so nice." Andi lowered herself onto a chair at the small dining table.

There was a quick knock on the door, and Hope reached out to open it.

"Hi, Hope. How is Andi?"

Hope backed up and motioned Birgit into the small space. "Come on in. We just got back."

"Hi." Andi gave her a little smile.

Birgit gasped and put a hand to her mouth. "Are you all right?"

Andi touched the bandage on her head. "Yeah."

"Oh, I forgot the ibuprofen." Hope disappeared into the bathroom and then was back again. "Birgit, could you hang out with Andi while I check on Maya?" She went past Andi to the sink, filled a glass with water, and brought it all back to the table.

"Ya, I have until two."

"Great. I shouldn't be gone very long."

They watched her go and then Birgit sat down across the table from Andi. "I'm so glad you are OK," she said. "Was your car badly damaged?"

"Yeah, they will probably total it. I guess I have to call the insurance company." Andi pressed a hand to her head and then leaned down on her elbow.

"Would you like me to check on that for you? Even when there is no problem, it can be a headache to call about insurance." She shook her head slowly. "I'm sorry. I did not mean that to be funny."

"It's OK." Andi exhaled trying to think where she had left the blue bag. She hoped it hadn't fallen out of the duffle. "Yeah, that would be amazing if you would call them for me."

"I brought some things for you from the library," Birgit said. "I thought you might need to rest after this morning." She took a brown envelope out of her bag and laid it on the table. "It is a study guide—to finish your homeschooling. I did my education that way as well," Birgit went on. "I went to an international school online. I have a certificate instead of an American diploma, but I think the testing to get there is very similar. I would be happy to help you, if you wish."

Her father had told her to keep to herself and not to take anything she couldn't pay for. Instead, she had made a lot of trouble for herself and everybody else, and she had to admit she couldn't pay for any of what Hope and Birgit wanted to do for her. But, here was another person wanting to help, wanting her to survive. More than just survive, to go on with life. Well, this morning she was literally sideways in a ditch. There wasn't any place else to go from there but up.

CHAPTER 13

Her head hurt so much. The medicine had helped some, but the ache still echoed day after day. Andi had stopped looking at the bruises in the mirror—what was the point of reminding herself how stupid she had been?

"Do you need anything before I open the café?" Hope asked, zipping her coat.

"No." She glanced up at Hope. "I don't know what I would have done without you."

"No worries. We girls have to watch out for each other." She picked up her bag. "I'll check in with you after the rush. Call me if you need anything."

"OK."

Andi lay back on the pillow. We girls. She had never had anyone talk about her like that. Andi was still checking that new look to decide if she liked it. She and her dad had been a group. They and the guys on the crew had been a group. She had always been the only girl, but they had never made her feel like an outsider. They always had her back.

There was one guy who had not. Thomás. Andi still shivered, thinking of the way she'd look up and find him watching her. Once, when she was under the hood trying to sort out a noise in the truck, he had come up next to her. When he ran a finger over her hand, it felt like a snake ready to bury its fangs in her.

She had gone into the motel room and washed her hands, soaping them again and again until the water burned away his touch. Then she pulled up her hoodie and crawled under the covers. It was the first time she had ever felt like she needed to hide from any of them. Thomás had never reported to work the next day. At the time, she was glad he left, but thinking back now, she knew the guys had enforced a code among brothers that also included her.

Her phone vibrated on the table, and Andi pressed one hand to her head as she reached for the device. The screen flashed the time: 10:30. She hadn't even realized she'd fallen asleep. The phone buzzed again, telling her that Hope had left a text.

Guy down here asking about you. Torres. Legit?

Andi texted back. *Yes. Do you mind if he comes up?*

Looks like there are two more out front. Send all?

Andi texted a thumbs-up. They had found her, even without the truck. Her heart jumped in her chest but then fell when she thought of telling them what happened and of why they were there to see her.

She stood up and then sat back down til her head stopped swimming. There was a knock on the door, and she tried it again, slower this time. "Just a sec," she called out and then whimpered in pain. Finally, she got to the door and opened it to find Torres, with Manny and Garcia behind him on the steps.

"Hi," she said. "Come on in."

"*Mija*, what happened to you?" Torres frowned.

"I had an accident—with the truck." She sank into one of the kitchen chairs to get her head straight.

"Are you OK?"

Define OK. "Yeah. Just...everything hurts." She frowned. "And the truck was totaled."

Manny swore in Spanish under his breath. Some of her first Spanish attempts had been words like that, but her father had shut that down real fast. "Oh, man, Andi."

"It's OK. I shouldn't have been driving it anyway." The guys still huddled by the door. "Do you want to sit down?"

"No, we have to go soon." Torres shook his head. "Gotta new job. Over by Detroit."

Hope had commented on the fakey-green hydro-mulch sprayed a few days earlier, so Andi figured the condos were done. Still, she hadn't wanted to think about the guys leaving. They had given her space, pushing her out of the nest like a baby bird, but she always thought they'd be there in case she couldn't fly on her own after all. And now, they were leaving.

"You doin' good, *chica*?" Manny asked.

"Yeah, I'm doin' good. I work downstairs, or I will when my face isn't bruised and I can stand up without falling down."

"Where you livin'? Here?" Manny looked around.

"No. I mean, I wasn't. Now with the truck...Anyway, I'll figure it out." She shrugged.

"You *lista*." Garcia looked at Torres.

"Smart. He says you're smart. You got this," Torres said.

Andi nodded, just a little. About as much as she believed the statement that she was smart.

"Your dad," Torres continued. "He was a great man. He loved you very much, and he was so proud of you, how you learned all those things by yourself. He wanted you to have a real life when you could be on your own, not just going from job to job like we did." He reached up in a grasping gesture. "You have a strength. Find it and use it." He dropped his hands. "OK, I'm done talking."

"*Buena suerte*," Manny said. Good luck.

"Thanks," Andi said. "For everything." She would not cry. She would not cry. "You guys have been my family."

They all stood there, not speaking, not wanting to move. Andi got back up, steadying herself with the table. "Adios," she said. She held out a tentative arm in invitation.

"Adios," Torres said, stepping into the hug. "Remember, you got the key." Then he backed away and made room for Manny and then Garcia.

Andi hugged them each in turn. "Bye," she said, squeezing her eyes shut.

Torres folded her into a second hug. "Te amamos."

And then they were gone.

Andi sat back down and held her head in her hands, the tears running down her face. She would give anything to go back to last year, or even last summer. To be with her father and Torres and the rest. To make time stop. But nothing would make that happen. No matter how long she sat there wanting to go back, the only way left was ahead.

She saw the brown envelope from Birgit across the table. She wiped her eyes, pulled open the flap, and took out the contents. Dates and locations for GED testing were in there with a booklet on how to prepare, and the form to fill out and send back with a hundred and fifty dollars.

Andi looked from the envelope to the apartment. Bright flowers, pillows scattered on the couch—it was like walking into a hug of Hope. The guys were her past, but these women were her future. The strength that Torres thought was hers, it came from them, but only if she would allow it. Andi slid the materials back into the envelope. She would start with asking Hope to help her drive.

How long would the future wait for her to get her act together?

Chapter 14

Andi closed the book. Her stomach was growling, and she couldn't focus on the Boston Tea Party without thinking about something to eat. Hope had been so nice to take her in and feed her and give her everything she needed, even during the weeks she couldn't work in the café. Maybe a way to pay Hope back would be to kick in for some groceries.

Andi pulled on the tall rubber boots she had got at Frank's. The puffy coat Hope had ordered for her wasn't due for delivery for two more days, so she layered another shirt under her hoodie. Dressing like that had been warm enough, even in the middle of winter, every-where else she and her father had lived. Andi got the plasticky reusable shopping bags from the closet, left a note for Hope, and went out the door.

When she lived in the truck, she had walked the ten blocks to the grocery store every few days with no problem. But today, the cold stabbed her, first in her nose and lungs, then her hands and arms. She pulled up her hood and crammed her hands into the front pocket on her sweatshirt. The sun's glare off the new-fallen snow was so bright, it burned just looking at it, but by the time she reached the library, her entire body was freezing. There was no way she could walk another mile, shop, and bring everything back in this cold.

She turned back, and icy air blasted her in the face. Andi ducked between the bank and jewelry store to get out of the wind and stood there, shivering violently. She couldn't stay put, but walking into the wind was no better. Finally, she pushed herself out onto the walkway that ran behind the businesses and back toward Hope's apartment.

After lying under three blankets for half an hour, she could at least feel her toes again. She got up and made some hot water in the microwave. The numbers on the read-out counted down not just the time left before tea, but also the time left before she had to make some major changes.

Not that she had a car, but maybe she could borrow Hope's Jeep for days like this. But before she could think of having a car she needed to take the driving test. More than once, she had started to ask for help, but Hope had done so much already. On the other hand, maybe her boss was ready to ditch the unintended roommate.

"Of course, I'll help you," Hope said that night. "I didn't realize you had never learned." She frowned. "Does that mean you were driving without a license when you crashed?"

"Yeah."

"Can you even get a license then?" Hope lifted her spoon and blew on the soup.

"The sheriff deputy said I could, but it would come with points." Andi held up the booklet. "I read through this, but I need an adult to supervise me in the car for thirty days. Then I can take the test."

"We can start tonight," Hope said. "We need some stuff from the store anyway."

Hope's Jeep was easier to drive than the truck, and the hardest part was to not go too fast. They drove around in the marina parking area and then to the grocery store. On the way back, Hope had her practice parallel parking on Main Street.

"This will be easier to learn now when no one's here. With traffic, it's kind of tricky."

Andi felt good as she carried up the bags of food. Her driving was pretty smooth, and she got the hang of checking mirrors and changing lanes.

"I think you did awesome today," Hope said. "Next weekend, we should go out on the state highway where there are more cars. We can road-trip!"

The memory of the seat belt squeezing her tight took Andi's breath away. Her heart beat in her ears. She couldn't move.

"Andi?" Hope set her bag on the table and came around to face her. "Hey. Are you OK?"

Breathe. Breathe.

"Oh, my gosh. I didn't even think. Do you need to sit down?"

Andi shook her head and blinked away the thought. "No, I'm OK."

"Maybe we should take this slower."

Andi let out her breath. "Yeah, that would be good."

"I'm sorry." Hope shook her head. "That was stupid."

"No, it's...it's OK." Andi gave her a little smile. "I'll probably have to leave here someday."

Hope shrugged and grinned. "Only when you want to." She opened the refrigerator and unpacked the bag of cold food.

Leave here. Grow up. What other things would she have to do on her own? Andi pulled a box of cereal from the second shopping bag. Really, she was not alone, which was so much more than she deserved. She took a deep breath. "How about two weeks? For the highway."

Hope closed the refrigerator. "Done."

Chapter 15

"I hope you like it," Hope said.

Andi looked at the wrapped present Hope held out to her. "It's not even Christmas yet."

"I know, but I couldn't wait. I've already been keeping it hidden for a week."

"Thanks." Andi peeled back the paper and opened the box. Under the white tissue paper was a light blue sweater. She ran her hand across the soft yarn and then held it up.

"It's a cowl neck," Hope said. "You can leave it down, or pull it up on your head. Like a hoodie."

"It's really pretty," Andi said. She had no clothes that anyone would call pretty.

"I thought maybe you could wear it today. With your jeans and my boots. The ones with the fur tops. Oh, and there's another surprise later." Hope got up from the chair and went into her room.

Andi laid the sweater back in its box. Her mouth went dry. What kind of surprise? Maybe she should back out of the driving, say her throat was sore or something.

Hope came back holding the boots. "I just need to put in an order and then I think we can go."

"OK."

Hope smiled. "This is going to be so fun."

Andi pulled onto Main Street, and after a few minutes, passed under the archway. She could do this; she *was* doing this. She turned on her signal, stopped at the light, took a deep breath, and turned onto the highway.

"Keep going on this road until I tell you," Hope directed.

"OK."

While Andi focused on keeping inside the lines, Hope talked about friends she had in high school, trips she went on with a singing group, and working at the ski resorts. Andi could relate to none of it.

"Here's the turn," Hope said. "You get a twofer today."

"Twofer?"

"Two for one. You're logging highway miles and city miles. We're going to Traverse."

Andi squeezed the steering wheel. What if she hit someone or caused an accident? What if she got them lost? Or got a ticket?

"It won't be *busy* busy at this time of the year," Hope continued, "but it's bigger than Frankfort." She glanced at Andi. "You can relax. You're doing great."

Andi took a deep breath and let it out.

Hope smiled. "Better?"

Andi followed each direction Hope gave: leave the highway, drive along the bay, turn from the center lane across two lanes of on-coming traffic, circle the mall. Finally, they turned onto a smaller city street, and Andi relaxed. With the older buildings, it felt a lot like Frankfort.

"Parallel park in that spot there," Hope said.

Andi pulled forward of the target, angled in, and scored the goal. No one honked a horn or yelled at her. It was, to use Hope's new phrase, awesome.

"OK. Here's the surprise. My friend Michaela just opened this tea shop. It's that one there with the green and white awning. Today, she's hosting a princess tea party, and I told her I'd come help, but I also want to get some ideas for the café. You have such a great memory I wanted your help taking it all in. And, it was a good reason for the road trip."

"Fun." This was a lie, but for Hope, she would fake it.

They walked back down the block to the shop. Hope held out both hands as she took it in. "This is so cute."

Once they got inside, Andi waited near the door while Hope and her friend hugged and talked. Pink and white balloons decorated the room. Each table was set with a different little flowered teapot and tiny cups. Stuffed animals were seated near the counter at a miniature table and chairs. Andi had experienced all of this cuteness exactly never, and the urge to run back to the car was excruciating.

"Michaela, this is my friend, Andi."

"It's so nice to meet you," Michaela said.

She had the same accent as the people on the *British Baking Show.*

"Hope has told me all about you, and she's so fortunate to have you at the café too."

Andi smiled. "Thank you." She waved vaguely at the room. "This is very sweet."

"We have twenty little girls and their mums coming in an hour. I want them to have so much fun."

Andi jumped on that. "I don't mind working so you two can be out here." There was nothing she wanted more than to be behind the door where she could breathe.

"That would be fantastic," Michaela said. "Thank you so much. Let me show you everything."

Andi followed Michaela back to the prep area. It wasn't huge, but it was more than Hope had with just her sink and metal counter. White boxes were stacked on the long table in the middle of the room, each with a coffee-colored swirl logo shaped like a cinnamon roll. She took off her coat and looked for a place to wash her hands.

"That sweater is gorgeous and the perfect color for you. It would be a shame to get icing on it." Michaela went to the hook on the wall and brought back an apron covered with big, round roses in different shades of pink.

Andi fingered the cowl, tempted to pull it over her head. Instead, she exchanged her coat for the apron Michaela held out. "Thank you."

Andi filled the trays with cookies and mini-cupcakes and carried them out to the tables of adoring mothers and girls in sparkly dresses. She had never lived in a little-girl world. It wasn't a bad place to be, but it was just not right for her. As she cleaned up afterward, she made a decision. She needed to get a life. One that fit her and didn't require her to be someone she was not. It was time.

Past time, actually.

CHAPTER 16

"My mom called today," Hope said as she stirred the pasta mix. "She's flying back to spend Christmas with my grandparents and wants to see the café while she's here."

"Where does she live?" Andi asked.

"Alaska. It's about as far from home as she could go without leaving the hemisphere."

"I guess so."

Hope laid down the spoon. "There's kind of a backstory. But, anyway."

"So, is that good that she's coming back?" Andi asked.

"Definitely. I haven't seen her for three years."

Andi looked at her pillow and blanket tucked beside the couch. Would Hope's mother want to stay here?

"Yeah," Hope continued with her back turned, "I'll probably close the café on the twenty-third for the rest of the week and drive down with her." She brought the saucepan to the table. "No pressure, but if you want to come with me, you're more than welcome. For Christmas."

The words hung in the air. Hope had a few lights up on the wall in the shape of a triangle, the only kind of Christmas tree that would fit in the space. The stores along Main Street, even the ones closed for the winter, had displays of wrapped presents. To Andi, it seemed like she was the only one not waiting for Christmas.

Christmas in the past had been quiet. The guys were either on the road to see their families, or holed up in their rooms doing videochats across time zones and borders. Her father might have given her a little gift, and pretended at the Goodwill counter not to see the things she picked out for him.

Andi played with the tiny pompoms on the pillow in her lap. Any way that she looked at it, going with Hope would make her twice as lonely for her father, and she would be crashing their party. She didn't belong in Christmas this year.

"That's really nice of you, but I'll stay here," Andi said. "If it's OK." Was that rude?

"Sure. And you can always change your mind.

Andi had gotten so used to the 24/7 togetherness that it felt strange being alone in the apartment without Hope somewhere nearby. Living in motels had trained Andi to entertain herself, but there was nothing she really wanted to do. During the three hours Hope had been gone, she had cleaned up, done the dishes, and washed the windows. She pulled one of Hope's business books off the shelf, paged through it, and set it aside. Hope had known what she wanted from life and made it happen. What did she want from hers?

Birgit had given Andi the study guides she would need to take the GED test, and she hadn't even opened them. Obviously, life moved on for everyone, so why did she think it wouldn't for her? She and Hope weren't that different, both orphaned in a way. The only difference was Hope could call her parent on the phone whenever she wanted.

Andi found her dictionary, opened it toward the back, and blindly pointed at the page with her finger. The word for the day: pretend. Once she had asked her father if her mother was dead. His answer had been, "I don't know, and don't ask me again." She never had, but always hoped he would fill in more of the blanks. Especially the one that read Father: Unknown.

She pulled her phone out of her bag and powered it up. It still seemed like some kind of magic lamp that would do something if she just polished it enough. Andi scrolled through the programs and found the Contacts icon. One by one she read the names, looking for one she recognized. Her eyes stopped on "Dee." Every other contact, even Torres, had a first and last name, and she had never heard her father talk about anyone named Dee.

She pushed the little telephone icon and held the phone to her ear as it rang.

"Nate, I don't have time for this," said the voice. "I told you last time—"

"It's not Nate. It's Andi." There was a deep bass beat in the background so she knew the call hadn't dropped, but the woman was silent. "Hello?" Andi heard the click of a lighter, then the sound of someone taking a drag on a cigarette, and finally a sigh.

"Whatever my brother told you about me is probably better than the truth." The music thumped, and the woman sniffed.

Her brother? If Andi could get her to just talk, or maybe they could meet. She took a breath. "I just wondered—"

"I can't do anything for you. You're better off staying with Nate," the woman said, and ended the call.

Andi dropped the phone into her lap and sat back. Dee, if that was her name, had said *Nate* and *my brother*. She had never said *your father*. The snakes coiled and uncoiled in Andi's stomach.

Over the years, she had tried to imagine a mother who was part of her life and not at the same time. She had pretended her mother was traveling or had amnesia when that was the dictionary word for the day. She pretended what it would be like if she was waiting for them when the crew went to the next job.

She pretended her mother would call, or write, or come back.

If what Dee said was true, Andi hadn't been the only one pretending.

CHAPTER 17

The loud knock scared Andi, and she bobbled the full glass of water in her hand.

"Andi, it's Birgit!"

She set down the glass and opened the door.

"I'm so glad you're here. I come bearing gifts," Birgit said. "Well, I guess, gift, singular. Is it all right if I stay for a few minutes?"

"Yes, come in."

Birgit kicked the snow off her boots and stepped inside. "Hope said you decided to stay here for Christmas." She pulled a small present from the deep pocket of her coat and handed it to Andi.

"Should I open it now?" Andi asked.

"Yes. I am not a patient person."

Birgit shrugged off her coat and perched on the Big Chair, what Hope called the second piece of furniture in her living room. Everyone always left the couch for Andi, like it was hers to claim.

"OK." Andi sat down on the couch with the present in her lap. She slid the ribbon off the box and ran a finger under the tape to open the paper. She lifted the lid and pulled out a key.

"It's a house key," Birgit said. "I have friends who go south for the winter, and they need someone to check the house while they are away."

"I don't understand," Andi said.

"Well, if you are willing, they would love to have you stay there until they return."

Andi frowned. "I can't pay—"

"You would be working for your board," Birgit said. "The city requires the drive and sidewalk be shoveled. With the snow expected this winter, you'll be *saving* them money in plowing fees."

Andi ran a finger along the sharp edge of the key. "Does Hope know about this?"

"Yes, we've all talked about it. She wants you to do what you're comfortable with."

She gave Andi one of those smiles that said everything would be all right. Andi nodded, trying to make sense of Birgit's words. "And the people would trust me with their house? They don't even know me."

"I know you. Hope vouches for your work ethic and your reliability as a roommate." Birgit paused. "Would you like to meet the Reuters and see the house before you decide?"

"OK. Sure."

Birgit stood up. "We can go right now, if you're ready."

After just a few minutes' drive, Birgit pulled her car into a driveway across the street from a school and playground. "You will be very safe here, and it's still within walking distance of the grocery store and the café."

Birgit rang the doorbell, and a little dog barked at them from inside the house. After a moment, the door opened, and the warm scent of baking cookies wrapped itself around them.

"Hello! Come in!" The woman smiled, looking from Birgit to Andi. A man joined her in the hall as she motioned them inside. "You must be Andi. We're so glad to meet you. Birgit has had simply wonderful things to say about you. Here, give your coats to Kurt."

The man hung their coats in a closet about the size of Hope's bathroom. After living in the apartment, and before that, in motel rooms as long as she could remember, the living room was, as Lainie would say, "gi-normous." While Mrs. Reuter and Birgit talked, Andi scanned all of the furniture trying to decide where to sit. She was relieved when Birgit patted the cushion next to her on the couch. The little gray dog that had been running around and panting finally stopped near her foot. Then it sat, stared at Andi, and raised one paw.

"Zoey really likes you," Mrs. Reuter said.

Andi smiled at the woman. "She's cute."

"Do you like dogs?" Mr. Reuter asked.

"I've always wanted one," Andi said, leaning forward to reach for the dog's paw, "but we...couldn't have pets growing up."

"Oh!" Mrs. Reuter jumped up like she had been stung. "I've got to get those cookies out before they burn! Kurt, why don't you show them the rest of the house?"

When Birgit dropped her off at Hope's apartment that night, Andi was stuffed with cookies and carrying three containers of food for her "Christmas" dinner. The Reuters had not only asked her to watch their house, they had decided to let Zoey, who got carsick, stay home with her. Andi understood now why people pinched themselves to see if they were dreaming.

She had put away the food and changed into pajamas before she noticed the light flashing on her phone. Hope had texted her an hour earlier, from her grandparents' house.

How did you like the Reuters?

They're really nice, Andi typed. *They have a dog, too.*

Hope answered right back. *What do you think about the housesitting?*

I'm going to take the job. Not because I don't totally appreciate all you have done for me.

No worries. I'm happy you'll have a safe place of your own. And a bed!

And a dog! Their dog sitter couldn't take her and she hates riding in the car.

Cool. She's a lucky dog to have you take care of her. Gotta go. I'll call you tomorrow.

What was happening? Three months ago, she had no place to live, no idea where she would go or what she would do. Now, at least until spring, she had three jobs if she included caring for Zoey. She had a place to live, even if just for a few weeks. She had purpose.

Mrs. Reuter had little messages all over the house, stitched on pillows, framed on the walls. Right by the door to the breezeway was a wooden plaque printed with the phrase "A friend closer than a brother." Andi's father had that with his crew, and now it looked like she had that with hers too. True, she was kind of their project but that's not how they made her feel. Also true, there was more nail polish involved than she wanted. But Hope and Birgit were her friends, there for her even before she knew she needed them.

CHAPTER 18

All of the snow in the world was in the Reuters' driveway. At least that's how it looked. Andi let the curtain fall and put on a second pair of socks. The boots were tall enough, but not warm enough. Neither were the "cute" mittens Hope had given her to match her winter jacket. Much more useful were Mr. Reuter's gloves and thick hat she found in a bin in the mudroom.

She took a deep breath. "Ready, Zoey?"

The little dog bounced up and down as she waited for Andi to open the door to the breezeway. She let Zoey into the backyard and went to the garage for the shovel.

Snow had blocked the breezeway door to the driveway, and Andi pushed hard against it until she could squeeze through the opening.

Up and down the street, fountains of snow rose and fell, arcing from snowblowers that all whined with slightly different pitches. Andi scooped some snow with the shovel and flung it far away into the yard, but after just five minutes of that, she was too warm from all the work.

She looked at what she had accomplished. The cleared part of the driveway was not even big enough to park a car in, and she had the rest of that plus the sidewalk to do before she could leave for the café. She stuck the shovel in the snow and turned to go inside to tell Hope she'd be late.

A truck pulled up at the curb and the door slammed.

"Are you Andi?"

She turned back toward the street. Who was this guy?

"Kurt called and asked me to stop by."

Andi waited as he clomped up the driveway.

"Hi. I'm Bryant Bachmann. We know the Reuters from church. I guess he saw the snowfall report this morning and realized he forgot to tell you about the snowblower."

"I didn't know there was one," Andi said.

He glanced at the pathetic square she had shoveled.

"Well, I'm glad Kurt called before you finished this all by hand. Do you mind if I open the garage door?"

Andi moved aside to let him pass, and a moment later, the big overhead door creaked up the track.

She stepped over the snowdrift into the garage where Bryant was poking around in the dark corner she had never gone into.

"Found it," he said. He gathered a tarp into his arms. "We're going to have to back the car out to get to it, though."

Andi looked at the car, so much bigger than Hope's, and her stomach sank. She didn't want to practice in front of someone she didn't know.

Bryant laid the tarp on the workbench. "If you don't mind grabbing the keys, I'll shovel some tracks."

"OK." Andi went into the mudroom and studied the collection of keys hanging on the hooks. Some were small like the house key. None of them looked like the fob Hope's Jeep used. She picked two she thought might be right, and went back to the garage.

"I'm not sure which one," she said, holding the keys out to him.

"It's the Buick." He looked into her hand. "'Grammie's ride.' Do you want me to do it?"

Andi nodded and handed him the key.

Without any hesitation, he backed the car out to the street and then walked back up the drive to her. "Have you used a snowblower before?"

"No," Andi said.

"First, we probably oughta see if there's any gas in it."

Bryant showed her how to check the gas, where more gas was in the garage, and how to start the machine. "You turn this to shoot the snow in whichever direction you want. And you'll want to be careful not to send it all into the neighbor's drive." He grinned and checked his watch. "I have to go get my daughter in a little bit. How about I do a strip down to the sidewalk, and you practice while I'm still here?"

Her stomach told her it was somewhere between breakfast and lunch when Andi rolled the snowblower into the empty side of the garage, glad that Bryant had pulled the car back in for her. She took off her gear and saw she had missed a text from Hope.

Going to be slow. I'll be OK alone today. Have fun with your snow day!

Andi looked down at the damp little dog. "I think we've had enough snow for the morning, huh, Zoey?"

She got out a pan and a can of tomato soup from the pantry. She started the soup and changed out of her snowy jeans and socks into dry clothes. Just as she was ladling her soup into the bowl, Zoey barked at the front door. Andi walked into the hall toward the stream of envelopes and fliers falling through the slot in the door. Andi scooped up the pile and dropped it into the basket Mrs. Reuter had laid out for mail.

A glossy cover caught her eye, and she reached back in for the small magazine. On the booklet's front were three high school kids who, according to the caption, were part of Early College. She didn't think the Reuters would mind her reading the catalog, so she used her nail to slit open the paper sticker that held it closed and walked back to the kitchen.

She brought her soup to the table and then opened the catalog. As she turned the pages, she realized it was a college brochure in two parts. The first was an alphabetical list of the course offerings for the spring term. The second was a write up of the programs offered at the college, located in Traverse. Andi turned to the M section of the Programs. Mechanic was not listed, but maritime engineer was. Could she work on a boat? She turned to A and found automotive technician, but also aviation, and page after page of programs she had never even considered.

She closed the booklet and looked out the window at the bird feeder. The snow on its roof made it hard to see the little house underneath, and a tiny bird flitted about, looking for a way to get through to the seed. Andi watched for a minute. "Little bird," she said, "I know exactly how you feel."

CHAPTER 19

Z oey barked and jumped at the door so furiously Andi was afraid her nails would scratch the paint. She let the dog into the backyard and went back to the dining room where she had been taking care of the vacuum before Zoey started her weirdness. Even though Andi had kept up while they were away, when the Reuters called to say they would be home the next day, she cleaned everything she could think of.

As she wrapped the cord around the plastic prongs, she heard Zoey barking at a higher pitch. Andi let the cord fall and went to the mudroom. She put on boots and her coat and stepped carefully onto the thick ice walkway that now connected the house to the garage.

The freezing rain in the night had made everything look like a scene from the movie she and Hope had watched with Lainie a few days earlier. Andi forced the song "Let It Go" out of her head and followed Zoey's bark coming from somewhere behind the garage. She walk-skated over to the dog, her boot occasionally breaking through the icy crust.

"What is going on, little dog?"

Zoey paused, her stubby little tail straight up, and then went back to her digging.

Andi moved closer in small, slippery steps. "What? What are you after?"

Zoey looked at her again, then pounced at the hole.

"It's cold out here," Andi said. "I think you should let it go." Had she really said that? "Come on, Zoey, let's go inside."

Andi went back to the house, retracing her steps as well as she could even though the boot shape punchouts in the ice were backward. Zoey pounced and barked until Andi called her again, then ran to the garage door and barked there.

"If a critter made it into the garage, it can stay there," Andi said. She grabbed the back doorknob, cold under her hand. It didn't move. She turned it harder, but the door would not open. "Are you kidding me?"

Mr. Reuter had told her the door did that sometimes, just locked them out, and that they left a key outside just in case. It was under the flowerpot next to the door, and at the moment, also under two inches of ice. No amount of kicking at the pot with her boot loosened it, although she did succeed in falling down in the process. Zoey had stopped barking and looked over at her, tail wiggling.

"Yeah, thanks." Andi sighed, slid on her knees to the garage door, and pulled herself up by the doorknob that opened easily when she turned it. She flipped on the shop light over the workbench, glad that the ice on the utility lines hadn't knocked out the power like the café customers described when they compared winter stories.

She checked the garage for something to use on the flowerpot to get it to give up its treasure, like whacking at the piñata at Lainie's birthday party. Andi smiled at the wall of tools, remembering how excited the little girls were at the candy waterfall. Rake? Shovel? What she needed was the sledgehammer they used in the house remodeling shows, but she didn't see one. Mr. Reuter didn't seem like the smashing type.

She really wished now that she had taken the time to put gloves on. Her pants were wet and clammy after falling on the ice, and the snow in her boots was melting onto her socks. Andi went to the doorway and looked out to the icy driveway. She would never make it down that.

"Come on, Zoey." She crossed the garage and opened the back door of Mrs. Reuter's car. Zoey eyed her from the doorway. "It's OK. We're not going anywhere fast." She scooped the dog up. "I need you to warm up my hands while I figure this out."

I need you. How many times in the last few months had she said that to her father, only to hear silence back? She shut the car door, pulled the dog onto her lap, and pressed her forehead into Zoey's neck.

I need Hope. She had said that to the ambulance driver.

I need hope. She had said that to herself when she shut the truck door every night against whatever was outside. When she shut the apartment door after Torres and the guys glanced back as they walked out of her life. And before that, when she shut the motel door, holding the box of ashes in her hands.

Now, she sat in someone else's car, in someone else's garage, holding someone else's dog. But this time, instead of wanting out, she wanted in. She wanted this life where people knew her name, cared about her, and treated her like she was one of them.

Andi closed her eyes. Whenever she needed to calm down and was out of folding paper, she would think about taking apart one of her projects. In her mind, see herself removing the screws that held it together, taking off the back to reveal what was inside, laying each piece out in order so she could put it back. The process, even though it was all in her imagination, usually helped get her straightened out.

Andi tried to visualize a clock, or some little electric gadget, but nothing came to mind. She opened her eyes and saw the rows of screwdrivers organized in size from large to small on the wall over Mr. Reuter's workbench. Then she moved her gaze to the back door of the house. Zoey squirmed and pawed at the car door.

"I guess we don't have anything to lose. Besides ruining the door, getting fired..." She looked at Zoey, who panted at her. "You know." Andi opened the door and went to the tools.

An hour later, she had all the parts of the knob on a cloth in front of her. Zoey barked, pushed open the door to the mudroom, and stood at the treat container looking back at her.

"You're welcome," Andi said to the little dog, "but now I have to put all this back together." She went into the house, giving Zoey a treat on the way, and got her phone and her house key. One time a day was her limit for getting locked out.

Chapter 20

When she came back inside, Mrs. Reuter's voice echoed from the kitchen answering machine. "So, we saw the weather and thought, 'We'd better just go home.' We're getting off the expressway now."

"Hello? Hi, it's Andi." That sounded stupid. Who else would it be?

Mrs. Reuter laughed. "Andi, hi. I was just saying, we decided to leave early. I guess it's a good thing. All the trees here are bent right over with ice."

"Yeah, here, too." Andi said. "At least the power didn't go out." She heard Mr. Reuter's voice in the background.

"I'm sure she already found it, Kurt. Did you, Andi? Find the salt for the sidewalks?"

She had not thought to look for it, even though she had sprinkled salt on the sidewalk in front of the café all through the winter.

"He says it's in a black and white bag. Over by the snowblower."

"I'll put some out," Andi said, then added. "I didn't do the driveway, because I don't have a car."

"That's fine. Well, we'll be about an hour."

"OK," Andi said, "drive carefully."

She put her boots and coat on again, double-checking for the key in her pocket, and went to the garage. There was the bag, just like Mr. Reuter said. Andi took a scoop and sprinkled it over the walkway between the garage and the house. Then she dragged the whole bag to the front of the garage, opened the overhead door, and tossed out wide arcs of the white crystals so they fell across and down the driveway.

She took the snow shovel and shoved it under the melted edges of ice on the cement, and after a few minutes, the walk was pretty safe to walk on. She nudged the flowerpot and it moved aside to reveal a gold-colored house key. "Traitor," Andi said to the pot.

She was clearing the bottom of the drive when she heard Zoey start her crazy bark inside the house. Not even a minute later, the Reuter's car slowed to a stop at the curb. How did Zoey know?

Mr. Reuter flung open his door, got out and stretched. "Hello!" he called.

Andi returned Mrs. Reuter's wave through the windshield. "Hi. Welcome home."

Mr. Reuter leaned back into the car and said something to his wife before closing the door. "Looks like you've been busy," he said. "I just thought I'd look it over before I drove up on ice and got the car sideways in the yard." He laughed. "That'd be a great way to end the trip."

"I'm glad you called, because that probably would have happened if you got home an hour ago," Andi said.

"Well, I think it's safe, thanks to you. I think just a little more salt on the sidewalk here and then you can quit. You're probably cold through and through."

"I've been out in it a few times today." Andi smiled. "I've lost touch with my feet."

"Do you want me to carry that?" she asked Mr. Reuter when she got back up to the house.

"No, you go on in," he said. "I can get this last bit."

Andi stomped the slush off her boots and went into the mudroom. She stripped off the coat and walked in her sock feet into the kitchen.

"It looks and smells so clean in here," Mrs. Reuter said. "Usually, I spend a few days after we get back every year baking just to take away the closed-up smell."

"You'll have to find another excuse to make cookies, I guess," Andi said.

Now that they were home, she didn't know what to do. Would they want her to go back to Hope's right away? Her bag was packed, but it was getting dark. Would it be rude to ask for a ride?

"I...something's different about that knob." Mr. Reuter pointed in the direction of the mudroom. "It always turned so hard, and I about overdid it just now turning it."

Andi chewed on her lip, debating what she should say. The words just fell out of her mouth. "I took it off."

"The doorknob?" Mrs. Reuter asked.

"Yeah." Andi pressed her lips together, waiting.

"Why?"

"I got locked out earlier, and the key was frozen under the pot, and I didn't know there was salt, and I've never lived in a house..."

"It's OK, Andi...you...that's amazing." Mr. Reuter looked toward the mudroom and back. "That you even thought of it, but also that you took it off *and* put it back on."

"And fixed it," Mrs. Reuter said. "Finally, those tools got used for something." She prodded her husband and then turned to Andi. "Why don't we sit down? I'll make some cocoa, and we have something we want to talk about with you."

"Maybe you should let her put on some warm clothes first," Mr. Reuter said. "By the sounds of it, she's been out in the snow for a long time."

As she changed and washed up, Andi thought about what they would say. Had they seen or heard something they didn't like about her work or how she took care of Zoey? Again, she wondered if they wanted to send her home ASAP.

"Here you go, sweetie." Mrs. Reuter slid a steaming mug in front of her.

"Must feel different being on the other side, huh?" Mr. Reuter smiled. "I mean, at the café, you're usually the one handing out the tasty drinks."

Andi nodded and took a sip.

"Andi," Mrs. Reuter said, "over the winter, we've had a long time to talk, and we feel strongly that we are to make this offer to you." She nodded at her husband.

"It's more than just the tools," he continued. "We've got whole *rooms* sitting around here going unused. Andi, we'd like to have you stay on with us."

"To live here, no rent necessary," Mrs. Reuter said. "We gathered from Birgit that you have faced some...difficult things, of late, and we want to help. If that's OK with you."

How was this happening? How could she ever repay this kind of favor? Zoey put her feet up on the edge of the chair and nudged Andi's hands where they lay in her lap.

"It looks like we all agree on it," Mr. Reuter said. "What do you say, Andi?"

She patted Zoey's head, and a fat tear rolled down her cheek. She brushed it away, took a big breath, and looked up at the Reuters. "I ... can't even find the words."

CHAPTER 21

The café bell jangled as Birgit came in. Andi found it so funny that Birgit the energizer bunny worked in a quiet library, but she made the paradox, today's dictionary word, work.

"Hi, Andi."

The way Birgit said her name always made her think of the crew.

"¿Qué pasa?" Andi asked.

Birgit smiled. "¿Me podrías traer un café, por favor?"

"I thought I could trick you," Andi said. "Maybe librarians really do know everything."

"We'll never tell," Birgit said. "Could you make it hazel-nut today?"

"Sure."

"Hey, Birgit." Hope came from the storeroom with a chalkboard. "How are you?"

"I am blessed," Birgit said, laying down her money in the shape of an origami heart.

Andi set the cup in front of Birgit. "Nice folding."

"I learned from the best." Birgit turned to Hope. "What do you have there?"

"I'm setting up a comment board. I'm going to put out a prompt and let the customers write their thoughts." She turned the board around to show the question, 'What is your favorite cookie?' "Not really life-altering, but kinda fun," Hope said. "Oh, and I found these chalk markers, too. They're just fun all by themselves."

"My vote is snickerdoodle," Birgit said. "And yellow."

Hope chose a pen from the container and handed it to her. "Have at it."

Andi's father had liked Oreos best. He always ate the white cream out and then dunked the rest in coffee. Andi could eat three of hers before he finished his one. He did the same thing with pie when they stopped at a diner on the road. He ate each cherry out of the inside one by one. By the time he finished the last bite of crust, Andi had hers gone and had used her finger to wipe the last of the whipped cream off her plate. She sighed at the memory and turned to empty out the grounds from the portafilter.

"I'll see you later, ya?" Birgit asked.

Andi turned back and nodded. "I'll be done at three."

"Sí. *Adios.*"

"Bye," Hope said. She moved around the room, standing in different places looking at the walls. "Do you think there, where people can see it when they walk in the door, or on that wall when they turn around with their orders?"

Andi leaned on the counter. "Well, when they get their coffee, their hands will be full, and they'll want to find a seat."

"Good point."

"What if you just leave it on the counter? It would give them something to do besides watch us."

"That's a good idea. We can even mention it when they pay."

Andi nodded.

"You have a talent," Hope said. "I think most people would look at a problem and see if there was an easier way to get around it. You track the different ways to solve it."

"Thank you."

"I mean, you're much braver than I was at your age. You figured out how to take care of yourself and all that."

"Kinda didn't have a choice."

"You know what I mean," Hope said. "And you've literally taught yourself, up to the college level."

"With help."

"But you didn't give up. I admire you for that."

Hope admired *her*?

"What *do* you want to do next?" Hope asked. "I mean, I'm pretty sure working at a café is not your life dream."

"I've never really had a life dream."

Hope tipped her head. "Still, there must be something you're interested in."

They had never talked about where Andi had been going the day of the accident. She didn't think Hope would understand the mechanic thing, but the woman did know something about having a plan and seeing it through.

"I'd like to be a mechanic someday," Andi said.

"No joke? That's awesome."

"You think so?"

Hope looked at her, incredulous. "Of course. I can totally see you rocking that."

"I don't know about rocking it."

"Go big or go home," Hope said. "Anyway, I can't see you doing anything a little bit." She came to the counter. "So, how does that work? Are there schools for that, or do you have to learn at a garage?"

"The mechanic I talked to said I would need to go to school and get certified before I could work anywhere."

"Are there schools here? Like in this part of the state?"

Andi rubbed her lips together. She could see the shiny pictures in the brochure from the college. Students walking on sidewalks, hanging out in front of buildings, watching instructors in labs. She would probably never be in any pictures, never in any of those classes. Her going to a school like that was definitely a paradox. "There's one in Traverse," she said.

"That's so close! Awesome."

It might be Hope's word for the day, but it was not an accurate description of the moment. College would take money. It would have to get in line behind food, rent, car, insurance, and whatever else stood between Andi and the future.

"Most colleges require you to live on campus your first year, but Traverse is close enough you could come back for the weekend, or whatever. So, are you going to apply to start fall semester?"

"I...don't think I can," Andi said.

"You're taking the GED test in a few weeks. The results should be back in plenty of time. Why wouldn't you be able?"

"Hope, I can't ..." She looked away and then back. "Pay for it."

"What?" Hope frowned. "College?"

"Yes."

"Oh, my gosh, Andi, you won't have to." Hope laughed. "You qualify for so much financial aid, they'll practically pay *you*."

Andi frowned. "I don't understand."

Hope waved her hands in the air like she was wiping the writing off her board. "OK. First, hardly anybody can afford college, so almost everyone applies for some kind of financial aid to help them pay for it. Sometimes it's a loan, or a scholarship...or a grant." Hope tapped her fist to her forehead and then stretched her hands wide. "The Sisters."

"What?"

"Candace and Carla have a foundation that gives grants. This is exactly the thing they want to support."

"Me going to college?"

"A hardworking woman going after her dream." She held her arms out wide like she was giving a speech, then let her hands fall. "So, now that we've got that settled, let's go on to more important things, like..." Hope sorted through the chalk markers on the counter in front of her, and held out a blue one to Andi. "What's your favorite cookie?"

Birgit looked up from the young boy showing her his book, and smiled. Andi nodded and found a table by the windows. In the channel the boats in their slips waited idly for the weekend. Sailboats, fishing boats with poles sticking up from their holders, cruising boats with flat swim platforms. They were fine, but the tug, docked farther down, was Andi's favorite. Not sparkly like the speedboat or self-important like the yacht. It was ready to work. It was her inspiration, as Hope would say, ready for whatever was next.

"Goodbye." Birgit waved to the family and came over to the table. "He's just discovered a series all about a boy with his name," she said. "Yours, too, actually. He is also an Andy."

Andi smiled. She had never thought much about having a boy's name. She just liked how short it was.

"So, this test is in one week. How do you feel?"

"I feel good," Andi said. "Nervous. I've never taken a test—I mean, in a room with other people like that."

Birgit smiled. "The secret is to pretend no one else is around. It is just you and the material, which you know so well."

Andi nodded.

"Now tell me what is really wrong."

How did she do that? It would have been a little scary the way Birgit could read minds, if she wasn't so great about not judging what was in there. "Hope has been talking to me about college and financial aid, and I don't know anything about that. My father always used cash. I never even saw him with a credit card."

"He was a wise man," Birgit said. "It is good to have access to credit, but as Hope told you, you will qualify for aid that does not have to be paid back."

"She talked about The Sisters."

"Yes, and there are government programs and scholarships through colleges that we can look at first."

Andi played with her fingers in her lap, trying to keep the snakes in her stomach calm. This was too much. She looked up when Birgit stopped talking.

"You don't have to move through this any faster than you want to, Andi. Never let anyone rush you ahead."

Andi nodded.

"Most adults will never in their lifetime experience the things that you have in just the last few months. You have survived great loss, and still, you push on. Hope and I, everyone who knows you, are amazed at your resilience and admire how you take on each next thing at your pace, in your way."

"I don't feel that amazing."

Birgit smiled. "Believe me, you are. So, why don't we treat this like everything else? Break it down into pieces, and take one at a time."

"OK."

"Now let's start with looking at the problem first."

The deckhand on the tugboat caught the cast off rope, and coiled it while the boat gained power. Steadily, the tug moved away from the dock and down the channel, to the lake and to its next job.

If you can, I can.

Andi turned to her friend. "I want to be a mechanic."

CHAPTER 22

The little bird held onto the flower stem, turned its head toward Andi as if listening to something, and then flew off. Andi felt just like that, clutching at her perch for just a minute more before flying away. Not too far, just to Traverse. All thanks to grants, including one from The Sisters. So much had happened since she met them on her first day at the café.

She knocked, and Carla answered the door. "Andi, come in," she said. "What a nice surprise!" They went into the tiny sunroom of The Sisters' cottage, and Carla waved her into a seat. "Candace ran out for a minute, but she'll be back. Now, when do you leave?"

"This afternoon. Hope's driving me up to the campus."

"We are so proud of you. To go from being rudderless to now sailing right into college, all in less than a year's time."

Andi smiled at the way Carla, like most of the café's customers, found a way to work the lake into the conversation. It was kind of a Frankfort thing. "I had a lot of help," she said. "That's kind of why I came over—to thank you again for the grant. It covered everything the scholarship didn't."

Carla gave a few small claps. "That's wonderful!"

"What's wonderful?" Candace's voice came into the room before she did. "Oh, hello, Andi. So nice to see you."

Carla turned toward her sister. "Andi's on her way to move into her dorm."

"I'm sure Carla has already told you, but I'll second it—we are so thrilled at what you are planning to do, and how hard you've worked to get there."

"Thank you, but I didn't do it alone."

"Well, we're certainly excited to be part of your 'pit crew.'" Carla made air quotes. "Will you let us know how things are going?"

"Sure. Yes."

"You'll always have friends here," Candace said.

"Thanks." Andi stood up. "Well, I have one more stop, so, I guess this is goodbye."

"For now," Carla said, pulling her into a hug.

Andi picked up her pack and walked to Main Street, past the inn, and the beach parking lot. She passed the artists' cottages and turned up the drive for the lighthouse. In the summer, there had been crowds, but today she was alone. Kind of.

She walked to the spot she had gone to a lot during her year in Frankfort. From where this tree stood, she could see over the water, see to forever. Andi wondered what her father would have done in life if he hadn't had a kid to raise. How far would he have gone?

She wasn't sure where he had grown up. Andi took out the one picture she had of them together and studied it. She tried to find some detail in his eyes or freckled face that they shared. But she didn't find anything, of course.

Hope had figured out that the strange key unlocked both a safe deposit box and Andi's past. The box had held two pictures. One of a brown-haired man in crew cut and uniform was dated 1980. The second, from 1986, showed the same man still in uniform with his arms around a little red-haired boy who had her father's birthmark on his cheek. There was a death certificate from the same year for Jared Thomas Collins. Deeper in the box was an Independent Living document for Nathan Collins, age seventeen. Under that was a note scribbled on a faded receipt: *Dee, Glass House Recovery.*

She had looked at all of those before opening the envelope addressed *Andi.* On a piece of notebook paper in her father's tiny block print was the story he'd never told her. Of living in four foster homes in seven years. Of the girl Dee from the last house who called him brother even though they weren't related, and the phone call a few years later when she asked him to "come get her kid for the night" while she was in jail for possession. Of his decision to pack up Andi's stuff into three grocery bags and never take her back to that house or that life.

She had kind of known all along that he was not hers, but she was his anyway. *Keep to yourself, and don't take anything you can't pay for.* He had paid his life, his future, to take her with him. Away from a life she would never have to know, thanks to him. *Don't quit til the job is done.* She had been angry, more than once. He had not taught her how to do all of the adult things that she had to learn on her own. How to take care of herself, how to know herself. But he had not quit on her.

Andi took a garden shovel from her pack and dug a hole just deep enough to hold the small wooden box. He would have approved its construction—good clean joints; everything square; simple and true. "You can see a long way from here," she said. "At night, the lighthouse will push away the dark. You can hear the wind in the trees and the waves on the shore."

She set the box into the hole and carefully covered it with the soil, then reached into her bag for a small crane made from paper the same blue as the faded jeans he'd always worn. Andi sat there for several minutes, looking at the crane and the water and the sky. She took a deep breath, let it out slowly, and then checked the time on her phone. She still had to go to the library to thank Birgit and tell her goodbye.

Andi had learned how to find her own crew, how to rely on them as much as she relied on herself. She had learned to know herself and to follow her road where it led, just as he had followed his here. "I'm going to do this," she said, laying the crane to mark the grave. "I won't quit on me, either."

Andi stood and shifted her pack on her shoulder. Somehow it seemed lighter by more than just the weight of the wooden box.

She had walked out of the motel almost a year before, so scared of what was next, feeling like she was trapped on the wrong side of the door. No lie, she was still a little scared, but now she felt like she was living out one of Mrs. Reuter's little sayings. True, the door behind her had closed, but the one in front of her, the door that led to the rest of her life, was wide open.

Liz

CHAPTER 1

Liz dried the plate and slid it onto the stack in the cupboard, turned the handle of one of the coffee mugs on the shelf below so that it lined up with the others, and closed the door. One cupboard the way it should be. She wondered if, when Bry drove away from her every morning and left their mess behind, it was the best part of her husband's day.

Liz pulled open the drawer to get out a new towel for the next meal's dishes and saw the card, decorated with a brightly colored butterfly resting on a leaf. She stood up with the card and laid it face down on the counter.

The tender sentiments and caring words did not belong with the towels or in the kitchen. She would need to clean the drawer now.

She pulled out an armload of towels and carried them to the laundry room. Hot pads, oven mitts, the aprons the girls had used on Cookie Saturdays, all went into the basket. Liz chose the hot wash, started the load, and went back and sprayed down all the surfaces with disinfectant. When the towels were done they would have a properly clean place to rest.

The card lay upside down on the counter where she had left it. She picked it up, wiped the counter with a sanitizing cloth, and took the card into the office to put it with the others. The clock in the room off the kitchen chimed the noon hour and Liz froze. Lunchtime. Her stomach was upset enough without adding more to it. No, she could eat dinner later. In the meantime, she only had a few hours to get the rest of the house cleaned up.

Liz straightened Lauren's jacket on its hook in the mudroom, then pulled the vacuum from its spot. She took the canister off the base, turned the hoses around to accept the hand piece, and went over each carpeted step a few times on her way upstairs. They needed attention after the dusty days of June.

The landing in a farmhouse had never made sense to her. There was always a dead-end corner too small for any decoration but too big to be empty. All it did was catch every bit of lint on the dark maroon carpet. They should just tear it out and put in a hardwood floor, one that you could see was clean.

Liz set down the canister and scrubbed the corner with the hand brush. Then she worked in sections down the length of the landing and around the stair opening until she got to the master bedroom. She had read an article about the number of house dust mites found in mattresses past a certain age, and their mattress was beyond geriatric.

She was running the hand brush over the seam on the edge of the pillow top mattress when the vacuum stopped.

"Liz!"

She spun around to see her husband in the doorway.

Bry held out the vacuum cord. "I guess you didn't hear me."

"No. I was busy." She motioned to the pieces of the bed around the room.

"I see that." He frowned. "Hon—are you OK?"

"Yes. I'm just cleaning."

"Yeah." He scanned the room and nodded. "Everything looks great. It's just that…didn't you do all this last week?"

What was he getting at? He had his things to keep him busy, and she never questioned where he went or what he did. "I think it's been longer than that," she said.

"Well, anyway. Do you want me to help you put it back together? It's already almost seven o'clock." He dropped the cord and came into the room. "Did you eat already?"

Dinner. She had not made any dinner. She had not thought about dinner at all. "No. Not yet. I can get this."

"All right."

He ran his fingers through his hair and down the back of his neck. Gave it a rub. Bry language. Liz waited for him to say something out loud, irritated by the interruption.

"Do you want me to go get some subs?" he said finally, rubbing the lower part of his chest with an open palm. "That's all I'd really want."

"OK. Sounds good." Her throat was tight, probably from the dust mites she had unearthed in the carpet under the bed.

"Sure you don't want help with the mattresses?"

"No, I'll be OK."

Bry nodded at the cord. "Want me to plug you back in?"

"No," Liz said. "I'm finished."

"All right." He took a deep breath. "Be right back."

Liz heard him thump downstairs in his socks. She wrestled the mattress pieces into place and put a clean set of sheets on them. She remade the bed and wrapped up the vacuum cord, all without opening the door to Lauren's room once. She lugged the vacuum back down to the mudroom, dropping the bundle of sheets on the floor by the washer as she went past.

As she measured laundry soap and added the sheets she could hear that the clock was off again, measuring time tick-tock, tick-tock. Liz closed the lid of the washer and cleaned her hands in the kitchen.

She took down only two plates and two glasses, then edged the cabinet door shut and blew out her breath. Dinner was one of the worst times of the day. Liz carried the dishes to the small table in the corner where they ate most of their meals now. Sighing, she went into the other room and adjusted the clock on the wall until its tick-tock rhythm was even.

The clock was eleven minutes out of synch with time. What she wouldn't give to have eleven more minutes with Lauren. Liz opened the glass front, moved the long hand ahead to the correct time, and latched the door. She listened to the clock ticking off time that never stopped, minute after minute, hour after hour.

And there was morning and there was evening—the thirty-fourth day.

CHAPTER 2

A nother tiny bead of condensation crept down the side of the glass. Why had they not put in AC when Bry remodeled the house? She knew the answer but kicked at it anyway—they couldn't afford it. At the time, it was more important to get his grandmother into her own room on the main floor so she could stay in the house, but in the end Camille had lived within her own mind, no longer aware of the sunny room Bry had built for her.

Liz pulled her hair up off her neck. If she stayed here any longer she would liquefy too. She washed and dried her glass, put it into the cupboard, and got her purse. There had to be some breeze at the lakeshore. At least she could have the air on during the drive to Frankfort.

She passed farms with wide tracts of tall corn and scattered plots of leafy bean plants. In one alfalfa field, an Amish man drove a horse-drawn rake around while the others loaded bales onto the wagon. Liz breathed deeply as she made her final turn onto the road that gave her peeks of Lake Michigan, but at the entrance to the lighthouse, she frowned. A bright red sign read Parking Lot Full.

She picked up speed, making her way into town. Maybe she could find a spot on a side street and walk to the water. At the last minute, she decided to try the beach parking and, surprisingly, found a space facing the water.

Every bit of the beach was crowded with people. She plodded across the sand, around families eating snacks on big blankets and clusters of teen girls laid out on their beach towels. At the water's edge, little kids splashed in the waves and packed their buckets with sand, watched by parents who sat nearby in submerged beach chairs. Liz stopped. She couldn't do this, be surrounded by all this normal life.

As she turned back, she felt the air crackle and a breeze wash across her face. Liz looked out across the lake and saw dark clouds churning and boiling over the water. In an instant, the parents were calling kids out of the water, folding blankets, shoving the day's detritus into giant, colorful bags. She was swept along with the migration to the parking lot, and made it into her car just as the first big fistfuls of rain thudded against the windshield.

She glanced in her rearview mirror and saw a line of cars snaking toward the exit. There was no point in going anywhere just then so she waited, watching the sky first through drops and then streams of water rushing down the other side of the glass. Liz winced as lightning streaked through the dark clouds and prepared herself for the boom of thunder that would follow. Her chest tightened, and she checked to see if the traffic had cleared.

In the time it took to glance in the mirror, the rain changed to sheets of water slashing at the car from every direction. All she could hear was the roar of the storm around her. She crossed her arms and hugged herself, remembering.

She had not wanted Lauren to go with her friends even though she completely trusted Aisha's parents, but Bry took their daughter's side, as usual.

"You can't keep her the same age forever, Liz. She's going to grow up someday. You have to let her do things. That's how it works."

But Liz had seen the storm, the big ferry breaking in two like the Titanic, all the cars sinking into the dark pit of the lake, and she couldn't shake the feeling.

"It was a dream, hon. That boat goes back and forth across Lake Michigan every day. She'll be fine."

So, for the three days Lauren was in Wisconsin with Aisha's family, Liz jumped at every loud noise, certain the storm was coming.

"How about we go meet the ferry?" Bry said that morning at breakfast. "We can run down to Ludington after lunch and get ice cream. It'll be like a date."

"OK." Liz mashed the eggs around on her plate. She glanced at the clock on the microwave; eight more hours to wait before the boat docked.

Bry had chatted all the way to Ludington about the progress he had made on the house, his first custom build. Liz let him talk and watched out the window as the trees thinned here and there, allowing teasing views of the lake. After Manistee, there was no more water. Instead, they drove by farm after farm, solid land bathed in bright, yellow sun.

Bry nodded to the line of people two blocks long that stood between them and the restaurant. "We've still got an hour or so before the boat," he said. "But it might take that long to get to the counter." A young couple passed them carrying cones piled high with ice cream. "I wonder if Lo would like to go there," Bry said.

"Where?" Liz glanced around.

"Ferris." He gave her a puzzled look. "For college. Those kids had on Ferris shirts."

"Oh."

"Even though neither of us got a chance, I want her to go to college."

No, they hadn't, aside from the business classes Bry had taken through Adult Education the year Lauren was born. Liz's dreams of conservatory had evaporated long before that.

"What do you think she'll study?" he asked.

"I don't know." She didn't want to think of that yet. Lo, the nickname Lauren now preferred, was eleven. She had plenty of time left to be a kid.

"She has so much she's good at," he said. "I could see her having her own business, though, whatever she finally decides on. She's pretty independent and driven."

Wasn't that the truth? Lauren didn't want Liz's input on anything anymore. The more Liz tried to be open to her, the less Lo wanted to share with her. It was like her daughter was slipping right through her fingers.

"Maybe we should get back to the car," Bry said. "Those clouds are getting dark fast."

Liz looked at the sky, and her stomach turned over. It was just like the dream. She turned back toward the ferry lot, needing to get to the car, to get to Lauren, to keep her safe. She and Bry had just pulled their doors shut when the sky dumped on them. She shrank from it as rain pounded at the car's roof trying over and over to force its way in.

This storm, too, quit in the same sudden way it had started, leaving an uncertain silence. All the cars but hers had left the beach lot and the only light in the still-dark sky came from the lighthouse. Liz jumped when her phone dinged, and she took it from her purse, expecting it to be a message from Bry, wondering where she was and if she was ok through the storm. Instead, there was the daily verse email he must have signed them up for.

If I say, "Surely the darkness will hide me and the light become night around me," even the darkness will not be dark to you; the night will shine like day, for darkness is as light to you.

Psalm 139:11-12

Liz put away the phone and started the car. In her darkness, there was no light.

CHAPTER 3

Liz wrinkled her nose; the strange burning smell was getting stronger. All she had set out to do after Bry left for work that morning was to drive from home to the store and back. Bry could look at the car later, but right now, she needed to get the bottle of disinfectant and get home. She could just imagine how many germs had been on the bottom of Bry's boots earlier when he walked through from the garden. Liz frowned at the spray bottle in the seat beside her, its 99.7 percent bacteria kill-off claim all false. Just an empty promise.

Fog slipped over the windshield. No, it was steam. From the engine compartment. Liz threw on her blinker and yanked the wheel to turn into the city parking lot. She stopped the car and fished in her purse for her phone, which wasn't in there. The white cloud swelled inside the car and the smell took her breath away. Liz pushed open her door and rushed from the car into the library.

"Liz, hello!" Birgit said.

Birgit was a friend and all, but there was really no time for this. Liz spied the phone just below the lip of the counter. "I have to call Bry. My car's...I don't know. Can I use your phone?"

"Yes, of course." Birgit set the black desktop phone on top of the counter and glanced at the girl standing beside Liz.

"I'm sorry. I didn't see you there," Liz said to the girl, trying to remember what buttons to push. The obnoxious tone sounded in her ear and then the message about the number she had reached being out of service. Liz banged the receiver into its base.

"Would you like to sit down?" Birgit asked. "You look like you should sit down." She came around the end of the half-circle desk.

"I told Bry about this," Liz said, feeling Birgit steering her to a chair in the large print area. "He was 'busy.' Busy." She turned to Birgit.

"Yes. Can I get you some water?" Birgit asked.

"What? No. Thank you." Liz shook her head. The lights were burning into her retinas, and she felt like she might vomit.

"My friend Andi knows about cars," Birgit said. "Would you like her to look at it?"

Liz breathed in for three and out for five. "OK." She searched her bag, and then felt her pockets for the keys.

"Andi, would you mind looking at Liz's car? At least see what you think?" Birgit moved back to the desk, and the girl nodded and said a few words.

Some people came to the desk with a stack of books, and Liz heard the beep of Birgit scanning their library card. Liz folded her arms across her middle and leaned forward. She really might vomit. The voices moved out the door, and a moment later Birgit was in front of her.

"Liz?"

"I'm...OK." She sat up, too fast, and closed her eyes against the dizziness.

"Andi goes to college in Traverse. To study auto repair," Birgit said.

Liz tried sitting up again. "That's good."

The girl came back, bringing the sticky smell with her. "You'll need a new radiator hose," she reported.

"Is that bad?" Liz asked, looking from Andi to her friend.

Birgit raised her eyebrows in question.

"I don't think so," Andi said. "I've read about it, but I've never done it."

"You could fix it?" Liz asked her.

Andi looked at Birgit who tipped her head. "I could try," Andi said with obvious hesitation. "I mean, I'm not a mechanic."

"Yet," Birgit added. "I am about to take lunch. Why don't I drive Liz to the auto parts store and get what you need?"

"OK," Andi said. "I have one more thing to do before I leave for school. I'll come back when I'm done."

There was no end to this. All Liz had wanted to do was mop the floor. Now, here she was, trying to get up the energy to care about some car part.

"Liz, would it be better if you stayed here and I went for the parts?" Birgit asked. "I can check with Andi to see the model of car to ask for."

"I'm sorry," Liz said. "No, I can go with you."

She had told Bry there was something wrong with the car, but all he seemed to care about was getting out the door in the morning. It was more than just the usual stuff that went with starting at a new jobsite. This was different, like he couldn't get away fast enough. From the house; from her, probably. Whatever. She would see to the house just like she had ever since—Liz pushed away the thought and followed Birgit. Forget the cleaner. Once the car was done, so was she.

Before she even got through the glass door of the auto parts store, Liz felt smothered by the thick, mixed smell of rubber, oil, and plastic, but Birgit, in her direct way, went right for the manager. "Hello. I need to buy a radiator hose for a...," she verified with the note in her hand, "2010 Ford Edge."

"OK. Let me check." He typed something into his computer. "Do you need the clamps, too?"

"Yes." Birgit raised her eyebrows at Liz as if to say, *Sure, why not?* "And a screwdriver," she added.

"Flathead? Phillips?"

"Whatever it takes to put on the hose."

"Sure. I'll, uh, get that for you."

Liz saw that Birgit was giving him her best principal look. The woman had probably missed her calling. "Thanks, Birgit."

"Of course. Should we have called Bryant, do you think?"

"No. He gets terrible service at this new job."

"OK." Birgit turned back to the manager. "Thank you."

He had brought back everything she asked for, which never would have happened if Liz had come by herself. Liz pushed her credit card into the reader hoping it would work. She didn't know if she could handle it if it didn't.

The bills had started coming that week. First the one from urgent care, then the ER doctor, and the lab. Already the co-pays were adding up. They hadn't gotten the hospital's bill yet, and she dreaded opening the mailbox every day.

"Would you like some lunch?" Birgit asked after the receipt was printed. "I was thinking of a quick sandwich."

"I could eat some soup," Liz said. She could try. Nothing tasted right anymore, but she would at least go through the motions.

At the restaurant, Birgit suggested Liz sit down and save a table. While Birgit listed what sides she wanted and her choices of bread and cheese, Liz watched out the window. A minivan pulled into one of the spots and a woman got out. She waited at the back of the van, and a moment later, a girl about Lauren's age came around the side. They had obviously had some kind of disagreement before the parking space, based on the way the woman marched up to the sidewalk of the strip mall. The girl rolled her eyes and slogged along behind her.

Liz wanted to pound on the window, to shout at the woman and tell her to go back. Make up. Do the things that make the girl happy before it's too late. Don't waste this day, this hour, this minute together, because you don't know if there will be a tomorrow.

"Here you are. Broccoli and cheddar." Birgit set the paper bowl and a plastic-wrapped spoon in front of Liz. "I'm so glad Andi came in today. She's going back to college this afternoon." Birgit smiled. "She has had quite a journey."

Between bites, Birgit talked about an accident the girl was in, and how the Reuters from church had let her "housesit" while they were in Florida when Birgit had told them she was looking for a place for the girl to stay. Liz nodded and played with the soup while Birgit told her story.

The woman and the girl came back to the van, still walking far apart, a large bag announcing they had bought shoes. Liz's stomach churned as she watched them, and she pushed her thoughts toward the woman with every bit of strength she had. *Don't waste the time. Don't let the music stop.*

CHAPTER 4

She hadn't been anywhere but to the store in weeks, but she wasn't up to going into town, not today. Liz scrolled through the "new" books on the library's app not sure what she was looking for. Not a romance. Not a classic. Not a memoir.

Secrets Your Body Wants to Tell but Can't

Liz twisted her mouth and then clicked on the book's sample button.

Your body has a lot to say, if only you could hear it.

Liz skimmed the lines about secret messages carried by courier service from part to part, cell to cell. In the text box off to the side, there was a list entitled *Cries for Help*. Liz read through the entries: itching, redness or swelling of skin, abdominal cramps, and headaches. She had all of them.

> *While a lot of the body's warnings are triggered by outside influences, there are several internal reasons as well. Of singular importance is repressed emotion. Whether guilt, anger, or sorrow, feelings are a potent source of inflammation. Many times, these emotions act as a three-headed dog, not permitting any living soul to leave.*

That was a little dramatic. Liz meant to click out of the book but her finger swipe turned the page instead.

Why won't you forgive yourself? The words flashed at her in an oversized font, and then the screen went black. A moment later the book's text reappeared in proper format. Liz shut off her phone and pushed it away from her. What was that?

The garage door opener hummed, and a minute later, she heard the truck door slam. She stood up from the table and faced the mudroom. Bry came in with his hands full but stopped short in the doorway like he might turn right around and never come back. "Hello?"

She frowned at him. "What?"

"Why are you standing there like you have big news?"

She shrugged a shoulder and shook her head. "I don't have any news."

"O-kay." He glanced at her sideways as he walked to the kitchen island and set down his laptop and a bag of take-out wrappers. "You all right?" he asked.

"Yeah. As all right as usual." For having a dead daughter.

He nodded. "I've got more to bring in."

"OK."

He gave her a long look and went back to the garage. Liz took a deep breath and exhaled. She should start dinner.

The question she had seen flash across the screen nagged at her as she peeled potatoes, diced onions, stirred the skillet. She thought about it as Bry went over the highs and lows of his day. She found herself mentally arguing with the electronic image. *It's Bry who needs to forgive, not me.*

"I'm not doing *that* anytime soon," Bry said.

Liz startled. "What?"

"Going to Canada."

"Why are you going to Canada?"

"I'm not." He frowned. "I just said that."

"Sorry." She took a deep breath and tried to shake it off.

Bry set his fork down and pushed his empty plate to the side. He folded his hands on the table in front of him. "What's going on there?"

Liz shook her head and took a drink of water.

"You've been wandering around here like something spooked you. What happened?"

"Nothing." She looked away and then back to him. "Do you blame me for Lauren's death?"

Bry scowled. "What? No, I don't blame you. Why would you—why would you think that?"

Liz rubbed the heel of her hand, thinking of the red slash on Lauren's palm. "I didn't tell you right away about her hand," she said. "Maybe if I would have taken her in—"

"Liz. Stop." He sighed. "I don't know why she died, OK? But it wasn't your fault. It was *never* your fault." He ran his hands through his hair and blew a breath out from pursed lips.

"I just...I need you to forgive me," she said.

"There's nothing to forgive, Liz. Don't do that to yourself." He exhaled again and stood. "Do you want me to clean up?"

"No, I can do it," she said.

He put his hands on the table and leaned in like he wanted to say something. Whatever it was, she didn't want to hear it. Didn't know if she could handle it. What if he...? Well. She stood up and reached across the table for his dishes.

"I have to turn in a draw tomorrow, so I'll be busy for about an hour," he said. "You gonna be OK?"

"Yeah. I'm OK."

She accepted his kiss on her cheek and watched him walk away with shoulders slumped. She had never seen that before. He seemed to be doing a lot of deep breathing, too, especially when she brought up anything about Lauren or that night they drove home from the hospital with Liz hugging the pajamas Lauren would never wear again.

Liz sighed and picked up the plates. She set them on the counter and turned the tap on to warm up. He could tell her he didn't blame her, but she could see what was going on. Bry was trying to move on, and she was like an anchor dragging along behind him, slowing his progress. She wondered how many times he had considered cutting the rope and letting her sink to the bottom by herself.

Liz put the stopper in and let the water fill. Her stomach turned as it did every time the dish soap began to bubble up. She forced herself to put her hands in the water and clean each plate and fork. *Forgive yourself.* She turned on the tap to drown out the words, but they were there anyway. *Forgive yourself.*

"I can't!"

"Liz, are you all right in there?"

"Yes," she called back. No, *you're not.*

She turned on the water again, rinsed the plate, and set it in the drain rack. Wash, rinse, repeat. Wash, rinse, repeat. She let the water out and watched it drain. How nice it would be to go with it, down and away, out of sight.

CHAPTER 5

Liz took the wood polish and a cloth from under the sink and blew out her breath. Maybe if there were less *things* it would be easier to keep the house clean. Honestly, how long after the woman died did they need to keep Camille's Hummels? Just because Bry's grandmother had spent her social security collecting them, did they need to stay in the Bachmann house forever? Liz stood up, sighed, and walked the few steps across the kitchen to the room they still thought of as Camille's.

The curio cabinet was in its original place in the corner. The walls were the same bright yellow Camille had chosen, along with the drapes that had hung on the windows for six years now. Liz looked at the open space on the same fifteen-year-old carpet where they had put the pack-and-play when Lauren was a baby.

Everything had changed in this room.

Liz remembered it all again. She had called Lauren out of the garden, of course. If she hadn't kept after her, the girl would have been in the dirt all day long, but you can't let one thing define your whole life. Lauren had walked back along the row she just hoed, then turned and surveyed the garden. All her little shoots and stems, urged to sprout in the portable greenhouse in the living room over the early spring, had transformed into their teenaged gangly selves once she planted them outside.

Lauren had stopped in the half-bath just inside the back door and washed the garden off her hands. Liz had put a scrubber in there hoping Lo would get the hint and clean under her nails. The grungy nails of her piano students were sometimes more than Liz's stomach could stand.

Then Lauren had come into this room, to the piano. "Go ahead and start with your scales," Liz had directed. "Steady and with good finger posture."

Lauren didn't have to say a word. The shoulder slump gave her away, although she turned it into an arm stretch. On the other hand, the girl had been in the garden for hours. She could have been stiff from all that repetitive action.

The notes came out in fits and spurts, most of them in decent tune. The E minor scale always tripped Lauren up, but Liz was a firm believer in knowing the basics. Everything built out from there. "Make them even, just like spacing your plants," Liz said. "If they get bunched up, nothing good will come of it."

She ignored Lauren's sigh, which she was sure was left over from their discussion a few weeks earlier about music choice.

"Why can't I play what I hear on the radio?" her daughter had asked. "None of these songs even have words." Which had been Lauren Code for Capital B boring.

"OK. Good. Let's work on the Prelude," Liz said, setting the music on the rack. "You've just played E minor scale, so it should be right there in your ear."

Lauren rubbed her hands on her pants, which Liz saw were not really that clean. The notes came out painful and slow. It wasn't an easy piece, but it was straightforward. The left hand had chords while the right hand played a single note. The beauty was in the expression, or it should have been if Lauren had any interest. At measure twelve, she stopped.

"I really hate this," Lauren said.

"The music?"

"No. I don't want to play the piano. I never have."

Liz looked at her daughter. "What?"

"I hate this. This is *your* thing, not mine. I'm done." Lauren slid off the bench. "I'm getting cleaned up for my 4-H meeting."

How could her daughter not share something that was such an important thing in Liz's own life? Now it was the only thing they *did* do together. Otherwise, Lauren was out with Bry in the garden or the barn. After twelve years of Liz's attention, Lauren was done with her.

Liz scratched her arm and then leaned down and closed the book. She gathered up all the music, lifted the lid on the piano bench and dropped it inside. Then she let the lid slam down. She wasn't going to fight this battle.

Lauren came back downstairs wearing clean clothes, her hair freshly braided.

"You still have dishes to do before you go," Liz said.

"It's like five glasses and two plates," Lauren complained. "We're going to eat again anyway. I'll do them later."

"You'll do them now," Liz said.

Lauren rolled her eyes and huffed into the kitchen. Liz heard her slam the lever, turning on the water full stream. The silverware clattered into the sink. After a moment the plates clunked into the water. Then the *chink, chink, chink* of glasses knocking against each other.

"Ouch!"

Liz sighed. "What happened?" The girl could chop off half her foot out in the dirt but pinch her finger inside and it was a major deal.

"The glass broke."

"No surprise there," Liz muttered and walked out to the kitchen. "Let me see. Did you cut yourself?"

"Yeah." Lauren held out her hand, blood turning the soap bubbles a strange pink.

Liz grabbed the darkest-colored towel from the rack and held it to Lauren's hand.

"Ow." Lauren tried to pull it back.

"Just let me dry it so I can see." There was a clean slice into the heel of Lauren's right hand, but it wasn't very big. The blood was probably due to the wound being in the meat of her hand. "OK. Rinse it to be sure there's no glass, and then we'll wrap it up."

"Am I going to need stitches?"

Liz remembered the words she said that day, had remembered them every day since she and Bry buried Lauren. "I don't really think it's that bad. You might have a little scar at most."

The phone rang, and Liz dropped the can of polish. She bent down to retrieve it from under the piano bench, and then sat down hard when she heard Lauren's voice. "Hi! It's the Bachmann house. You can talk after the beep."

"Hi, Liz. It's Deidre. Hey, I was wondering when piano lessons might start back up? We're trying to get the fall schedule on the calendar. Liam's got soccer and Caitlyn's in the play...We miss seeing you guys at church. If there's anything...Well...just know we're praying for you."

Liz looked down at her arm and the marks she had made from scratching it over and over as Deirdre had talked. She should get up and put some cream on it. So it wouldn't get infected. No. Liz touched her nails to the marks and slid them back and forth, back and forth, pushing harder each time. Back and forth.

"Babe?"

Bry stood in front of her with the mail envelopes in his hand, mid-sort. He laid them on the piano bench and squatted in front of her.

"What's going on, Liz?" He reached out and took her arm in his hand, then reached for her other hand.

They both looked at her nails. Liz kind of liked the way blood filled and turned the underside of each nail red.

"Liz," Bry said.

"It's a rash. That's all."

"You're hurting yourself, honey. I—" He rubbed her hand with his thumb. "I want you to call someone. To talk."

"I'm OK," she said. She pulled her hand away and reached for the can of polish. She held it up like it was a prize and smiled. "Really."

Bry stood up, bringing her with him. Liz felt trapped in this tiny room with its huge memories that replayed bits of her life over and over. Bry looked around, like there was something he wasn't saying. She reached for her arm to scratch it.

"Let me get some cream for that." He seemed relieved to have words to break the silence.

Liz dropped her hand. "I can do it." She gave him a bright smile. "I'm good."

He brushed her cheek with his fingertips and studied her for a long minute with hollow eyes. Then he reached down for the envelopes.

Liz snatched the cloth from the music rack. She walked with purpose to the closet and put away her things. She heard the slap of envelopes against the piano and then Bry's boots thumping behind her into the kitchen. She hesitated, fighting the urge to see what dirt he had tracked in. She closed the closet door and went upstairs, leaving Bry at the kitchen table, knowing he was watching every move she made.

CHAPTER 6

Whenever she went past the dining room windows, she could see Lauren's garden waiting to lure someone, anyone, behind its fence. The pumpkins along the edge were just turning orange, their color punching through the green of tangled vines. The stalks of Indian corn were in the final stretch, and Bry had laid some of the ears on the porch to dry out. Liz reached up and pulled the blinds down over the windows, one by one, blocking it all out.

Her head ached, today a dull thudding on the top of her head, different from yesterday's feeling of being shot right through the eye with an arrow. Maybe a nap would help. Liz went upstairs, lay down on her bed, and closed her eyes.

She saw Lauren in the hospital bed, growing smaller and smaller right in front of her. She saw the drip, drip of the antibiotic going into the tubing. She heard the beep of the monitor slower, slower. She felt the nurse brush past her to Lauren's side. Liz snapped her eyes open. She could not watch that again. Once had been more than she could bear. She sat up, waited for the dizziness to fade away, and then went back downstairs.

She wandered through the living room and into the kitchen where her toast from the morning sat on the table, untouched. Liz picked up the plate and dumped the toast into the trash. Then she thought of Bry opening the mail, throwing out the envelopes and fliers, seeing another meal in the garbage. She picked the toast out and closed the cupboard door. The bird feeder. Let the squirrels be useful for a change.

Out in the yard there was the thick, primordial green of growing things and she could feel it wrapping itself around her. She hurried back into the house, closed the mudroom door, and leaned back against it. It was ridiculous to be chased by the smell of tomato plants. She needed to change the air, to take control of these 'fears.' She could go out and pick the tomatoes whose blood red wounds made the garden look like it had been sprayed by gunfire. Bry had said just the day before, "Those tomatoes are so ripe they're about to roll up to the house on their own. Peppers, too." The subtext was, of course, *look what Lauren and I did.*

Well, she could do that, too.

She went to the pantry and pulled out cans of toma-toes—diced, paste, sauce. She took an onion from the bin and a jar of chilis off the shelf, and carried them to the counter. She turned on the stove, heated the pot, and browned the burger and onions. As she broke the meat into smaller and smaller bits she thought about herself crumbling into tiny, unrecognizable pieces. Liz drained off the grease with a paper towel and threw it away. She opened the cans, caressing the sharp edges of each metal circle with her fingertip. She rinsed the beans and spooned them into the pot with the meat, tomatoes, and peppers.

Lauren had loved chili. She had come up with what she thought was the perfect spice mix. She even printed it out neatly and taped the recipe to the inside of the spice cupboard door. Liz ran a hand over the ink, resting on the three exclamation points after the words "8 *Tbsp chili powder. I'm serious!!!*" Liz poured the spices into the pot one at a time and stirred until they were mixed in. She covered it and turned down the burner.

"That chili is gonna be good," Bry said. "I could smell it all the way outside."

Liz imagined miming licking her finger and giving herself a point. *Take that, garden beast.*

"Did you use up the tomatoes?" he asked.

"No."

"We really have to get those off the vines, Liz. They're nearly on the ground as it is."

Liz liked that image of the garden running red with tomato blood. It was very satisfying.

Bry rubbed his chest with an open palm. He'd been doing that a lot lately, probably some new signal she was supposed to know. "I can get to that this weekend, maybe," he said. "I was afraid they wouldn't be ripe on time for the fair, but I guess we didn't need to buy such mature plants. We would have finished too soon, with the tomatoes anyway." He blew out his cheeks and exhaled. Rubbed his chest again.

"The chili's ready," Liz said. She ladled some into a bowl and took it to the table with a spoon and some crackers.

"Aren't you eating?" he asked.

Usually he washed his hands and went right to the table when he was late, but this time Bry stood at the island.

"I ate already." Not chili, but he didn't need to know that.

"Yeah, I'm sorry. I had a laborer MIA today, and I had to go back to the site in Thompsonville…"

Liz went to the cupboard and pulled out a couple of plastic containers. She ladled the chili into them, and into a small one for Bry to take in his lunch the next day. The others would go into the back of the freezer. She wouldn't eat it. How could she eat when her daughter was dead?

Behind her, she could hear Bry pull out the chair and sit down. He opened a package of crackers, the plastic crinkle loud in the stillness of the kitchen. She set the empty pot into the sink and turned on the water to let it soak. She added a squirt of dish soap and watched the red froth gather as it had on Lauren's hand. She sighed.

"I'm sorry," Bry said. "I can't eat."

Liz pushed down the lever, stopping the water's flow. She dried her hands and went upstairs, each step a prayer.

Let me die. Let me die. God, let me die.

CHAPTER 7

"I'm getting ready to go." Bry touched her cheek.

"OK," Liz mumbled. "Have a good day." She smiled but kept her eyes closed.

"Liz?"

"Mm-hmm?"

"Did you make an appointment with the counselor? I left her card on the table."

"No, but I will." She opened one eye and then closed it. Bry stood there, and Liz was tempted to see what he was doing.

"I'll call *for* you," he said finally. "And I'll be back to take you."

She opened her eyes to that. "You don't have to come home. You have a schedule to keep."

"We're doing fine on time, and this is more important than someone's second home. I'll call you with the details. OK?"

"OK."

"All right. Well, get some rest. You look kinda pale."

"Mmm," Liz said. "Bye."

She waited until his truck pulled away before she sat up. It took longer than usual for the dizzy feeling to settle, and she stumbled a little walking from the bed to the bathroom. She checked in the mirror, ran her fingers through her hair, so thin now it didn't even cover her ears.

Liz went to her closet and pulled out a few shirts. The first was a loose, dark-green blend. She put it on at her reflection. She swam in it, so that wouldn't work. The second was a knit that was usually a little too formfitting. She studied herself again in the mirror. Her skin looked lemon yellow against the cream fabric, and the sweater was too big on her. She frowned, trying to think of something else she could wear.

She remembered buying Lauren a bright blue running shirt that was a little big but one she would grow into. Liz went into her daughter's room and pulled open the closet doors. She stepped forward, put an arm on each side of the collection of hanging clothes, and hugged them to her. Liz buried her face in them and breathed deep as Lauren's scent rose off the clothes.

Tears started in her eyes, but she willed them back. She would not ruin this gift by crying.

Liz stood like that for a long time not wanting to pull away for fear the magic would be broken. She shifted her weight and felt something under her bare foot. She noticed some small, dried particles on the carpet. Strange how the carpet looked gray, and the room was so quiet.

"God, no—Liz!" Bry's voice sounded so far away.

She would call out to him so he would know where to find her. "Bry." Her voice sounded so small. "Bry." It took so much effort, and she was so tired.

"Liz, can you hear me?"

Bry was by her side now, his fingers touching near her jaw.

"Yes." She thought she was talking, but she couldn't hear herself. Her eyes would not open.

Bry was saying something and then he was gone.

Something smooth and sweet was on her tongue, and Liz moved it around in her mouth. It was...honey.

"Liz." Bry's voice was much closer now.

"Yes." She opened her eyes at the sound of her own voice. Bry's look was intense and what else? Scared. He looked scared. "What's wrong?" she asked.

"It worked. Thank you, Jesus," he said. "Liz, do you remember how you got here?"

Liz moved her eyes. She saw the purple of the carpet and, farther away, Lauren's bed. Why was she lying on the floor? She turned her head to the clothes hanging above her. She remembered hugging them and then looking down.

"There was something on the floor, I think," she said. Liz realized she was holding something in her palm. She opened her hand and saw a yellow kernel of corn and a dried bean. "These."

"OK, I don't know what you're talking about, but I'm taking you to the hospital. Can you sit up?"

He slid a hand under her shoulder and pulled her up to a sitting position. The dizzy swimming feeling started, and she closed her eyes.

"OK, not so fast," he said. "Liz, did you eat today?"

Did she eat? "No. I don't think so." She squinted and then willed her eyes to open.

"Did you eat yesterday?"

She wrinkled her forehead, thinking. "I don't know?"

Bry pulled out his phone and dialed. "Hi, this is Bryant Bachmann. I made an appointment earlier for my wife, Elizabeth. I'm going to take her to the ER instead. I found her passed out. She doesn't remember eating for a few days." He listened for a few minutes. "OK, I'll let them know. I should have seen what was going on." He listened again. "I will. Thank you."

Bry reached up and pulled down something from one of the hangers. He worked her arms into it and zipped up the zipper. "All right. I'm just going to carry you. Ready?"

"Yes."

He put an arm behind her back and one under her legs and stood up. As he turned his face away, Liz watched a tear track down the side of his nose and drop onto the unicorn Lauren had asked her to appliqué to the sweat jacket. He cleared his throat.

"Here we go."

Bry loaded her into the truck and buckled her in. He went back into the house, and a minute later set her purse on the seat between them. As he drove out of their driveway, Liz opened her hand and saw the seeds were still there. These had meant life to Lauren. She had planted seeds like these in darkness, with faith and hope they would grow. Liz closed her eyes and let the movement of the truck take her far away.

She felt Bry put the truck in park.

"Liz, stay here. I'll be right back." He disappeared into the door marked Urgent Care and came back out with a wheelchair.

"I can walk," Liz said as he opened her door.

"No, I don't think you can," he said. He released her seatbelt and then held her gaze for a long minute. "Let me help you, Liz. Please."

CHAPTER 8

"We have both inpatient and outpatient groups."

Liz recognized the counselor's name from the card Bry had left out for her.

"Although right now," Mira said, "there is a waiting list for inpatients."

"I want to be at home," Liz said. She saw the counselor's quick glance at Bry.

"I'd like to see you again this week," Mira continued. "Then we can decide which group sessions will best work. Good? So, let's plan Thursday morning at nine thirty."

"OK," Liz said.

Mira smiled. "It's going to be *more* than OK. There's a prescription waiting for you downstairs at the pharmacy for a vitamin mix. Think of this as fresh air for your body—little bits of things it's been missing over the last few months. I think you'll find you like the boost the B vitamins will give you too. Bryant, you may want to pick that up now. I'm sure you both want to get home."

"I can do that."

"The nurse can give you directions to the pharmacy," Mira said. "I'll just keep Liz company for a few minutes longer."

"OK, thanks, Mira."

When the door closed, she turned to Liz.

"Liz, I want us to be honest with each other. You have been through a major trauma, and there are very likely some other situations also in play. It takes time to see how all of the pieces *have* come together, and to figure out how they *should* come together. It might seem like it happened overnight but that is not true. Nor will it disappear, get fixed, or return to normal. We can get you to healthy, but that will not be overnight either."

Liz nodded. Lauren had gone from healthy to dead overnight.

"For now, I want you to look not at the big picture, but at what's right in front of you. What is here and now that you can control? Maybe it's just steadying your breathing. Maybe it's deciding how you will spend the next five minutes. Small is OK. It might even help to have a small token in your pocket, like a worry stone, that you can touch to remind you to stay in that moment."

Liz knew exactly what she would use. The seeds on the closet floor, originally destined for the soil, she would plant in her own darkness.

Bry brought the truck around and, for the second time in three months, they drove home alone from the hospital. What should she say to him? What could she say? *I'm sorry I have given you more to worry about. I'm sorry I have been selfish. I'm sorry we have even more hospital bills to pay.* Or, would she say, *I'm sorry I didn't die.*

Ahead she could see the line of traffic stopped on the road.

"What is all that?" Bry said.

Liz shook her head. Then the smell of deep-fried onions seeping into the truck made her stomach churn.

"It's fair week," Bry said, his voice thick and raw.

He slowed to a crawl behind the line of cars turning one after another into the fairgrounds. They both stared out the window at the campers lined up inside the fence, the cows standing at the bathing stanchions, the signs of life moving on. Bry reached over and took her hand. "Like Mira said, more than OK."

They should have been there this week, celebrating Lauren's first 4-H exhibits and encouraging her to live out the 4-H pledge. Maybe later she would have considered the Leader Dog project that Liz had done the legwork for. They might have camped at the fairgrounds as a family. But no more. From now on, Liz and Bry would be outsiders looking in.

Bry pulled into their driveway, and Liz peered out her window at the garden as they passed. He parked the truck in the garage, and Liz got out. Instead of following her into the house, Bry walked down the drive. Liz stood on the porch and watched him unlatch the garden gate and walk along the rows as if he was searching for something. Then he stopped, squatted down, and lifted a pumpkin. He went a few steps farther and chose a second.

He juggled them in one arm as he closed the gate and then brought them up to the porch. "I figured we could harvest some. Maybe give them away."

She hadn't helped at all with planting and tending the garden. Actually, it seemed like Lauren and Bry were fine without her. Liz hadn't helped Bry keep it going, and to be honest, she was glad that it had taken him out of the house. But now she saw that Bry was doing it not for himself, but for Lauren. Lo would have wanted to share this with others. Liz was the one being selfish here.

She remembered taking photos in the spring of Lauren staking the beans, and some close-ups of the plants for a poster project Lauren meant to display with her vegetable fair entries. Liz gave Bry a small smile, then unlocked the door and went inside. She set down her purse and got her camera from the other room. She pulled out a rag from under the sink, got it wet and soapy, and took it all to the porch.

Bry tipped his head and watched her wash the pumpkins. When she settled the strap of her camera around her neck he understood. "Do you want them on the steps where the light is better?"

"We'll take a few different shots," she said.

"They're pumpkins, Liz, not graduating seniors."

She stared at him, unblinking.

He nodded slowly. "Tell me where you want them."

For the next hour, she took portrait-quality shots of everything she could find that had to do with the garden. Produce, withered stalks, the rake, the latch on the gate. Even the scarecrow that Lauren had made but never set out. Liz wasn't sure what she would do with the pictures. She just knew they had to be taken before it was too late.

CHAPTER 9

M ira had encouraged her to find a focus. "It could be for just a few minutes, or maybe a day. Look for a place you can spend some energy in a way that fills you." Liz took a deep breath and pulled open the door. Once inside the lobby, she could hear barking coming from behind another door to the right.

"Hi. Welcome to Blanche's Friends."

Liz smiled and moved closer to the girl at the desk. "I wondered if you ever needed anyone to walk the dogs. Not to get paid, just—to volunteer?"

"Sure. Yes. We definitely welcome volunteers. Do you know about our shelter?"

"Not really," Liz said. "I kind of found you by accident."

"Well, I guess that's lucky for us," the girl said. "I'm Kacee. If you like, I can show you around."

Liz smiled. "Great."

"So, this is Blanche." The girl pointed to an oversized photo on the wall behind her of a perky-faced little black and white dog. "She was the first dog adopted by our major sponsor. Some people had come up on her after a car hit her. They took her to the vet and had her leg casted before turning her over to a shelter. Our sponsor named her Blanche because of that line from the play, something about relying on the kindness of strangers."

Liz nodded.

"Some of our friends were strays like Blanche," Kacee went on, "and some are surrendered to us. They can stay here for as long as it takes to find them their forever home."

"Wow," Liz said.

"Yeah, it's pretty awesome."

They went through the door and down a hall of rooms, each one with a big window in the door. Some rooms held kennels; others were some kind of free-play area where dogs ran loose. Farther down was a room with cats—on benches, in the window, on carpeted towers.

"These are some of their stories," Kacee said, pointing to the wall next to the doorframe.

Liz studied the cluster of cards, each with a photo and short bio.

"The ones for the dogs are on their kennels. I'll take you in there, but be ready. It's kinda loud." Kacee smiled. "They like visitors."

Liz followed her into a room where rows of floor-to-ceiling fencing made kennels that lined both sides of a walkway. Large and medium sized dogs, one or two per kennel, came to the front or stood up and got a drink. One black dog brought a toy to the gate.

Kacee motioned her to another door at the end of the room and closed it behind them. "This will be a little quieter. These are some of the newer dogs. We give them some time in here to kind of get used to everything before they join the party in there."

Most of the dogs hung back from greeting her. One small, brown dog lay on a bed in the corner of its cage, and Liz could just feel the sadness coming from its eyes. She read the bio.

> Billy was a true friend to his first owner, spending time on his lap and later next to him on his hospital bed. Billy came to us when no suitable home could be found for this shy but sweet friend.

Liz looked at Kacee. "Could I pet him?"

"Of course. Here." She reached for a can of spray cheese and a wooden tongue depressor. "Sometimes this helps break the ice."

Lauren would love this little dog. Would have loved him.

For the rest of her life, Liz would refer to her daughter in past tense. Lauren was part of the Life Before, like the shadow behind her that Liz couldn't catch hold of. The weeks she had lived without Lauren had passed one day at a time, moving Liz farther from the life she wanted back.

As she drove home, she thought of the little dog and all the memories of his previous owner he had stored away. Did he think about the man? Did he recall the day they met? The day that they said goodbye? The days in between that passed unnoticed? Would he want another life with someone else? Did he even want to go on?

That night, Liz could hardly wait for Bry to take off his boots before she pulled out her phone. "I did what Mira suggested," she said.

"Great. What did you decide on?"

"I went to a rescue out on Park Road called Blanche's Friends. I'm going to walk dogs and help socialize them."

"That sounds good. One of the plumbers just adopted a dog from there. Had all good things to say." He went to the sink and washed his hands.

"I wanted to show you this." Liz queued up the shots she had taken of Billy.

"What is it?" Bry came to the table, drying his hands on the towel. He took the phone, flipped through the pictures, and handed the device back to her. "Liz, I'm glad you found a place, but I'm not interested in a dog."

"He's very sweet. Just lonely. We could—"

"Liz. You can't bring home every dog that is lonely."

"It's one dog."

"No."

"Bry."

He held up a hand and turned away, his sign for needing space before talking again. Liz waited.

"I'm not hungry," he said. "I'm just going to get ready for bed."

Liz sighed. They were exactly the kind of home Billy needed. He could be with her during the day and at night curl up in Bry's lap. She could already see his little dog bed next to the piano. Bry was just tired. She was sure in the morning he would be ready to talk about it

CHAPTER 10

Liz woke up to her alarm. She hadn't set one for months, hadn't had a reason to for months. But this morning, she wanted to catch Bry before he left and before the day wore on him. "Hey," she said from the bathroom doorway.

He wiped the last of the shaving cream from his neck with the towel. "You're up early."

"I thought I'd get up with you, for once." Liz smiled. "Where are you working today?"

"I've got to go down to Hart. You know we did that remodel back in March? Now they want to put up an outbuilding and asked me for a bid."

"You're going all that way to build a barn?"

"Sounded like more. They wanted me to look at the plans and the site before I bid." He rinsed the razor under the water and set it aside. "I'll humor them. They were a nice couple."

Liz nodded. Was it the nice-ness or the nine-ty-minute drive that he liked better? "Do you want some eggs for breakfast?"

"No, I want to get going. It's gonna be a long day already." He looked in the mirror and rubbed a spot on his left cheek. "I still have to finish up on the Weick project. Get some of this stuff off my plate." He hung the towel on the rack, straightened the edges. "I could use a sandwich for lunch, if you want to make that."

"Sure. Turkey all right?"

"Good."

Liz went to the kitchen and washed her hands at the sink. She breathed some deep breaths just as Mira had told her to do when she felt the panic starting. She closed her eyes and imagined a level horizon, then turned to the refrigerator to get out the sandwich fixings.

Bry came downstairs and went out to the truck. By the time she got the sandwich boxed up he was back. She put a container of applesauce and a spoon in the bag, added a cheese stick, and then froze, looking at what she had done. It was Lauren's lunch, the one Liz had packed for her for years. Liz zipped up the cooler bag and pushed it away from her to the far edge of the counter.

Bry sat on a kitchen chair lacing up his boots.

"I wondered if we could talk about the dog," she said.

He continued pulling the lace tight up to the top of his boot.

"It's just that he's suddenly all alone. Someone in his world has gone away. He's grieving, Bry."

"Welcome to the club," Bry said to his boot. Then he stood up and turned toward her. "I already said no. I said no months ago when Lo asked. I'm saying no now." He pulled his jacket off the chair. "I'll be back after six."

He went out the door, closing it hard behind him. A moment later, the truck started, and Liz followed the sound of it down the drive and out onto the road. Her eyes found the bright blue of the cooler bag still on the counter. She backed against the refrigerator and slid to the floor. She pulled her knees up and buried her face in them as hot tears pricked her eyes and then ran down her cheeks.

When they were young marrieds, she and Bry went river rafting. Liz had been tossed out of the boat in some white water and got mixed up in the churning. Water had pushed at her, tugged her backward, smashed into her from every side. She couldn't find the way up, couldn't tell where to go. Her chest hurt from holding her breath. She remembered kicking out, grabbing at anything, knowing she would die. The current had carried her along and spit her out in calm water on the edge of the river. She had not wanted to get back in the boat, but it was either that or get left behind.

She cried now, her sides heaving, her mind seeing again the swirling waters pulling and pushing her under. She couldn't breathe. She was drowning in all of this. She wanted to give in and give up. But then the tears ran out, and she was sitting on the floor in her kitchen, the clock on the wall quietly counting the seconds away.

Liz wiped her face, listened to the *tick-tock-tick-tock*. She was not dead. She had come out in still water.

"I don't want to do this," she said out loud. "I can't do this." But what was the alternative?

She pushed her hair away from her face and stood up. She emptied the lunch bag into the refrigerator and put it back in the pantry. She forced herself to put bread in the toaster, spread it with peanut butter and then eat it in slow, measured chews. Controlling what she could control for that moment, just as she had learned. Liz went back upstairs and made the bed, got dressed, started the laundry. Each time the feeling rose in her, she pushed it back down and kept paddling.

On the river, the guide had told them how to prepare for each new set of rapids, what side to paddle on, where to go in the water to keep the boat afloat. "The worst thing you can do," he said, "is to hunker down. The raft will flip for sure. When you hear the roar coming, anchor your feet, lean out over the edge, and paddle like crazy."

Liz went down the stairs looking for some dust to wipe away or some reason to get out the vacuum. She walked through the dining room and let her gaze go toward the garden. She could hear the roar coming.

Liz went out to the garage and grabbed a garden rake. She let the current carry her to the gate and down between the rows all the way to the end where she raised the rake and smashed it down on the bright orange pumpkins, over and over, until every one of them was broken and bleeding. Then she turned her focus to the plants.

She ripped down the sorry remains of the second harvest beans. She chopped at the fall greens and what was left of the basil and cilantro. Tomatoes, peppers all fell under her rake. She swung and hacked, paddling like crazy, until the roaring stopped.

She was back at the gate. The garden lay decimated, the vegetables mixing with the dirt in a giant, disgusting salsa. Liz threw down the rake and walked out through the open gate, her steps matching her breathing. One-two-three-four, one-two-three-four, all the way up to Lauren's room. She pushed open the door, lay down on the bed, and curled up into a ball.

CHAPTER 11

L iz lay there facing the wall. She had not changed out of her muddy shoes or even taken off her gloves. Her heart hurt so much. *She* hurt so much. If Bryant wanted a fight when he got home, she didn't care. Let him think he'd won.

Images filled her mind. Of Lauren as a tiny baby, Liz's first glimpse of their "impossible" child, the one they were not supposed to have had. Then Lauren as a toddler with a big Kool-Aid grin. At the beach. In front of the Christmas tree. Blowing out birthday candles. Riding her bike with her silly unicorn helmet and training wheels. Speaking her part in the class play. Hanging upside down from the monkey bars, her arms touching the ground.

One by one, Liz set them in front of her like a collage. All of those moments pasted in the scrapbook of her memory. She turned the page and found it blank. There were no more photos to add. No ribbons from the fair, no first dance, no sweet sixteen party, graduation, wedding, grandchild. That Lauren would never be, maybe was never meant to be. In her mind, Liz closed the memory book, ran her hands over the cover, and hugged it to herself.

"Liz?" Bry's voice came from the hall. "Are you in there?"

He pushed the door open and padded across the purple carpet they had put in when they made over Lauren's room as a present for her tenth birthday.

"Hey." He sat down on the end of the bed.

Liz was silent. She had nothing left to say. She heard the scratch of his chapped hands rubbing over his chin. Then she felt him double over.

"God, Liz," he whispered. Then a sob.

Liz rolled over and saw him, elbows on his knees, head clutched in his hands. His back jerked again and again, and Liz realized he was crying. Even when they were the last ones at the graveside, he had only had tears in his eyes. But he had never cried.

"Bry?" She sat up and swung her legs over the edge of the bed, careful now to keep the dirt off the comforter. She took off a glove and laid her hand on his back, and when he didn't shrug it off, she rubbed in soft circles like she had done with Lauren.

After a few minutes, he sat up and wiped the back of his hand across his face. He turned to her with pain in his eyes.

"I couldn't do it," he whispered.

"What?"

"The garden. I couldn't till it under. It was like—it was like if the plants were there, so was she. And burying them was like putting her in the ground all over again."

Tears stung Liz's eyes. She squeezed her hands between her knees. "I was jealous," she said. "Of you and her together. You were so into the garden, working in it, talking about it. There was no place for me anymore."

Bry gave her a weak smile. "It was the first thing in a long time that I could share with her. You did all the girl things. I guess I felt like there wasn't much left for me, of either of you."

"I didn't know," Liz said. "I'm sorry." When had she pushed Bry away? When had she stopped seeing him as her husband and started seeing him as her competition? Like Lauren was some prize to fight over?

"I need you," he said. "I've tried to do this by myself, but I can't. I can't."

She reached for him, and he buried his head in her neck. For several minutes, he cried, letting out the sadness he had kept dammed up for months. Then he sat back and wiped his eyes.

"I love you so much, Liz. I can't lose you too."

"I'm not going anywhere."

"But you did. You're so thin, Liz. I know you wanted to be dead rather than live through this."

She looked down at the carpet and nodded. "I didn't think there was anything left."

"I'm left." He laced his fingers through hers and squeezed. "Please come back to me."

She squeezed back. "For better or worse."

It had been a long time since they prayed together—years—but they prayed then. For each other, for their marriage, and they prayed Lauren's spirit into God's hands. It was never theirs to hold anyway, she knew, at least not in the way they once had hoped.

When they were done, Bry lay back on Lauren's pillow with one arm over his face, and after a few minutes, Liz heard his soft snore. She knew the feeling, to be emptied by grief. She got up and closed the door quietly behind her.

Liz washed off the dirt and debris of the garden and changed into clean clothes. She went downstairs to the kitchen but found herself drawn into the yellow room and to the piano. Music had been her life once, before it got put aside again and again. She came back to it each time, changed by what had happened, around her, to her.

She pulled out the bench, sat down, and opened the fallboard. Lauren's fingers had been the last to touch the keys, playing out of frustration, pushing the notes away from her. Liz should never have set the music in front of Lo. It was not hers to play.

Liz positioned her hands above the keys and held them there, suspended. Then she closed her eyes and played the opening note, then the second, then the E minor chord of the prelude. A tear slipped down her cheek as she played through the thirteenth measure, and then another and another. She paused at the fermata in measure twenty-two, the hold before the final chords of the piece. The place she had been living in for three months. The end that is not the end.

CHAPTER 12

Liz could hear the barking as soon as she got out of the car. She walked across the gravel drive and took a deep breath before pulling open the door.

"Hi, welcome to Blanche's Friends. I'm Kacee." The girl hesitated. "Wait, you came on a tour a few weeks ago." Liz nodded. "Yes."

"Welcome back! Did you still want to volunteer?"

"Yes, if that's OK."

"Of course. There's always room for more. Let me get you set up."

Liz followed Kacee to the quiet room, just as before. She noticed Billy was still there, still hiding in the back of his kennel on his bed. "He didn't move out yet, huh?"

"No, not yet." Kacee shook her head. "I know you had an interest in him before. Do you want to walk him first?"

"Sure."

"OK." Kacee took a leash from the hook near the door and handed it to her. "Just out that door. Take as long as he needs. Oh, and the treats are up on that shelf."

"OK," Liz said. She chose a treat from one of the bags and turned to the kennel. "Hey, Billy." He moved his eyes toward her but did not stand up. Liz inched open the cage door and held out her palm with the treat. He turned his head away.

"That's all right. You don't have to eat it. I'll put it here for later." She set the treat near his bed. "Do you want to go outdoors?" She slipped the looped leash over his head as Kacee had shown her last time. Billy rose to his feet, resigned, and came to the front of the cage. Liz set him on the floor and took a step.

"Ready? Let's go." The dog hesitated and let the leash pull on his neck. "It's OK. Let's go outside," she said again. Then she remembered to use his words. "Billy, come." He moved toward her, and she led him out into the yard.

The other dogs barking in the runs startled him, and he waited at the edge of the grass for a moment before venturing out. Liz let him take the lead, and after a long pause, he sniffed a clump of grass. They moved around the yard at a snail's pace, stopping for new noises or brown patches in the grass.

Liz squatted next to the dog, and when he didn't shy away, she reached out a hand to pet him. Billy sat down. "Good boy." She rubbed behind his ears and then down his back. He seemed to relax as she petted him. "Good boy."

When it seemed like he had lost interest in the yard, Liz stood up and led him back inside. He stopped on the floor under his kennel and waited. "OK, I guess you're all done." She picked him up and put him into his kennel. "Don't forget your treat is there," she said, closing the door.

She walked all of the dogs in the quiet room and then slipped into the cat room for a few minutes. A proud black cat rubbed around her ankles and meowed up at her. "I see you." She reached down and petted his sleek coat. When he wandered off, a small gray cat came and sniffed her shoes, then put its paws up on the carpeted post and scratched away. The cats didn't seem to need her attention, so she got her bag and went out to the desk.

"All done?" Kacee smiled.

"Yes. Could I come tomorrow?"

"Tomorrow's perfect."

Liz had volunteered at Blanche's Friends for a few hours each week. She liked the rhythm of going to the shelter and had hoped that it would give her the momentum she needed to get past this day, but it wasn't happening. Lauren should have been turning thirteen. She should have had cake, and presents, and an overnight with the girls. Liz could see it all happening behind her closed eyelids. If she didn't open her eyes, maybe it would be real. She could hope.

"Hey." Bry sat down on the edge of the bed.

Liz turned toward him. "Hi. Are you home early?"

"Yeah. I just couldn't make any headway."

Liz nodded. That made two of them.

"Did you eat?"

It was his standard question any time she was at all quiet. She was a little tired of it, but she knew he meant well.

"A little cereal this morning."

"Good. Can I come in?" Liz moved over on the bed, and Bry stretched out beside her. She reached for his hand, and he squeezed hers back. They lay like that for a long time, not talking.

Bry sighed. "This sucks."

"Yeah." Liz swiped at the tears with her hand. "Yeah, it does."

"What are we supposed to do?"

"Keep going," Liz said. "That's what they say, anyways."

He sighed again. "Some days, I just..."

Liz nodded. "I know."

Neither of them said anything. There was nothing to say. Their daughter was dead. It happened to people all the time, but that fact did not make them feel any less ragged and torn apart. They were raw and hurting and lost.

The image came to her of Billy lying in his bed, turning his face away from the world, and Liz was jealous that she could not do the same.

CHAPTER 13

"Hi, Liz. It's Kacee from Blanche's Friends. Hey, I just wondered if you were planning to come in this week to volunteer."

There was a pause and Liz thought the answering machine message was done.

"I mean, we don't want to pressure you, but...well, Billy isn't eating. And we thought...Um, OK. Have a good day."

Liz looked at her watch and then at the bags of groceries on the counter. She could put away the perishables and still have time to go to the shelter for a little while. Billy had seemed to open up to her a little during her visits. He never wagged his tail or anything, but maybe she had made a difference.

Pulling open the shelter door, Liz had a sense of urgency she hadn't felt in a long time. "Hi," she said. "I got your message. How is he?"

Kacee smiled. "I'm glad you came. I don't know. He just isn't like he was when you were here a few weeks ago."

"I'm sorry. I...I—"

"It's OK," Kacee said. "Do you want to see him?"

"Yes."

They went into the quiet room, and Liz took down a treat before opening the kennel. Billy didn't even look up. "Hey, buddy. I'm back." She set the treat by his bed and put a hand on his head. He didn't flinch, so she petted him in her usual way. Liz glanced at Kacee. "He does feel thin."

"We thought so too."

"Billy, do you want to go outside?" Liz asked. She looped the leash over his head and reached under him. He stood and let her pick him up. "I'll just carry him," she said, and Kacee nodded.

In the yard, Billy made his rounds and then went back to the gate. It was a start, anyway. Liz squatted down to give him his "good boy" pets. "I'm sorry I ditched you," she said. "I was having a hard time, and I...well, it wasn't an excuse for leaving you alone. I'll do better." Billy looked at her and then at the gate. "OK, point taken." She took him back to his kennel and then went out to the desk.

"Thanks, Liz," Kacee said. "I was sorry to bother you at home, but I thought you'd want to know."

"I did. I'll be back tomorrow."

Kacee was on the phone, so Liz waved and went back to the quiet room. Liz gave herself a pat on the back for the fact that over the last two weeks everyone but Billy had transitioned to the other rooms. Billy, her Billy as she secretly called him, was making progress, but he still hesitated at the doorway if the big dogs were barking.

Liz unzipped the treat bag and took one of the crunchy bits that Billy seemed to like better. She turned to his kennel and found a plastic smiley face hanging from it. Her heart sank.

"Isn't it great?" Kacee leaned on the doorframe. "A couple came this morning to see him. They were going to talk about it and get back to us tomorrow or Wednesday."

A forever home. The whole goal of the rescue, of course, but this was Billy.

"How did he do for them?" Liz asked.

"Well, he would be a pet for an older man, like Billy knew before. His daughter and her husband are the man's caretakers. We had them meet him in the guest room with the couch, and Garret told me Billy sat on her lap the whole time."

"What did they think?"

Kacee tipped her head. "They'll bring her father next time, but it sounds like a good match."

"That's great," Liz said. Not great, actually, if she was being honest. "Should I still exercise him?"

"Of course, yeah. They just visited. They didn't go outside with him."

Liz opened the kennel door, the smiley face clattering against it. She dropped the treat by his bed and rubbed his ears. "Do you ever let the volunteers meet the for-ever families?"

"I don't know if it's ever come up before," Kacee said.

"It's probably not necessary," Liz began.

"No, I'll totally check on it," Kacee said. "I know you guys have something between you. To be honest, I was kind of surprised you didn't take him home yourself."

"I would have, but...well, there's a lot to the story."

"I get it. Let me make a call."

"OK," Liz said. She looped the leash over Billy's head, and he stood up. She set him on the floor and walked him out to the yard for the last time.

"The little dog I've been working with is probably being adopted today."

Bry set down his coffee. "That's good, right?"

"Yeah. I asked if I could meet the new family."

"What did they say?"

"It's fine."

Bry ran his finger up and down on the handle of the mug.

"You want to say something," Liz said.

"This is kind of why I said no. This is the same dog you wanted to bring home, right?" Liz nodded. "They don't live forever. I didn't want you to get hurt."

"It's probably best this way." Liz said. "He's a man's dog. He'll be company for an older man with dementia."

Bry nodded. "Nice."

He stood and came behind her chair. He rubbed her shoulders, and she leaned her head on his hand, wiping away a tear.

"I guess I'll go get ready," she said. "They're coming in at nine thirty."

Bry slid his arms around her and held her for a minute. "We're both lucky dogs," he said, "to have you."

Mr. Taylor smiled vaguely, his eyes shifting toward his daughter's voice whenever she talked. When she took her father's arm, he walked beside her with short, shuffling steps. Kacee settled them in the guest room and then gave Liz a thumbs-up on the way back through. They had agreed Kacee should bring Billy out to the family, so Liz pretended to tidy up the counter while she waited.

This was not about Liz. This was Billy's day. This was a celebration.

Liz watched through the guest room's picture window as Kacee carried Billy in and set him in the man's lap. Her breath caught when Billy fidgeted. Was he nervous? Did he want down? Then Billy slid off onto the couch, turned round and round, and lay down next to the man's leg. Mr. Taylor reached out a hand, took one of Billy's ears between his thumb and finger, and rubbed it as Liz had.

Kacee chatted with the couple but Liz focused on Mr. Taylor. She watched the uncertainty and haze fall away, as if Billy's calm traveled up the man's fingers, up his arm, to turn round and round and settle in. Billy glanced up at the man once and then put his head down on his paws.

Liz was stunned. All this time she thought Billy was afraid or shy, when he was just doing what he did best. His job was not to jump around and be animated like the other dogs. His job was to be a place to lay a hand. To replace concern with care. To be near when needed. Just as he had been for her.

Kacee came across the lobby to the desk. "He looks good, don't you think?"

Liz smiled. "Yes. They both do."

"You should give yourself some credit for this, you know." Kacee nodded. "You took things at his pace, let Billy be Billy."

I never wanted to play the piano, Mom. That was your dream, not mine.

Liz rubbed her finger over an invisible spot on the counter. "I guess that's all anyone can be, right? Whoever they are inside." She breathed out. "So, he'll be Billy Taylor from here on?"

"Looks like it." Kacee picked up the folder of paperwork. "Did you want to say hi?"

"No, it's OK. Thank you for letting me watch this play out."

Kacee smiled. "Hopefully you'll see this many more times. Will you keep coming back to volunteer?"

Liz nodded. "As long as you need me to."

CHAPTER 14

L iz tried the visualization, the small questions, the small steps, all of it, but nothing got the words onto the paper. She was supposed to write letters to someone with whom she needed to settle things about her grief, although Mira packaged it differently.

"You can do this as many times as you need to, Liz. What we're going for is that place where you feel you have said and heard everything that you need to move on to the next level of healing."

They had talked about her father's months of slow death that brought her home from the music conser-

vatory for good. They had talked about the miscarriage. They talked about Lauren. So many ways Liz's
life had unraveled. She was such a jumble of things
that didn't end well. Was it her fault? Was there more
she could have done, should have done?

Mira had helped her understand that those were
the questions she was always asking herself, no matter the form—with words, with anorexia, by isolation.
Mentally, physically, and socially punishing herself.
Over and over again. Before, she had always moved
on to the next thing because someone needed her.
Her mother, Camille, Lauren. Who needed her now?

"What about you?" Mira had asked. "We are often
our worst critics, and our strongest enemies against
change. Is it possible that one part of you is the
resistor to the part that longs for healing and peace?
What will that part of you need to hear in order to see
the battle is over? That, in fact, there was no battle at
all, just sadness and the basest of all emotions—loss.
The denier angry part needs to be heard, but so does
the part that wants healing. They are all parts of you.
All parts that need to be heard, to be cared for."

Liz still didn't know who to write to. The baby she
never held in her arms? Her father? Lauren? The loss of
each of them contributed to who she turned out to be
and would affect her for the rest of her life. But did the
regrets and missed moments need to travel everywhere
with her, whisper into her ears, crowd her thoughts?
Or was she the one keeping them gathered around her?
Could she let go? Maybe the real question was the one

she didn't want to answer: when those parts of her life were peeled back, would there be anything left?

I have created you.

As the words filled her mind, a peace came over her.

There is nothing you need to do to make you more you. Don't be afraid. Don't be afraid for the dry husk of your grief to fall away and let the seed sprout. See, I have begun a new thing. I give beauty for ashes, joy for mourning, peace for despair.

Liz pulled the paper to her and began to write.

Bry sat across from her, waiting. She had asked him that morning if he would help her with a project after dinner. They had eaten and cleaned up, and now, it was time.

"Mira gave me some homework, and I need someone to listen to what I've written," Liz said.

"OK." Bry smiled. "Do I need to do anything else?"

"Not yet. Maybe at the end."

"All right."

Liz took a deep breath and let it slip past her lips. *One. Two. Three.* "OK," she said. "So, the homework is to write three letters to someone I am grieving." She looked up and Bry nodded.

"The first is to say what I *wish* I would have said. The second is what I *think* they would say back. The third is what I would *like* them to say." She exhaled again. "I thought for a long time about what I would want to say and to hear. And I thought even longer about who

I would write them to. Mira has helped me see that I have more than one option. There are a lot of things that didn't get said."

Bry nodded but kept his focus on a spot on the table in front of him.

Liz unfolded the paper and cleared her throat.

"*Dear Bry.*"

She could feel him look up at her, but she kept her eyes on the words on her paper.

"*When I think about the hard parts of my life, I see that you have been with me for all of them. Even though you didn't know my dad, you knew me when I was sad from losing him, and you loved me through it. When our baby died before we got a chance to watch its little heart beat, you loved me through it. Now, losing Lauren, and wanting to die myself, you loved me through it. So, when I think about what to say to you, all I have is 'thank you.' And what I would ask is, will you forgive me?*"

"Liz, I—"

She held up a hand. "I have two more letters."

He took a deep breath and put his hands in his lap, and she unfolded her second letter.

"*Dear Liz,*

I would do anything you need me to do. We'll get through this. We always have. God put us together to do this together."

She looked up. "I have one more. This is what I wish I could hear you say."

She paused before going on.

"*Dear Liz,*

I *forgive you. For making me feel left out, for feeling left out yourself. For shutting me out. For making me do this alone. I miss Lo every day just like you do, and always will. I love her, and I love you.*"

Liz slowly folded the paper. Bry's face was contorted, and he shook his head side to side, again and again. He closed his eyes, brought a clenched hand to his forehead and pushed hard against it. After a moment, he dropped his hand and opened his eyes.

"Do I get to say something now?" he asked.

"If you want."

"First—yes. I forgive you. I love you—always, forever, no matter what. But I also want to say, I'm sorry. I'm sorry for what I did."

"What are you talking about?"

"I'm sorry I let your life slip away. I was all about my business, my goals, and I never made room for yours. And when you should have been allowed to grieve our baby, I let my grandmother's care fall on you. By the time we had Lauren, there was very little of your dream for your life left. And now you don't even have her."

"That's not your fault."

"I know. But the point is, I never made room for *you* in our life together. You gave everything, any time anyone asked, but I never gave back to you." He shook his head and clenched his fist again. "When I think of what you could have done, could have been...Music was your life, Liz, and I didn't even get you a *piano.*"

His voice rose. "You could have been on any stage, anywhere in the world and you're playing on a cast-off instrument in a little room that I built *for someone else.*

I'm sorry. I am so sorry, Liz. I let you settle for a second-hand life."

Liz shook her head. "I got Lauren out of this life. I got *you* out of this life."

"But don't you see?" Bry said. "There's more left to live. Like those seeds you keep, there's more of you that needs to send out roots, that needs to see the sun." He reached across and took her hand. "That's my letter to you."

Liz thought about his words. She agreed she had put aside her dreams, more than once, but didn't everyone? On the other hand, putting them aside and packing them away forever were two different things entirely.

CHAPTER 15

L iz turned off the vacuum. She had moved this box around Lauren's room every time she cleaned, but it was time to open it.

Linda Harris had brought it to them herself. "I'm so sorry for your loss," she had said. "Lauren was the perfect student, always kind, a hard worker, polite to the teachers and staff. Her locker, I'm sure you remember, was just outside my office. I...thought you might want to have these."

Liz had accepted the box, thanked the principal, and set the box in Lauren's room. If she never opened it, then she could tell herself, "Lauren's at school. That's why she's not here." Thanks to Mira, Liz had done a lot of unpacking in the past few weeks. Liz had learned things about herself that she didn't want to know, as well as some good things she had never thought were very special.

"Not everyone has the depth of compassion that you have, Liz. For you, it's innate, so you don't see it. But it's that same level of investment in others that hurts so much when you can no longer offer it. The tendency is for the pain and longing to make you cling to another person or project right away to try to shrink the hurt. Instead, that is the time to pause and let the moment surround you.

"Journal, or even say the words out loud to yourself. There is no shame in feeling deeply for another, and you need to do that, but it takes time to be able to properly begin again. If you do not give yourself time, then the next thing will feel inadequate—a poor substitute for what you need—and unfulfilling, leading to a need for another thing and another."

"Like the eating disorder," Liz said.

"Exactly. Was that satisfying?"

"It seemed like it, but...no. It was like the hurt expanded instead."

"Give proper closure to the heart-bond. You have experienced something special and profound. It has helped shape the talents, abilities, thoughts, and dreams that make you *you*. Liz, you are not deficient *without* Lauren. You are *richer* because of her."

Liz took the lid off the box and looked inside. On top was a light sweatshirt. Liz held it up to her face and breathed in the laughter and the sunny smile she imagined on Lauren's face as she flung off the shirt after a warm May recess. The next things in the box were the miscellany of her school day: pencils, erasers, a discarded sheet of math problems. Unicorn shaped magnets. A photo booth strip of the three girls caught in crazy expressions.

Liz touched their faces. Aisha, Lauren, and Nikki had been friends since kindergarten. They had such plans for their last year in middle school made during many Cookie Days and tent sleepovers. They had a fierce competition for predicting the annual first beach day, when the Lake Michigan water temp finally reached sixty-five degrees, and then for who could stay in the water the longest. Lauren had missed that, had stayed in suspended animation while the other girls figured out how to keep going. Liz laid the photos aside.

The last thing in the box was a piece of notebook paper folded in a square. Liz smoothed it out on her lap. 'Write Your Story' it said, in large letters across the top. Along the side column were the words 'Beginning,' 'Middle,' and 'End,' in a fat tire font. There were some cross-outs and erase marks in the first couple of lines, as if Lauren had changed her mind about how to start.

My name is Lauren Camille Bachmann. The coolest thing about me is I love roller coasters. *I am an only child.*

That was Lo: so many ideas and plans, it took her a few attempts to land on what she wanted to do first.

Sometimes I think my parents give me more because there is just one of me and they weren't even sure they would get that.

Liz would never forget the dread she felt during those first months of pregnancy. Was that twinge the beginning of another miscarriage? Would this food or that make the difference between a healthy baby or none at all? Even after the routine ultrasound where they saw for themselves the little arms and legs moving, the tiny heart fluttering, Liz still could not rest.

She had read about women delivering full-term stillborn babies or having them die after just a few days, or minutes, or breaths. Every day that she waited to feel her baby's heartbeat was another day that could lead to heartbreak instead. On the other hand, one day closer to holding her baby meant one more day her baby was still alive.

At one time, Liz had counted down the days until she could hold Lauren. Now she counted how long it had been since she lived.

I've been to Disney, Cedar Point, and California. Some of my friends have never even left Frankfort. I have my own room, but since I'm the only kid I have to do all the vacuuming. So that sucks.

Sometimes I don't love being the only child. If my friends are busy with their families I don't have anyone to do stuff with. I feel like my parents either forget I'm around or they stare at me like I might suddenly disappear, which is creepy.

It had taken months before Liz could sleep without waking up terrified that newborn Lauren had died while she slept. Bry was more relaxed, especially as Lo went through the bumps and bruises of toddlerhood. "She's gotta fall sometime. That's how she'll learn." But Liz had never fully reached that point of letting go.

I sleep with a stuffed unicorn, kinda baby-ish, but I pretend it's a dog. My dad said I couldn't have a real dog. I don't know why. Maybe because his dog died when he was a kid. I told him there are other dogs in the world. He might like one if he would just try it, but he said no he wouldn't. I guess that's why I picked a unicorn. They're one of a kind, just like me.

I don't like Endings. I always want movies to keep going. I want the popcorn bucket to stay full. I want fun days to be like a roller coaster ride where you never have to get off. So, I'm NOT writing my End. I'm going to be a unicorn and live forever.

Liz folded the paper and put everything except the photo strip back in the box, thinking of Lauren's wish. If only. She sighed and pushed the box into the closet. She closed the door and sat on Lo's bed holding the stuffed unicorn to her while she debated. It had been six months since their last Cookie Day. Would the girls be ready for another? Was she ready?

CHAPTER 16

Liz had made the dough the night before, glad for the familiar rhythm of measuring and mixing. The last sheet of cutouts had two minutes to bake when the doorbell rang. She went to it, wondering who would be at the front door on a Saturday morning.

"Hi, Mrs. Bachmann."

"Hey, Aisha, come on in." She smiled at the girl and held the door open wide. "You didn't have to ring the doorbell. You could have come in through the garage like normal."

Aisha pulled on a braid and gave her a small smile, then glanced toward the drive where Nikki was climbing out of Justin's red truck. Liz stepped out onto the porch and waved at him. He waved back, and the diesel lumbered down the drive out to the road.

"Come on in, you two. Oh, no, the cookies!"

Liz rushed to the kitchen and threw open the oven door. The unicorns were several shades darker than usual but not quite burned. She set the tray on the stovetop and quickly moved the cookies over to the rack to cool. The girls stood at the counter watching, still wearing their jackets. "So, what colors today?" she asked, like she did every Cookie Day.

Aisha glanced at Nikki. What was typically a several minute argument over the pros and cons of each color, the frequency of their past use, and the contemplation of trying something new, was over in three words.

"Blue and purple."

"OK," Liz said, her voice rising a pitch. "Do you want different shades of each?"

"Sure."

"Well, get comfy. The aprons are in the drawer. It'll just take me a minute here."

The girls silently hung their jackets on a chair and got out the aprons. There was a moment of hesitation as Lauren's tie-dyed apron got tangled with Nikki's red one. Aisha pulled it loose, folded it, and quickly slid it back in the drawer.

"Can you get down the sprinkles and stuff?" Liz asked. She added a drop of purple and then another to the bowl and stirred it in. She held up the spoon and saw the frosting was not quite the color she envisioned, but it would be fine.

The girls got out the plates and the spatulas they each had claimed over the years. Liz turned on the playlist called Cookies and hummed along to the song. "Tell me about school," she said, spreading a lavender stripe on the cookie star on her plate.

"We have the same home room," Aisha said, "and math."

"I'm in choir," Nikki said.

Lauren and Nikki always took choir together and had planned to sing a duet in the annual middle school talent show. Liz waited for more, but nothing came. "What about sports?" she asked. "Did either of you go out for cross country?"

"I did," Aisha said. "We had our first away meet this week, and there's an invitational next Saturday."

"Is that with a bunch of other schools?" Liz asked.

Aisha nodded. "Six, I think? It's in Traverse."

"Wow," Liz said. "The big time."

The girls spread and sprinkled in silence for several minutes.

"How's your mom, Nikki?" Liz calculated the twins were about four months old.

"Tired. But OK."

"Good." Liz held up a unicorn that she had tried to swirl with different colors. "Well, that didn't go quite like I wanted," she said.

"It will still taste good," Nikki said. Their answer for any decorating mishap.

Liz noticed that neither girl was actually doing any decorating. Aisha was rolling a stray sprinkle around under her finger, and Nikki was twisting a spoon in the blue frosting.

"This whole day isn't going quite like I thought," Liz said. The girls both gave her sad smiles. "Do you want to just talk?" Liz asked.

"OK," Nikki said.

They all took off their aprons and laid them on the counter next to the five cookies they had decorated. Liz poured glasses of water and brought them to the table. After several sips each, she cleared her throat. "Do you want to go up to her room?"

They nodded with more energy than she had seen the whole visit.

"You can go ahead. You know the way."

Without a word, the girls slid out of their seats and left the kitchen. She heard their feet padding up the stairs, and mentally tracked them into Lauren's room. Liz put away the frosting and bagged the cookies to go into the freezer. Maybe later there would be a need for three dozen assorted mythical creatures.

Liz washed up the dishes and, when she had run out of work, followed the girls upstairs. She pushed open the door to Lauren's room and found them sitting on the floor, leaning back against her bed looking at the strip of photos from Lauren's locker.

"Where were you when you took those?" Liz asked.

"Michigan Adventure," Aisha answered. "We had a blast that day."

Liz sat down in the bungee chair across from them. "Which rides did you go on?"

"We couldn't decide, so Lauren voted donkey tail," Nikki said.

"That's where we close our eyes and point at something," Aisha explained.

Liz nodded. She listened as the girls told her of a Lauren different from the one she and Bry had held by the hand on the kiddie rides at the fair. This Lauren waited for the front seats, rode with strangers so her friends wouldn't have to, and ate her weight in caramel corn. Lauren had lived a lifetime with these girls in just a few short years. They were just as much a part of her growing up as she was of theirs. Lauren would live on in their memories.

"Would you like to have those?" Liz motioned to the strip of pictures.

"Yes, please," Aisha said.

"Is there...anything else you would want of hers?" Liz saw her words had surprised them as much as her.

The girls looked at each other and then at Liz. "Her socks?" Nikki asked.

"All of them?" Liz couldn't understand what they would want with socks.

"Her crazy socks. The tie-dye unicorn ones."

Liz laughed. Lauren had insisted on the socks in a Chicago novelty store, six pairs in all. It was the only thing she bought the entire trip. Liz went to the dresser and searched through the top drawer. There were four pairs in various degrees of wear, and two others unopened. Liz pulled them all out of the drawer and dumped them on the bed.

The girls both reached for the broken-in, some-what faded socks.

"You should take all of them," Liz said. "Lo would never want a good unicorn sock to go unworn." She sat down on the bed. "I'm really glad you guys came over today. I thought maybe the cookies would make it seem like she was…"

"In the other room," Aisha said. "I pretend that a lot."

Nikki nodded. "Me too." Tears gathered in her eyes. She laughed and swiped them away.

Liz felt her own tears spill over. "Do you guys mind if I hug you?"

The girls stood up and they group-hugged. Their scents were a mix of baby powder, strawberry Chap-stick, and cookies, like a teen version of sugar and spice. Liz gave them a final squeeze.

"I'm going to miss having you over," she said. "But I still want to hear all about you. Send me a text every once in a while, OK?"

"OK," they said together.

"She was a lucky girl to have such amazing friends. Thank you for being in her life."

"She'll always be part of ours too," Nikki said, and Aisha nodded.

A phone chimed. "My dad's here." Nikki checked the phone and slid it into her pocket. "My mom needed me to be back by noon. We can take Aisha home, if you like."

Liz smiled. "Thanks for coming. It means a lot."

The girls were at the front door when Liz remembered their jackets. "Hang on a sec." She went to the kitchen and grabbed the coats, then went to the counter and added the aprons to her arms. "Here you go," she said as she handed each girl her apron. "Now you can carry on the tradition at your houses too. Maybe with the twins in a few years." She hugged each of them again. "Bye. Be well."

She watched them go down the walk, lined up in their usual way: Aisha on the left and Nikki on the right with a small space between them where Lauren would always be.

CHAPTER 17

Liz woke up to the thought, *Where is Bry?* His side of the bed was empty, and so was the bathroom. Why hadn't he said goodbye? She felt the panic rising. *Breathe in. Breathe out.* She pushed back the covers and hurried downstairs.

"Could be a little crazy next year." Bry stood, coffee in hand, looking out the dining room window. "There are seeds all over the place."

Liz started to say, "I'm sorry," but he stopped her with a squeeze of her shoulders.

"Nope. Not going there." He slid his arm down around her waist. "It'll be fun. Lauren would have loved it."

Liz wasn't so sure of that. She remembered the careful planning Bry and Lauren had put into the garden when she decided on it for her first 4-H project. They had sketched out on paper where the rows would go and what would be planted in each one. Neither her husband nor her daughter was what she would call random.

"Hey, I got us a little something. Saw it on my way home yesterday."

"What?"

He held up a finger. "After we eat."

Liz dressed while Bry set the table. They ate their first "big breakfast" in months and then did the dishes together.

After Liz dried her hands and hung up the towel, Bry said, "And now, if you'll come with me, ma'am." He took her hand and led her out to the garage. "Ta da." He waved his hand over the bed of the truck filled with white plastic bags.

"Dairy Doo?"

"Manure from fancy cows. I bought it to put on the garden. Wanna help?"

They spent the morning "setting the garden to rights" as Bry called it. Raking the debris into a compost pile, tilling the soil, and shoveling the bagged manure over the whole thing. Bry tipped his head. "Might as well give the seeds a leg up," he said.

After lunch, Liz tidied the kitchen and found her camera on top of the refrigerator. She went into the office to put it away, but the image of a pumpkin popped into her head. She opened the little door on the side of the camera, ejected the SD card, and pushed it into the port on her laptop. A few clicks later, she had almost a hundred pictures laid out in a grid on her screen.

"Hey," Bry said from the doorway. "I'm going to go get some gas. We used up everything I had in the cans."

Liz turned to him and nodded. "All right." She smiled. "Hey, thanks for today."

"What?"

"Breakfast. No judging. All that. It's more than I deserve."

"You deserve so much more than that, Liz." He walked into the room and kissed her. He nodded at the pictures on her screen. "Those came out great. Back in a few."

Liz turned to the computer and scrolled through the images one by one. Most of them were pretty good, especially considering the frame of mind she had been in the day she took them. Although she wasn't sure why, she created a file to store them.

The date at the bottom of her screen reminded Liz that school had been in session for six weeks. For a minute, she felt the darkness coming back, but she saw the photos of seeds and centered herself on them. Bus schedules, homework, and normal rhythms of life still happened for other people.

Liz closed the photo program and opened the file of her piano students. She put her hand on the phone receiver, sighed, and then held it up to her ear. She dialed the first number on her list.

"Hi, Jordan, this is Liz. I'm going to start piano lessons back up. Let me know if you guys are still interested. Once I hear back from everyone, we can talk days and times. Thanks, bye."

She set down the receiver and closed her eyes. *In, out. In, out. In, out.* Then she dialed the second number, and the third, leaving her messages. She had her finger ready to dial again when the phone rang. "Hello?"

"Liz, it's Trista. How are you?"

"I'm good. Yeah," Liz said.

"It's great to hear you are starting lessons. I've tried to keep Caleb on track, but you know how much I know about the piano. My playing is a little like two-finger typing." She laughed. "We are absolutely interested, and we have a pretty open schedule. No fall sports for him this year."

"OK, thanks." Liz typed a plus sign next to Caleb's name. "I'll let you know. I haven't gotten very far down the list yet."

"Sounds good. So, kind of along the same track, I did have a question for you."

"O-kay," Liz said. She hoped Trista wasn't offended by her hesitation.

"Would you be at all interested in playing keyboard for the praise team? Miranda's work schedule has her on call a lot of Sundays, and she doesn't want to chance having to leave in the middle of a worship set. I mean, we could probably make it work, but..."

Liz sat back in her chair. The image of Lauren standing on the sanctuary platform singing looped in her memory. It would be hard enough just going back to church, seeing the concern on everyone's face. What if she had a breakdown and was trapped at the keyboard? What if she couldn't make it through the songs? What if? She took a deep breath.

"Liz?" Trista's voice was quiet. "If it's too much or too early..."

Liz reached out and took a kernel of corn from the small bowl of seeds on her desk. She rubbed it with her finger, thought of the tiny shoot that would come from it when it was buried in the soil. Until it was planted, it was just dried up, not dead but not really alive either. Lauren would want this seed to grow and do what it was meant to do.

"I can do that," Liz said. "It will be good to play in public again."

Trista exhaled. "I'm so glad. Not only because it keeps us from having just a flute and a bass guitar as our praise band, but, well, I'm glad you're feeling up to it. I can't even imagine how hard this has all been. But, we're here for you. Whatever pace you want to go, we'll go with you."

Liz wiped at a tear. "Thank you."

"OK. Well, I'll let you go, but call me if you need anything."

"Thanks, Trista." Liz set the phone in its charger.

She had done it. Like Bry said, it might be kinda crazy, but she had planted her seed.

CHAPTER 18

I t wasn't as often anymore, but there were times when the dark thoughts tried to surface, and she had no interest in talking to anyone.

"Hon?" Bry's voice echoed from the answering machine. "Hey, pick up if you're there."

Liz crossed the kitchen and picked up the receiver. "I'm here."

"Good. How's your day?"

"OK. Yours?"

"It looks like I'll be done earlier than I thought, and I wondered if you'd like to go on a date."

"Right now?" She looked down at her worn leggings that really needed to be replaced.

"How about at one? I thought we could meet at that Café Hope in town. We've never gone there yet, and it's been open almost two years."

"Sure. Sounds good."

"OK, love you."

"Love you, too." Liz pushed the button and set the receiver down. Where had that come from? She couldn't remember the last time they had done something together. Something that didn't include Lauren. It was sweet, strange, and sad all at the same time, and just what she had needed.

It had been a long time since Liz had walked along Main Street, altogether different now after the summer T-shirt shops and ice cream places closed. The café had a little table outside decorated with tiny pumpkins and ears of corn. Liz sighed. Thanksgiving. Christmas. Could they just skip over that this year? Maybe every year?

Bry pulled into a space, and she waited for him to cross the street.

"Hi," he said, kissing her cheek.

"Hey." She motioned to the tiny storefront. "This is cute."

"I did some work on the apartment upstairs for the two ladies who own the building. I haven't been in since it became the café. Ready?" He pulled open the door and stood aside for her to go in first. They moved the few steps to the counter to read the hand-lettered sign and decide on their drinks.

"We just got a new batch of pumpkin muffins a few minutes ago," the barista said. "They don't last long!"

Bry looked at Liz. "Do you want one?"

"I'll split one with you," she said. She was distracted by the sign propped up on the counter that said, *We're looking. Part-time with variable hours.*

They gave the barista their drink orders, and Bry asked, "How much do I owe you?"

"At Café Hope, you pay what you can," the barista said.

"All right." Bry paused, took some bills from his wallet, and laid them on the counter.

The barista slid the plate toward him and took the money. "OK, give me a minute," she said, "and I'll bring your drinks right over."

It was a tiny room, with just a few tables plus the usual narrow counter and barstools along one wall. A series of prints of a finch clinging to a single flower stem caught Liz's eye. The little bird was hanging on for dear life, or hoping to. She could relate.

The sound of frothing milk gave kind of an audio barrier between them and the barista. "I didn't expect that," Bry said when they sat down. "The 'name your price' thing."

"It must work. They're hiring."

"That's great. We can use more local businesses down here, especially during the off season."

The barista brought their drinks over on a tray. "Here you go. Enjoy."

Liz smiled and thanked her while Bry took the two bright blue cups. He passed one across the small table, and Liz took a sip of the latte while he used a plastic knife on the muffin. Since he had asked her out, she would let him start talking.

"A lot of times when I drive to the sites, I leave the radio off," Bry said. "The quiet helps me process."

Liz nodded.

"So, I've been thinking about...a lot of things." He gave a quick glance to the counter, but the barista had gone out through a door in the back of the room. "I know we have to let her go, but I also know she'll always be a part of us. I've been trying to work that out."

Liz nodded again and took another sip. She couldn't talk this through, not here.

"I wanted to find some way to, I guess, talk about Lauren out loud. To people who didn't know her, I mean. I want to create something living that will help us share Lo—her spirit, her energy, her life." He reached into his jacket and pulled out some glossy catalogs.

Seeds. She felt the darkness coming up from her gut.

"Liz." Bry was laser-focused on her. "Hear me out."

She looked away and then back. "OK."

"I'm thinking we could start a CSA. It's like a garden that people subscribe to. They buy shares, we do the growing, and they pick up their portion as each vegetable and herb is ready."

She nodded.

"We could work on it together," he continued. "You can do as much in the garden as you want, but the website is what I thought you might like. You're really good with organizing and talking to people. We could include recipes to go with what we harvest," he said. "There's a lot to do that doesn't involve dirt."

A little bird peeked out from the front of the flower catalog. Probably not a coincidence that it was also a finch.

"We could call it 'Lauren's Garden,'" she said quietly, then met Bry's eyes.

He smiled in relief. "I like that." He gestured at the catalogs. "I brought these, but if you want to think about it first—"

"No. It's a great idea. I can use some of those 'pumpkin portraits' for the website."

Bry laughed. "I did call them that, didn't I?"

"It's going to be a rough next couple of months," she said. "I think it will be good to have something like this to work on and do it together."

Bry smiled and took her hand. "That's what I was hoping for."

"I'm thinking, too, that I would like to get out of the house some. The last job I had was at Dairy Queen before we got married, so maybe it's time I got back out there."

"What are you thinking?" he asked.

Liz smiled. "Well, I read there's a cute little café downtown that's hiring."

CHAPTER 19

Liz held out her fist. "You did it!" Tyson bumped her back. After three weeks of being stuck on a phrase, he had played it flawlessly. "All right," Liz said, "we better wrap it up, or you'll be late for baseball. See you next week?"

"Yeah."

"As a reward for this awesome job, why don't you pick what *you* want to work on next? Anything in the next five pages."

"OK."

She could tell by his sideways glance that he had already looked ahead. Probably why he couldn't get past this page in the book. Liz walked Tyson to the door and waved at Cara waiting with the baby in the car.

Liz stood on the porch, breathing in the newly washed air. Out of habit, she checked the garden. This was just what it needed to get those seeds sprouted into their first harvest of peas, beans, broccoli, squash, herbs, and flowers. Now she just needed something to bring her out of her darkness into the light. Mira had told her to expect these feelings to surface, especially this week. The first anniversary would be rough.

The phone rang, and Liz went back inside. It was Hope's cell number.

"Liz, hi. Hey, my mom's flight was delayed, and I'm still at the airport. Nita just called—she's got a sick baby. I know it's super short notice, but could you fill in for her at the café, just for a few hours until I get back?"

"Yes, I can do it. I just finished with my student."

"Awesome. OK, I'll be back soon. Thanks!"

The community, the downtown, Hope, everybody seemed to win from the café being there. She and Hope got along great, and Liz liked working for her. The building itself was tiny, but the café was so much more than just a coffee shop. The 'pay what you can' mantra seemed to apply to more than just money, something Liz had tried to explain to Bry, but she could never get the right words.

Liz parked in the public lot near the channel and soaked up the last few minutes of afternoon sun before she went inside. She put away her purse and slipped on her apron, green in honor of the garden, and went out to relieve Ava. When Liz first started at the café, they were scheduled together, and she liked Ava. She was young but a good worker. Liz pushed aside the question, would someone one day have said that about Lauren?

"Hey, thanks for coming in. I have finals the rest of the week, and I really need the study time."

Liz worked her face into a smile. "No worries. How was the afternoon?"

"Pretty steady until just a few minutes ago. I'm gonna go, if it's all right with you." She was already stripping off her bright blue apron.

"Sure. Good luck on your exams," Liz said. "I know you'll do great."

"Thanks. See ya."

Liz checked over the café and found Ava had tidied everything. She bent down to look at the stock under the counter, and the bell jingled on the front door. As Liz stood up, a young woman came in looking around the room, not in the confused way new customers usually did, but like she was reconnecting with it somehow.

"Welcome to Café Hope," Liz said.

"Hey," the woman answered. "Um, is Hope here?"

"Not right now." Maybe the woman wanted to leave a résumé or something. "She should be in a little later. Can I give her a message for you?"

"I kind of wanted to surprise her. Maybe I'll just wait."

"Sure," Liz said. "Can I get you anything?"

The woman studied the display case. "Do you have any monster cookies? I always loved those."

Liz sorted through the trays and found two cookies speckled with M&Ms and chocolate chips. "Looks like we've got two. Do you want both?"

"Yeah, and a mocha latte, please." She slid a five-dollar bill across the counter.

"At Café Hope—" Liz began.

"You pay what you can. I used to work here."

"Really? How long ago?" Liz asked. She ground the coffee into the portafilter, tamped it, and put it into the grouphead.

"It seems like forever ago, but it will be three years in the fall. Then I went away to college. I just finished my second year."

"Oh, where do you go?" Liz asked. She frothed the milk and set it aside.

"Northwestern Michigan. I'm in the mechanic program."

That was not something she had heard very often. Liz stopped and turned around, still holding the empty cup. "I think I met you before," she said, the memory of that awful day coming back to her. "At the library. You worked on my car."

The girl frowned in thought and then her face cleared. "The radiator hose, right? That was you?"

"Yes," Liz said. "Oh, my gosh, I never paid you or anything. I am so sorry."

"It's cool. You were having a pretty rough day." She tipped her head. "I'm Andi, by the way."

"Liz." She held out the cup in her hands. "Let me at least finish your coffee."

Andi smiled. "OK."

"Did you want to sit down?"

"Oh, yeah. I forgot I was the customer." Andi turned and chose one of the small tables with the blue chairs.

Liz topped off the frothy milk and put on the lid. She set the cup on a tray and then plated the cookies. "How did you meet Hope?" She carried the tray over to the table and set it out for Andi out of habit.

The girl traced a circle on the lid of the cup. One thing Liz had learned, everyone had a story. Sometimes they shared. Sometimes they didn't. "I'm sorry," Liz said.

"No, I'm good. I have to learn to talk about it sometime." She looked up at Liz. "You can sit down if you want."

Liz pulled the chair a little away from the table so she could get to the counter if anyone came in. Maybe this girl had been helped through the women's shelter. People had really responded to the "Pay what you can" idea, and the café was now one of the shelter's regular supporters.

"So, my dad and I traveled around. He did construction with a crew, and they were hired when the condos were built down the street." Andi paused. "One day, he was too sick to go to work. He went to the hospital the next day, and the day after that, he died."

"Oh, my goodness." Liz covered her mouth with her hand, holding back her own memories.

Andi nodded. "The short story is that Hope gave me a job, and later, a place to stay. Her friend Birgit, from the library, got me a housesitting job. The Reuters let me stay on until I went to college. And The Sisters gave me a grant to pay for school. All because Hope unlocked the café door one rainy morning and let me in."

Liz laid her hand across her heart and shook her head.

Andi exhaled. "Yeah." She took a sip of her coffee. "In my lit class this year, we read a poem by T.S. Eliot, and there's one line that talks about how endings are beginnings. That really made sense to me."

"Yes, it does."

"I know from working here and hearing other people's stories, that everybody goes through something like that. Maybe not as young as I did, but eventually they get plopped down in a different world, and they don't have a clue what to do next."

"That's exactly how it feels," Liz said. "You are so right."

They both turned at the noise coming from the back room, and Liz stood up just as Hope came through the door.

"Hi, Liz. Thank you so much for being here."

"It's been good," Liz said. "We've just been talking about you." She moved aside so Hope could see, then watched her boss's face light up.

"Andi!" Hope rushed forward and gave the girl a hug. "Oh, my gosh, look at your hair—I love it! When did you get back?"

"Just this afternoon."

Liz moved back to the counter, but the room was so small she could hear everything.

"And, how did everything go this semester?" Hope asked, eyebrows raised.

Andi gave her a slow grin. "4.0 all around."

"That's awesome! I *knew* you'd kill it." Hope went on asking about favorite classes, how Andi had liked her new roommate, things on the radar of any college student.

Liz thought about their stories. Hope had told Liz hers, about The Sisters reaching out. Now, here was Andi with another version of someone coming alongside and just being there. Liz had her own experience of being helped out of the pit. The three of them were not so different, really. Each of them stuck, not knowing what to do or where to go.

Like Andi said, there were a lot of people like that, for different reasons. Each of them clinging like a little bird to the stem of the flower that they think is all they have left. But then hope turns their head and shows them another way, one they hadn't even known could be possible.

Liz glanced at the colored prints of the finches and back to the two women. Maybe that was the point: for hope to be shared on repeat, over and over and over. A tune without words, like the poem said.

Never stopping, at all.

ACKNOWLEDGMENTS

"Thank you doesn't seem like enough."

I agree with Hope here. So many people played a part in getting this book from my first handwritten page to what you see today.

I've learned the craft of writing and the business of publishing from countless authors who have generously shared their tips and tricks.

I so appreciate my first ever beta readers, Melinda and Teresa, who gave such valuable feedback and wanted to know, even back in 2021, when they could buy the book.

Special thanks to my sister, Kim Venema, for her sensitivity reading of Liz's section.

I want to thank my editors: Colleen Tomlinson for showing me how to look more deeply into my characters, and LaVerne Clark for editing the revised manuscript and giving it wings.

My newsletter subscribers have been so encouraging as I spooled out my plans to finally publish this novel.

Indie authors are incredibly supportive, and I'm so proud now to be part of the community.

Finally, my family, especially my husband Roger, deserves my gratitude for so many things: fending for themselves, politely listening to my thinking out loud, waiting for me to write down an idea before it flew away, and, most of all, for their confidence that this "hope" would become reality.

A Thousand Thanks,

Brenda

DISCUSSION QUESTIONS FOR A TIME TO HOPE

1. Which character did you relate to or empathize with the most and why?

2. Who would you consider the most courageous character? Why?

3. Discuss the different ways each woman has a crisis of faith. If comfortable, discuss a personal crisis of faith that may be similar to one of the women.

4. What secondary character would you want as a friend? Why?

5. How does community play a role in the lives of the three women?

6. What are the ways the characters demonstrate their grief?

7. Discuss the time frame of grief. When is the right time to reach out to someone who is grieving?

8. What are ways the secondary characters show their faith without 'witnessing' in the traditional sense?

9. What makes this book faith-based or 'inspirational?' Discuss how faith should be woven into fictional stories.

10. Discuss the phrase, "Pay what you can and have hope for the rest."

11. How did this book relate to your own life? Did it evoke any memories or create any connections for you?

12. How relevant or relatable are the themes or messages of the book to your own life, or to society today?

Dear Reader:

Thank you so much for choosing A *Time to Hope*. It has been truly been my pleasure to share this story with you.

Please consider leaving an online review, which will help share my work with other readers.

Brenda Lobbezoo

About the Author

Brenda Lobbezoo writes about life from the inside out,
bringing the reader on a deeply emotional journey. She is an
empath and an optimist, holding out hope to the very end.

Brenda credits her people-reading skills to her career as a
small animal veterinarian, and to clients who shared
incredibly personal stories teaching her that out of deep pain
can come deep trust.

Brenda lives with her family in West Michigan.
Her passions include animals and music, and both often find
their way onto the page.
A *Time to Hope* is her first novel.

Get updates and sign up for her newsletter at
www.brendalobbezoo.wordpress.com

Find Brenda online at:

www.ingramcontent.com/pod-product-compliance
Lightning Source LLC
Chambersburg PA
CBHW022004050726
47499CB00002BA/287